VAMPIRES DON'T SPARKLE!

Here are some vampire stories that don't suck. Enjoy!

edited by

Michael West

Copyright © 2013 by Michael West
All rights reserved. No portion of this book may be copied or transmitted in any form, electronic or otherwise, without express written consent of the publisher or author.

Cover art: Matthew Perry
Copyright © 2012 Matthew Perry & Seventh Star Press, LLC.

Editor: Michael West

Published by Seventh Star Press, LLC.

ISBN Number: 978-1-937929-60-2

Library of Congress Control Number: 2013934357

Seventh Star Press
www.seventhstarpress.com
info@seventhstarpress.com

Publisher's Note:
Vampires Don't Sparkle is a work of fiction. All names, characters, and places are the product of the author's imagination, used in fictitious manner. Any resemblances to actual persons, places, locales, events, etc. is purely coincidental.

Printed in the United States of America

First Edition

J. F. Gonzalez: "A New Life" ©2013 by author. Originally appeared in *Dread*, issue #10, January 2000. Reprinted by permission of author.

Tim Waggoner: "What Once Was Flesh" ©2013 by author. Printed with permission of the author.

Elizabeth Massie: "The Darkton Circus Mystery" ©2013 by author. Printed with permission of the author.

R. J. Sullivan: "Robot Vampire" ©2013 by author. Printed with permission of the author.

Gord Rollo: "Beneath a Templar Cross" ©2013 by author. Originally appeared in *The Downward Spiral* collection, October 2006. Reprinted by permission of author.

Kyle S. Johnson: "The Weapon of Memory" ©2013 by author. Printed with permission of the author.

Stephen Zimmer : "The Excavation" ©2013 by author. Printed with permission of the author.

Joel A. Sutherland: "Skraeling" ©2013 by author. Printed with permission of the author.

Bob Freeman: "Dreams of Winter" ©2013 by author. Printed with permission of the author.

Gregory L. Hall: "Dracula's Winkee: Bloodsucker Blues" ©2013 by author. Printed with permission of the author.

Lucy A. Snyder: "I Fuck Your Sunshine" ©2013 by author. Printed with permission of the author.

Maurice Broaddus: "A Soldier's Story" ©2013 by author. Printed with permission of the author.

Douglas F. Warrick: "Rattenkönig" ©2013 by author. Printed with permission of the author.

Jerry Gordon: "Vampire Nation" ©2013 by author. Printed with permission of the author.

Gary A. Braunbeck: "Curtain Call" ©2013 by author. Printed with permission of the author.

For two of the bravest women I have ever known, Sara and Stephanie.

Promises to keep...

"Here's what vampires shouldn't be: pallid detectives who drink Bloody Marys and work only at night; lovelorn southern gentlemen; anorexic teenage girls; boy-toys with big dewy eyes. What should they be? Killers, honey. Stone killers who never get enough of that tasty Type-A. Bad boys and girls. Hunters. In other words, Midnight America. Red, white and blue, accent on the red. Those vamps got hijacked by a lot of soft-focus romance."

—Stephen King, *American Vampire*

TABLE OF CONTENTS

Taking Back the Night, Michael West 1

A New Life, J. F. Gonzalez 5

What Once Was Flesh, Tim Waggoner 21

The Darkton Circus Mystery, Elizabeth Massie 33

Robot Vampire, R. J. Sullivan 53

Beneath a Templar Cross, Gord Rollo 75

The Weapon of Memory, Kyle S. Johnson 93

The Excavation, Stephen Zimmer 103

Skraeling, Joel A. Sutherland 121

Dreams of Winter, Bob Freeman 135

Dracula's Winkee: Bloodsucker Blues, Gregory L. Hall 145

I Fuck Your Sunshine, Lucy A. Snyder 161

A Soldier's Story, Maurice Broaddus 167

Rattenkönig, Douglas F. Warrick 181

Vampire Nation, Jerry Gordon 197

Curtain Call, Gary A. Braunbeck 205

About the Editor 225

TAKING BACK THE NIGHT

An Introduction
by Michael West

The 1988 concert film *Rattle and Hum* opened with a familiar sounding tune. Lead singer Bono took the microphone in his hand and announced to the crowd, "This song ... Charles Manson stole it from the Beatles. We're stealin' it back." And the band then proceeded to rock a huge arena with their amazing rendition of the classic *Helter Skelter*. It was a powerful moment—taking something wonderful, something that had been corrupted, and legitimizing it once more.

They made it *cool* again.

For years now, I've had the same feeling about the vampire. That supernatural creature of the night—a dark being who once struck fear in the hearts of mortal men and women—has been corrupted. In movies, in television shows, and in fiction, this fearsome demon has been "defanged." Instead of viciously preying on the blood of the living, today's vampires are meek "vegetarians." They have the gift of limitless power and eternal life, and how do they choose to spend their time? They go back to high school and sit in the same classes year after year; they sulk in corners, brooding and fawning for students who are centuries younger than they are, and in the face of these young, nubile bloodbags, these symbols of raw sexuality, these fearsome killers, these *animals* are suddenly neutered...

MICHAEL WEST

weak, more frightened at the thought of going dateless to the prom than a cross or a wooden stake through their black, soulless hearts.

Well, enough is enough.

Stephenie Meyer stole this monster from Bram Stoker. We're stealin' it back!

In this anthology, my fellow horror and dark fantasy authors will take you down some very twisted paths, each putting his or her own unique spin on the age-old legend of the vampire. Some of these tales are fanciful, some humorous, and some as black as an endless night. These are stories that will once more strike fear into your heart and make you dread sundown. These are tales to make the vampire cool again.

There is one person who would have loved these stories. Her name was Sara Larson. She was a wonderful writer and an even better friend. Sara was diagnosed with a rare form of breast cancer, and earlier this year, she lost a long and courageous battle against the disease and passed away, but not before all of us that knew and loved her made her aware of just how special she was.

Several months later, my own wife, Stephanie West, was also diagnosed with cancer—a slow-growing tumor that had taken root in her bone. Thankfully, she did not share Sara's fate, and as I type this, she is cancer free. Others, however, will not be as lucky, and more will become victim to this real-life monster until a cure can be found.

That's where you come in, faithful reader. By purchasing this anthology, you have made a donation to the American Cancer Society. You have helped to one day win the war against this dreaded disease. And hopefully, one day, we can say that cancer stole away the gift of life for far too long, but we are stealin' it back.

Thank you!

Michael West
December 7, 2012

CREATURES OF THE NIGHT

"Listen to them - children of the night. What music they make."
—Bram Stoker, *Dracula*

A NEW LIFE
J. F. Gonzalez

J. F. Gonzalez is the author of several novels of horror and suspense including *They, The Corporation, Back from the Dead*, and *Primitive*. His latest collaboration with Brian Keene – *Clickers Vs. Zombies* - is the fourth installment in his *Clickers* series (with Mark Williams and Brian Keene). His short fiction has appeared in numerous magazines and anthologies including *Shroud, Doorways, Dark Discoveries, Hot Blood: Strange Bedfellows, Dark Arts, Shivers III* and *IV*, and elsewhere. He currently writes a column on the history of horror fiction for *Lamplight Magazine*.

He doesn't dig what passes as vampire fiction these days. He prefers vampires from the old school. Therefore, he considers the best vampire novels ever published to be *Dracula* by Bram Stoker, *'Salem's Lot* by Stephen King, *They Thirst* by Robert McCammon, *Some of Your Blood* by Theodore Sturgeon, *Progeny of the Adder* by Leslie Whitten, *The Light at the End* by John Skipp and Craig Spector, *Midnight Mass* by F. Paul Wilson, *Live Girls* by Ray Garton, *I Am Legend* by Richard Matheson, and *The Passage* by Justin Cronin. He also likes *The Historian* by Elizabeth Kostova and *Fevre Dream* by George R. R. Martin, and has a soft spot for Poppy Z Brite's *Lost Souls*. He also considers *30 Days of Night* by Steve Niles to be the ultimate in vampire comics. His favorite vampire movies are similar - *Let the Right One In, Martin, Let's Scare Jessica to Death, Nosferatu* (both the 1922 silent and the 1978 remake), and *Near Dark*. He also has a soft spot for the Hammer *Dracula* films with Christopher Lee.

Those vampires definitely *don't* sparkle.

When Sammy Valentine popped the lock on the door to the large RV at the end of the street he was working he wasn't even thinking of getting caught. He had been working the Rose Parade and the New Year's Eve parties along Colorado Boulevard for the past seven years. He had never been caught. There was no reason to think about getting caught now.

The minute the door was open he was in. He closed the door softly behind him, then moved down the cabin toward the kitchen galley. He could tell an RV motor-home was vacant by two ways: for one, no interior lights would be on within the living area, and two, when his rappings on the door brought no signs of life. He had the perfect explanation for the few times people actually answered his knocks: *oops, I'm real sorry sir/ma'am. I've been celebrating a little too much and I got the wrong RV. Sorry.* Then he would move across the street and down the block a ways to make the next hit. It worked every time.

This particular RV was one of those huge monster trailers. Sammy always wondered how people could drive the damn things. They were like houses on wheels. The curtains were drawn in this particular trailer, providing little light, but Sammy had a penlight that he flicked on deftly. He cast its narrow beam quickly through the kitchen galley, moving it over mounds of clothes stacked on chairs. He moved toward the clothes and quickly riffled through them. No wallets or purses here. The back sleeping chambers were the next likely target.

He was just heading down to the sleeping chambers when the door to the RV suddenly opened. Sammy spun around, his heart leaping in his chest at the sudden fright. Dim light from the New Year's Eve night beyond stabbed into the RV, illuminating the man that had just come in. He looked in surprise toward the rear of the RV where Sammy was standing. "Who the hell are you?" the guy asked.

Sammy held up his hands in surrender. "Oh wow, man," he said, feigning drunkenness. "Shit, I must have the wrong trailer. I'm sorry... I'm *so* fucked up..." He made to stumble past the man, cringing slightly as he approached him. This had never happened before, and he thought that quickly reverting to the ruse he used when casing RV's would work. Not so this time.

The guy grabbed him by the lapels of his denim jacket the minute he tried to squeeze by. "Not so fast, guy." He leered at him. "You ain't going nowhere."

Sammy reacted instinctively, going out of his fake drunken mode to fight-or-flight. He tried to pull out of the guy's grasp but the guy held on tight. He tried shoving the guy into a closet set along the far wall of the RV, but the guy held fast. The guy grabbed him roughly in a bear hug, pinning his arms to his side, and Sammy thrashed wildly. Christ, but this guy was strong for such a skinny runt. Sammy yelled at the top of his lungs: "*Let me go you little—*"

The guy threw Sammy, sending him sprawling into the opposite wall where he crashed hard, rocking the RV. The blow knocked the breath out of him, and as he sank to the floor, trying to gain his equilibrium, the guy loomed before him with a mad grin on his face. He reached down for Sammy, locking strong fingers around his throat. Sammy tried to fight him off but it was no use. He was out like a light in seconds.

He had no idea how long he was out, but when woke up he saw that the RV's owner had been joined by five others. They were all standing around him in a rough semi-circle, staring down at him as he lay on a bunk that also served as a sofa.

Sammy tried to collect his senses. He must have been placed on the bunk when he was unconscious. It was still dark, and judging from the noise that emanated faintly from outside, the New Year's Eve bacchanal was still in full swing on Colorado Boulevard. Was it the New Year yet? He had started working around ten p.m., and had only been at it for an hour or so when he was caught. Surely he couldn't have been out for that long.

As if reading his mind, one of the new people that had shown up to peer down at Sammy answered his question. "It's almost two a.m. Now maybe you can tell us something." He leaned forward. It was an older man, probably in his mid-fifties, grizzled and bearded, long gray hair tied back in a pony-tail hanging down his back. He spoke in a smooth voice, like an FM disc jockey. He was dressed in biker leathers and boots. "Who the hell are you?"

Sammy swallowed, and decided to try his first ruse. "Look, man, I didn't know this was your RV. I-I-I was partying a little too heavy out there, and I was trying to find my trailer and yours looks a *hell* of a lot like mine and—"

The woman standing next to him raised her foot and nudged him with it. She leaned forward, her piercing eyes hooking his. "Try to come up with something better than that. Gus told us everything."

Sammy looked at her, taking her image in; she appeared to be roughly the same age as the man, standing about five foot two, her voluptuous figure clad in a black leather jacket. She was dressed in tight blue jeans and a T-shirt with a Harley Davidson logo on the front. Her hair was wavy, blonde, and cut to the shoulders. Was this the older guy's wife? "Listen, man, I'm telling ya the truth."

"Why did you go through our stuff then?" This came from one of two other men, both of whom appeared to be in their mid-thirties. The guy that asked him this was tall, bearded, with light brown hair and gray eyes, wearing a black leather jacket, blue jeans and a chambray shirt. The second was clean shaven with long black hair that fell to his waist with a hoop earring dangling from his left ear.

How the hell did they know I went through their stuff? Sammy thought.

A NEW LIFE

As if in answer to this silent question, the last of the five newcomers answered him.

"We could tell you went through our stuff because it's placed differently than it was when we left it." Sammy turned to this fifth person, a young woman who appeared to be in her early twenties. Tall, her body clothed in what resembled a blood red evening gown that clung to every curve of her body like a second skin, she had a fair complexion, long black hair, full red lips, and wide dark eyes that held him entranced. There was something about her that seemed familiar. Had he seen her before? Perhaps he was entranced with her because she was the most beautiful woman Sammy had ever seen.

They stared at each other for a moment, Sammy and the woman, the others staring back at Sammy. The older man broke the spell by nodding at Gus, the guy who had caught him. "We're done. Let's head out."

Gus nodded and headed toward the cab of the RV. He started the engine.

It took all of his effort to sit up, but Sammy did it. He tried to ignore the five crowding around him, especially the young woman. "Listen, everything's cool, I didn't take anything, okay? I'm just gonna walk out of here right now and let you guys go on your merry way."

"You're staying right here." The command was barked by the older man, who held him with his fiery gaze.

Despite trying to hold his ground, Sammy was scared to death inside. He felt a chill race through his body. "Come on, man, it's cool."

The older man turned to the two younger men. "Take him down."

The two younger men were on Sammy in a flash, pinning him down to the bunk. One of them produced a coil of rope, and within minutes they had trussed him up tight. Sammy's arms were pinned to his sides, held fast by the coarse rope. Likewise, his legs and feet were tied together, rendering escape impossible.

The RV pulled away from the curb and began cruising slowly down the residential street, heading north toward the 210 freeway.

Sammy tried to remain calm but it was hard to do with his heart beating so fast. He watched them as they took seats on the make-shift sofa/bunk opposite him, and along the chairs in the dining area. Their eyes were on him as Gus piloted the large RV down the residential street, braking slowly as he came to the intersection.

They were silent for a moment as Gus made a right turn down Walnut Street and then waited at the intersection of Walnut and Allen to make a left, which would take them to the 210 freeway. Sammy's mind was spinning, trying to think of something to say that would help him get out of here. He didn't want to piss them off, but he also wanted to get the hell away from them as soon as possible. He had first taken them to be another mid-western family that had driven out to view the parade like the hundreds of other tourists that descended to Pasadena, California every New Year's to camp out along the parade route to view the spectacle. It was those people—and the thousands that drove out to camp out along the sidewalk on Colorado Boulevard in their sleeping bags—that Sammy preyed on every year. New Year's Eve along Colorado Boulevard was like a mini Mardi-Gras, with drunken revelers doing their best to ring in the New Year. As a result, people let their guard down more, and for Sammy it was a thief's paradise. Long an expert pick-pocket and sneak thief, Sammy had perfected the job. He could be in and out of an RV in under thirty seconds, and he could rifle through an unattended sleeping bag and make off with whatever cash was in a discarded purse or wallet in half that time. He had never been caught, and the financial returns on returning to Pasadena year after year were greater than the few risks involved. He could average fifteen hundred bucks over New Year's Eve and New Year's Day alone, and he could always count on every other year of hitting somebody unwise enough to guard their jewelry or cash more stringently. The most he had ever made was a cool five grand.

This was certainly the first time that a would-be victim had turned the tables on him. He thought about this as Gus made a left on Allen and headed north toward the 210 freeway. He swung the huge vehicle up the east-bound on-ramp. Why would these guys risk being charged in felony kidnapping over being pissed off about a guy committing misdemeanor breaking and entering?

And what in the hell were these people doing *leaving* six hours before the start of the celebrated Rose Parade?

The answer was that there was more to this bunch than the typical mid-western tourist family. At least that's the impression Sammy was now getting. The impression grew stronger as he regarded his captors from his spot on the bunk. They were appraising him with a penetrating gaze that Sammy found uncomfortable. The worst of it was the young woman's. Sammy found it hard to resist gazing back at her.

Their silence was broken when the ringleader—Sammy assumed he was the ringleader because he was the oldest male of the group—suddenly burst out laughing.

The rest joined in. They laughed hard, as if sharing some secret joke among themselves. Even Gus laughed from the cab of the RV as he drove. Sammy looked around at them, the tension easing somewhat but not nearly enough for comfort. They weren't making any attempt at assaulting him further; they were just sitting in their respective seats laughing their asses off at him.

Sammy smiled and tried to laugh with them. This made some of them—the two young guys in particular—laugh harder.

The old man stopped laughing, shaking his head. He looked at the older woman and chuckled. "Who would have thought that out of all the years we've been coming out here to work the parade route we'd be preyed upon ourselves by a common criminal."

They laughed harder at this and then suddenly Sammy understood. They weren't typical tourists out to watch the parade. They were crooks like him who had come out to work the parade. The question was, what kind of racket were they working?

Sammy mustered a smile. "So you're not tourists then, right? So what kind of work do you do along the parade route?"

There were still some chuckles floating around the cabin. The long-haired guy shook his head and leaned back in his seat, looking out the window as they rode down the freeway. The old man and his lady leaned back, the woman taking out a nail file and working her nails. Sammy felt better as he saw the others relaxing. They weren't planning on hurting him. If that was the case, what the hell were they doing kidnapping him?

"You could say that we converge upon the parade route every year like yourself to prey on the tourist population," the older man said. His voice was deep and compelling. Sammy now pegged the ages of the older couple in their late forties or early fifties. The woman chuckled at that, and the man smiled and looked back toward Sammy. "Why don't I back up a bit. My name is Frank. This is Melissa," he indicated the woman beside him, who Sammy assumed was either the man's wife or Significant Other. He introduced the long-haired guy as Jason, and the quiet bearded guy as Robert. The young woman was Olivia.

Sammy nodded at each one as they were introduced and kept his gaze on Olivia longer than he should have. She smiled at him and Sammy felt a stirring in him, a sense of yearning. That familiar feeling was now easily explainable. He had obviously seen her before on previous New Year's Eves while working the parade. They had probably passed each other countless times on the crowded streets of Colorado Boulevard while each one worked through the long evening.

"And your name is?" Frank asked, looking at him questionably.

"Sam," he said, grinning. "But you can call me Sammy."

"Sammy it is then." Frank leaned back in his seat and regarded him with those steely cold eyes. Appraising him. "You didn't really stumble in here by accident, did you Sammy?"

They already knew the answer to that. Especially when he had basically confessed to it by asking what line they were in. His best bet was to lay all his cards on the table. He nodded. "No, I didn't."

Frank nodded, then glanced at Melissa, who was regarding him the way a mother would if she had caught her son doing something he shouldn't have been doing. Jason and Robert were relaxing, caught up in the ride, paying scant attention, but Olivia was closely watching the exchange. She gave an encouraging smile to Sammy.

"The question is, what do we do with you?" Frank asked. He seemed to be thinking out loud, tossing the question out for his posse to digest. "We could very well let him go."

"Let him go?" This came from Robert, who swung his gaze to the center of action. "We've never let anybody go before."

"True, but Sammy's a special case." Frank leaned his grizzled form forward, leaning his elbows on his knees, peering at Sammy. He was looking directly at him. "How long have you been doing this Sammy?"

Sammy swallowed a dry lump. What Robert had said—*we've never let anybody go before*—was hanging in his mind. "Seven years."

"And how old are you?"

"Twenty-four."

Frank nodded. "You ever been busted for this? Don't lie to me, because I'll know."

"No, I haven't." Frank didn't have to tell him that he would spot the lie. Sammy seemed to get the sense that Frank would. "I usually knock on the RV doors to make sure nobody's around, then I break in. If somebody answers the knock, I usually pretend I'm drunk and that I got the wrong RV. Works every time."

"Pretending you're drunk," Frank mused. "How many times has that happened?"

Sammy shrugged. "It happens at least once a year."

"But you've never been caught red handed in somebody's RV before, is that right?"

"Right."

"That's not bad." Frank rubbed his grizzled chin. "You been busted for other things?"

"I spent time in reform school when I was thirteen for shoplifting," Sammy said. "Other than that, no. I've never been busted."

"You do residential breaking and enterings primarily?"

"Yeah," Sammy nodded.

"And fencing?"

Sammy nodded.

"Anything else?"

"Credit card fraud. Identification theft. Some computer hacking."

Frank seemed to think about all this. Sammy's heart was racing in anticipation. What the hell were these people in to?

"Why do you do this? Surely you could support yourself through legal means. You said you've done some computer hacking; surely you could get a legitimate job in the computer industry. Why prey on people?"

"I suppose I could ask you the same question?" Sammy said.

"*I'm* the one asking the questions." Frank regarded him menacingly.

Sammy licked his lips, his eyes moving from Frank to Melissa, to Robert and Jason, then to Olivia, who smiled at him. Christ, but she was beautiful.

"People haven't been much use to me if you want to know the truth," Sammy said. "I never knew my dad, and my mom left me with my grandmother to raise me when I was six. My grandmother and her husband used to beat me up. They were real shitty people. When I was twelve my grandmother told me that I would have to fend for myself by buying my own food and clothing, so that's why I resorted to stealing. They were so abusive, though, that I ended up running away from them five times. And in all the times I been in and out of different foster homes and detention centers, the more I saw how fucked up the system was and how people were so fucked up. At first I needed to survive, so I stole things. I shoplifted, I learned to pick pockets, snatch purses. Yeah, I had to survive, but when I got to be pretty self-sufficient and knew I could make it by getting a real job, I decided I didn't want that. People out there, society," he nodded outside toward the city as they drove down the 210 heading toward Interstate 10. "They never gave me a chance, never so much as gave a shit about me. Fuck them. I'm stealing from them what they stole from me."

A NEW LIFE

They were silent for a moment, Frank appraising him, stroking his chin with long fingers. Sammy returned his gaze defiantly. Frank glanced at Melissa and the other two men, and the four of them seemed to share some hidden communication. Even Olivia nodded along, as if tuning into the subliminal conversation. Frank turned to him. "What you just said sounds pretty convincing and harsh. Have you ever had any second thoughts, any regrets?"

"Regrets?" Sammy spit the word out like it was a bad taste in his mouth. "The only thing I regret right now is being caught by you guys."

Frank smiled. The others laughed. For a moment Sammy was afraid that he had said the wrong thing; it had been on his mind and he had let it slip out before he could stop it. But now he relaxed as the laughter warmed him, making him feel better. He had a better feeling about these people now. They were renegades, outlaws like him, that much. But he was still unsure of their game.

"And I'll be honest with you now, Sammy," Frank said. "Normally, we would have killed you on the spot. But there's something about you that we feel that tells us you're different. Am I correct in that, Sammy?"

Sammy nodded. "You bet."

Frank watched him, the smile playing at the tips of his mouth. "We're a nice, tight unit here, Sammy. We've been doing this for a long time now. More years than I'd care to imagine. And we're good at what we do. We're the best. You seem like the best at what you do as well. I'd like to give you the chance to join up with us. To be with us."

Sammy was stunned. Frank was asking him to join them? To do what?

As if to answer his question, Frank responded. "Gus has been our good and faithful servant to us for many years. He's one-of-a-kind. We've had a lot of men and women in his place, but they never were ready to take that next step. They were simply content to live with us, work in keeping us safe and moving along. Gus is ready for the next step. To become like we are. In order for us to help Gus, we need another one like him. A man who is strong, who is witty, who knows that he is superior to the rest of mankind. We need a man with a brilliant mind, one who can get out of any jam, one who can manipulate the system. I see that in you, Sammy. You're that man. Am I right?"

Sammy nodded. "Yeah, you're right." Everything Frank said about him was true. He had beat the system time and time again. In fact, other than his juvenile record, society had no knowledge of him.

"I realize that when I say that we need another servant, that the term itself may not seem attractive," Frank continued. "Think of it as a man who makes sure things get done. A man who makes sure things look legitimate and legal, that makes sure that all things appear normal to the mindless human herd. You with me?"

Sammy was nodding. "Yeah." He was beginning to get an idea on what they were into now. The five of them were scam artists. Gus merely acted as a gofer, a chauffeur, a personal assistant who worked the day-to-day trivialities.

"You're probably thinking, 'what's in it for me?'", Frank continued. "That is easy to answer. All of your needs will be taken care of. Food, shelter, money, whatever you want, it's yours. All that we ask for in return is your devotion to us in moving us along, helping us create safe passage as we move from city to city. You give up whatever life you had in the outside world and live for us. Of course, you won't be a prisoner. You'll still be able to enjoy the same things you had before, and you'll hardly be chained to us. But we do insist on a strong loyalty to us. In return, we will protect you. We will make sure no physical harm ever comes to you. All of your needs will be taken care of." He locked those steely gray eyes on Sammy's. "You get me?"

Sammy nodded. "Yeah." This was actually sounding pretty good.

"Of course, one of the most important things to consider is you will get to live." Frank said this with a rather sarcastic tone, the inflection in his voice suggesting that it wasn't beyond their means to snuff him out of. This brought the feeling of dread back to Sammy's gut again, but it dwindled a moment later when Frank nodded toward Olivia, who rose

A NEW LIFE

from her seat and moved across to join Sammy. "And then again, you will also have the pleasure of knowing our company." He smiled.

Olivia began undoing his bonds. She was smiling at him, and Sammy was suddenly thrust into her sensuality, into her very being. He tried to smile at her and was immediately drawn to her. He could barely hear Frank as he said, "For now, why don't you relax. Let Olivia entertain you." He thought he heard laughter after that. If there was, he wasn't aware of it. All he was aware of was Olivia.

Everything was like a dream then. Olivia untied him and led him toward the rear of the RV to a bedchamber. She drew the curtains, closing them off from the rest of the vehicle and gently pushed him onto the large king size mattress that rested there. Sammy fell into the depths of her eyes, her touch, her caress, as she joined him in bed.

She was everything he had hoped she'd be.

When he woke up the first thing he noticed was that the RV had stopped. For a moment Sammy almost didn't know where he was, but then he turned and saw Olivia lying beside him, her creamy skin flush, her black hair spread out behind her head like a fan. Sammy's body felt weak with fatigue. He looked down at his nude body, trying to remember the events of last night. It had all become blurry when Olivia seduced him, but the pleasure of being with her last night was a distant memory. He smiled. Frank's invitation loomed in his mind. If one of the benefits of joining up with this clan was more of what transpired with Olivia, then he'd be a fool to pass it up. Last night was simply too wonderful!

Olivia stirred and opened her eyes. She smiled as she rose. "How you feeling?" she asked.

"Great," Sammy said, yawning. Actually he felt like shit, like he had just jogged five miles, but he wasn't going to tell her that. What mattered was last night and how great that had been.

A rapping on the wall outside the bedchamber snapped his attention away from Olivia. Frank's voice issued from behind the curtain. "Rise and shine, guys. The Vegas Strip beckons!"

"We're in Las Vegas?" Sammy asked bewilderedly as he grabbed his jeans and pulled them up his legs. Olivia covered her gorgeous body with a towel and exited the sleeping chamber, heading toward the bathroom in the middle of the RV. Sammy poked his head out of the bedchamber and down the RV where the others were exiting their sleeping chambers. Melissa was already dressed and ready to go, looking like she had last night. Ditto for Jason and Robert. Frank himself was ready to go as well.

"If you're hungry there are a ton of restaurants along the strip," Frank told him. "Have yourself a bite to eat. We'll be back in a few hours."

Sammy nodded, still trying to move past the murkiness of his mind. Olivia exited the bathroom looking as radiant as she had last night. How did she get ready so fast? Sammy smiled at her as she exited the RV with the others and she returned it.

And then he was alone.

It took him awhile to get dressed and look halfway presentable. He exited the RV and closed the door behind him, automatically reaching for his pockets and stopping the door before it latched with his other hand. His hand touched a key and he brought it out, looking at it. It wasn't his own; Frank must have slipped it into his pockets last night. But how could he have when he had been—

He didn't want to think about it. He fit the key in the lock of the RV and it slid through effortlessly. He locked the door and pocketed the key, his mind a whirling chain of thoughts. Leaving him with the key to the RV was an incredible effort in building trust in him. Was this a test?

He looked up at the sky. The grayness that he at first assumed were clouds was now giving way to darkness. Sammy glanced at his watch and with a rising sense of alarm saw that it was now five-thirty p.m.—the following day! Christ, had he really slept that long?

The rumbling in his stomach snapped him to attention. First things first. Get some food in his stomach. Then a walk was in order to clear his head.

After having a hearty meal at a steak house, he took a walk along the

A NEW LIFE

strip, not paying attention to the people as they wove their way around him. The Vegas evening was cool, and he hunched his shoulders against the cold. He tried to think about the events of last night and for the life of him couldn't come up with a plausible explanation. Maybe they had stopped somewhere last night so Gus could sleep, and then they had continued on until they reached Las Vegas. But Olivia was still asleep beside him when he woke up. Surely she couldn't have slept for that long?

Sammy reached the RV and let himself back in.

The first thing he did was go into the bathroom. He washed his face and then looked at his reflection in the mirror. He noted his pallor, his sunken eyes. He looked at himself closely, paying close attention to his mirror image for the first time in years. And then when he found what he was looking for he looked at himself in the mirror some more, then let himself out into the main living quarters of the RV.

He sat down on one of the front bunks and thought long and hard. He was still thinking about things when they returned, talking and laughing as if they didn't have a care in the world.

Sammy looked up at them as they entered and noticed Gus seemed a little different; he was more loose and relaxed. Melissa had her arm around him, and his was around her waist as they entered the RV. Frank cast him a baleful glance as they piled in the RV. Only Olivia made any lasting eye contact with him as they gathered around, taking seats in the RV. They all looked flush and healthy. Sammy took a deep breath, psyching himself up to ask them what had been turning over in his mind.

"I just have a few questions for you before I make my decision," Sammy said, the sound of his voice getting their attention.

"Of course," Frank said, speaking slowly. "Go ahead."

Sammy nodded and swallowed a lump in his throat. "You said that the other...servants, you called them...didn't want to go to the higher level, yet they remained faithful, lifelong servants. How long did they stay with you?"

Frank and Melissa glanced at each other. Robert and Jason grinned and Olivia merely looked at him. Sammy tried his best to resist her gaze, but it was hard. Finally Frank answered him. He frowned, as if trying to remember. "Well, Gus has been with us for, how long now?" He looked at Gus. "Fifteen years?" Gus nodded. Frank turned back to Sammy. "And before Gus there was Carlos Espinoza, a nice gentleman that was our friend and servant for about forty years. Before him it was a couple, Marion and Lemuel Jones. They were with us for thirty-seven years."

"You forgot Mike Johnson," Melissa said, rubbing Frank's neck. "That bootlegger we ran into in Alabama just after the Great War."

"Oh yes," Frank said, grinning over at Sammy. "I almost forgot about him. Fellow used to be a sharecropper. I seem to remember that we saved him from a Klan lynching."

Sammy nodded. He looked at them all, wondering how they all came to be in their state, but then figured he would find out soon enough. He looked over at Olivia, who smiled at him, and he knew right then that as long as he stayed with them Olivia would keep him company for as long as he decided to remain with them in this physical state.

"You said you had more than one question," Frank said. "What's the second question?"

Sammy grinned. "Provided I serve you well, and I mean to do so, how long do I have to wait before I take the next step?"

There was silence for a moment. Jason chuckled and Melissa smiled. Olivia's smile was wide and triumphant. Frank laughed and the tenseness lifted. Frank reached across and clapped Sammy on the back. "As long as it takes to find another unique human like yourself, Sammy. As long as it takes."

As Sammy took the wheel of the RV to take them out into the desert, Melissa took Gus to the rear of the RV to take him to the next step. The night was endless and black, the highway unwinding before them like a long snake, and as he piloted them along to the next town Olivia joined Sammy in the cabin of the RV and told him what it was like to live through the sinking of the Titanic.

WHAT ONCE WAS FLESH

Tim Waggoner

Tim Waggoner's novels include the *Nekropolis* series of urban fantasies and the *Ghost Trackers* series written in collaboration with Jason Hawes and Grant Wilson of the Ghost Hunters television show. In total, he's published close to thirty novels and two short story collections, and his articles on writing have appeared in *Writer's Digest* and *Writers' Journal*, among others. He teaches creative writing at Sinclair Community College and in Seton Hill University's Master of Fine Arts in Writing Popular Fiction program. Visit him on the web at www.timwaggoner.com.

His favorite type of vampire is the relentless, feral-at-the-core blood beast that, regardless of outer appearance, is the true embodiement of all-consuming darkness and evil: Christopher Lee's *Dracula*, Jerry Dandrige in the original *Fright Night*, Marvel Comics' *Dracula*, Stephen King's Barlow in *'Salem's Lot* and the corrupt inhuman thing in his story "Night Flier," the Master in Skipp and Spector's *Light at the End*, Prince Vulkan in Robert McCammon's *They Thirst*, the monstrously gluttonous creature in Kim Newman's *Anno Dracula*, among others. Soulless, merciless, remorseless and insatiable ... that's what makes a truly great vampire.

"You got some blood on the corner of your mouth," Al said.

An unnaturally long black tongue slithered out of Dylan's mouth to lap away the excess gore. He smacked his lips when he was finished.

"You gotta watch little details like that. That's the sort of thing that'll give you away."

"You telling me someone will see a smear of red on my mouth and think, 'Holy shit! That guy's a vampire!'" Dylan smirked. "I doubt it."

"Human senses may be duller than ours, but they can recognize a predator when they spot one – at least on a subconscious level. People start getting suspicious of you, they'll call the cops. That happens, and you'll have to find new a hunting ground. As it is, we can only stay in the same area a few months. A year tops, if we're careful. Why make life harder on yourself if you don't have to?"

"Yeah, I guess so," Dylan said grudgingly.

The two men sat in the front seat of a red-and-white van with the words *Community EMS* painted on the side. There was nothing to identity *what* community, which was exactly the way Al wanted it. In a town of any decent size, people – even police – didn't look twice at emergency medical vehicles. Not only was it a great cover, it was a damned good lure, too. The blue uniforms Al and Dylan wore put people immediately at ease, and it wasn't uncommon for someone to approach them with some sort of medical emergency and ask for their help. Talk about having your food delivered! And if a cop ever did pull them over, they had a plausible reason for why someone was strapped down to a gurney in the back. *Just transporting a patient, officer. Acute anemia. Real serious.*

Al had parked the van outside a UtiliMart, two rows away from a fluorescent lamppost. He wanted their vehicle to be visible, but not *too* visible. He'd been running the EMS scam for four years now, moving from town to town as necessary, and if there was one thing he'd learned, it was that, as in real estate, success was spelled location, location, location. And an extra-large helping of patience didn't hurt, either – especially when it came to breaking in a new partner.

WHAT ONCE WAS FLESH

Dylan was in his late twenties, stocky, with a shaved head, stubbly beard, expanders in his ears, and tattoos over much of his body. He looked like a tough customer, but when it came to vampirism, he was about as green as they came. He'd been turned less than a month ago, not by Al, but by some bitch working the prostitute angle, a scam as old as the Pleistocene. She hadn't stayed with Dylan. Why would she? Most humans didn't turn after they'd been drained, and most vampires had a "feed or die" mentality when it came to any progeny they might unwittingly create. Al had found Dylan working a rest stop in Kentucky, doing his best to subsist on the occasional sips of blood he managed to steal from truckers. He'd been half-starved and half-crazed when Al took him in, and they'd been traveling together ever since while Al showed him the ropes.

The first thing Al had taught the dumbass: It's not just blood they fed on, but blood *and* death. For blood to be truly nourishing, their prey had to die. Not right away, but eventually. There was something about having your teeth buried in the flesh of your prey as they died – being so intimately connected as the life fled their body – that charged the blood in your belly and turned it into fiery liquid more potent than rocket fuel. If your victim didn't die, you might as well be drinking water.

Speaking of victims, they'd had good hunting tonight. They'd picked up a jogger in a suburban neighborhood soon after sunset, and they'd each drank from her, although Al had let Dylan finish her off. He was still hungry, but he didn't feel deprived. He was saving his appetite. The jogger's corpse was in the back, strapped to the gurney, covered by a sheet. When he could, Al liked to wait a bit before disposing of his empties, just in case they turned. But it had been a couple hours since the jogger had died, and she hadn't so much as twitched in all that time. He decided to give it a little longer.

He settled back against his seat and watched the shoppers outside come and go from their cars, much as a lion watches animals move across the Savanna. Not necessarily hungry, but still alert for an opportunity too good to pass up. Al looked to be in his sixties, although he was far older.

His skin was sallow, almost jaundiced, and he was thin to the point of being gaunt. He wore his brown hair short, and although he'd sported many hairstyles over the centuries, he liked his current haircut best. It didn't get in the way, and it didn't give prey anything to grab hold of. His eyes were brown, too, although when the hunger was upon him, they appeared jet black. Like now.

Dylan lit a cigarette and took a long drag. He cracked the passenger window and blew the smoke out. Regardless of their habits in life, most vampires didn't smoke. Their heightened senses rendered all forms of tobacco noxious to them. But Dylan was still a child in darkness, his senses nowhere near as sharp as they could be.

"I got a question for you, Al."

"Yeah?"

"A lot of times you talk about us like an announcer in a nature documentary. To hear you tell it, we're apex predators, the very tip-top of the food chain. But we're more than that, aren't we?"

Al frowned. "I'm not sure what you mean."

"Well, we're ... you know. *Evil*, right?" He grinned, displaying elongated incisors. He hadn't yet learned how to conceal his fangs without concentrated effort.

Up to this point, Al had kept his gaze fixed on the people passing by. Now he turned his head to look at Dylan. "What exactly do you mean by evil?"

His smile widened too far, and tiny fissures opened at the corners of his mouth. Clear fluid beaded forth from the wounds, but Dylan seemed unaware of them. Vampires were so strong they could easily injure themselves, but since they were so resistant to pain, they often didn't realize it. *Good thing we heal so fast*, Al thought. And as if the thought gave birth to reality, the fissures in Dylan's mouth closed, though the beads of liquid remained.

"Evil," Dylan repeated. "Princes of Darkness, Lords of the Night, that kind of thing."

WHAT ONCE WAS FLESH

Al's smile was smaller and more controlled than Dylan's. "So melodramatic. Did you read too many comics as a child? Yes, we are creatures of evil, for lack of a better word. It's why we shun daylight, avert our gazes from holy objects of all sorts, and why our flesh burns if it comes in contact with them. And of course, it's why we must feed as we do. But all of these qualities are symptoms of our true condition. We have no souls."

From the bemused look on Dylan's face, Al knew he wasn't following.

"Human beings are born with souls. It's what sets them apart from all other creatures on Earth. When a human becomes a vampire, the physical body reanimates, but the soul is no longer present. This is why our kind can kill without hesitation or remorse. No soul, no conscience. It's a very useful adaptation. You can't be an effective predator if you're burdened by a conscience."

Dylan took another drag on his cigarette and stared out the window for several moments before speaking again.

"So where does it go? The soul, I mean."

Despite his long years of practiced control, Al had to fight to keep from grinning so wide that he ripped his own cheeks wide open. Dylan had finally asked The Question, the one every vampire came to eventually. And he had asked it at precisely the right time.

"Some self-styled experts in the occult believe that a vampire's soul is damned to Hell until its body is destroyed, thereby freeing the spirit to enter Heaven. But this is nothing more than a fairy tale concocted by humans. The truth is far more interesting. Do you really want to know where your soul is now?"

"Yeah."

Al turned and pointed at a man walking past their van. He wore a faded army jacket, old jeans, and running shoes on the verge of falling apart. His head was shaved, his body tattooed, and the holes in his earlobes were held open by large metal rings.

"It's right there."

"This is so freaky!" Dylan said.

The two vampires stood in an aisle in Utilimart's electronics department. The other Dylan was less than thirty feet away from them, examining a cell phone display with a vacant, almost lost expression on his face, as if he wasn't quite sure what he was doing here.

"Keep your voice down," Al hissed. "As long as you stay close to me, I can use my powers to conceal your presence from him, but he isn't deaf. Once you attract his attention, I won't be able to hide you again."

Dylan whispered this time. "You say that's my soul, but he looks solid enough. Is he some kind of ghost? If I walked over and tried to poke him, would my finger pass through his body?"

"He would feel like flesh and bone to you, but I wouldn't advise getting that close. He might not look dangerous, but he's the closest thing to a natural predator that our kind has. Or should I say, that *you* have."

"I don't get it."

The other Dylan turned away from the cell phones and headed to the aisle where the DVD's were kept. Al and the real Dylan followed at a discrete distance. The other Dylan paused before the comedies as if he might browse them, but he just stared at the titles with the same blank expression on his face.

"If you think of vampirism as a spiritual disease, then beings like him are antibodies," Al said. "When a new vampire is created, the mortal soul is cast out of its body and remains earthbound. Eventually, the soul – the Animus – is compelled to seek out the corrupt creature that stole its body and attempt to destroy it. It never tires, and it will not stop until its mission is complete ... or until it is neutralized."

"What's the big deal?" Dylan said. "He doesn't look so tough. I'll just walk over and tear his head off, and we'll call it a night." He took a step toward his other self, but Al grabbed hold of his arm and stopped him.

WHAT ONCE WAS FLESH

"Don't be fooled by his appearance. He's just as strong and resistant to damage as we are – and he has none of our weaknesses."

Dylan looked skeptical. "If you say so. But even if it's true, so what? There are two of us and one of him. All we have to do is tag team him."

"It's not that simple. Killing one's own soul is the final act of evil that completes our transformation. Once you do it, you'll be truly immortal. Otherwise, even though you are a vampire, you will age and die just as any mortal. But *you* have to do it. Your Animus can only perish at your hands. No one else's."

The other Dylan moved on from comedies and was now standing in the children's section. Al and the real Dylan could still see him, so they stayed where they were.

"Did you kill your soul?" Dylan asked.

"Yes. And it was the toughest battle I've ever been in. I'd rather face a dozen of our kind in combat than a single Animus."

Dylan continued looking at his other self for a few moments, and when next he spoke, he sounded overly nonchalant, as if he were scared and working hard not to show it. "So ... what do I do?"

Before Al could respond, the other Dylan's head snapped up and turned in their direction. His eyes narrowed, as if he were trying to see them but had trouble focusing his vision. Al grabbed hold of Dylan's arm again so they would be in physical contact, the better to extend his glamour over the other vampire.

"Don't move," he breathed.

They stood absolutely motionless in the way that only the dead can do, and after a few moments, Dylan's Animus looked away and wandered off to another section of the store.

Still keeping hold of Dylan's arm, Al led him toward the exit.

"Come on. We have work to do."

"Why didn't you warn me about him before?" Dylan asked. He tossed another shovelful of earth out of the hole he'd been digging, hurling it with such strength that it flew a dozen yards away to join the rest of the soil strewn there. The hole – a small pit by this point, really – was square, four feet deep and six feet across. Dylan stood inside, doing the excavating, while Al remained topside, supervising.

Dylan sounded pissed, and Al supposed he couldn't blame him.

"You're not the first vampire I've mentored. Ever heard the phrase 'Seeing is believing'? Why do you think we've spent so much time hanging out in parking lots the last couple weeks? I've been waiting for your Animus to track you down so I could show it to you – and I wanted to give you more time to grow stronger, so you'd have a better chance of defeating it."

"The least you could do is get in here and help me dig," Dylan said, sounding like a sulky child.

"I told you, I need to keep watch. We don't want your Animus sneaking up on us, and since I'm so much older than you, my senses are stronger. I'll know when it's within half a mile of here."

The two vampires were in a field beneath a clear night sky. A crescent sliver of a moon hung overhead, nestled in an ebony expanse dotted with glittering stars. Nights like tonight, it was good to be undead, Al thought. An abandoned farmhouse and barn sat on the property, two black shapes silhouetted against the horizon. The Community EMS van was parked inside the empty barn, lights off, of course.

Dylan removed a couple more shovelfuls of dirt before speaking again.

"I don't see how this is going to work. You said my Animus is just as tough as we are. How is falling into a pit going to hurt it? And really, do you think it's stupid enough to fall for a trick like this?"

"It's not intelligent, per se. As I said earlier, it's like an antibody. It doesn't think; it just acts and reacts. I stopped cloaking your presence over an hour ago, so your Animus is undoubtedly on your trail and headed

WHAT ONCE WAS FLESH

this way. Once it sees you, it'll make a beeline straight for you, and as long as you're standing on the other side of the pit, it'll tumble right in. Hell, by that point, it'll be so excited that we probably don't even need to cover the pit, but we'll put some trees branches over it and lay some sod on top, just to be sure. When you finish digging the pit, we'll put sharpened stakes in the bottom. They won't kill the Animus. It's not a vampire. But they will hold it in place long enough for you to jump in and sink your fangs into its neck. The only thing that can kill your Animus is the bite from a vampire. But not just any vampire: you."

Dylan flung another shovelful of dirt out of the pit, and then looked up at Al, a skeptical expression on his face.

"Are you sure about this?"

Al smiled. "Have I steered you wrong yet?"

"It's close," Al said.

He stood next to Dylan at the edge of the pit. They'd waited like this for several hours, during which Dylan had run through all of his cigarettes. The stink of tobacco hung heavy in the air, but Al didn't complain. He had been in Dylan's shoes once, and he understood how nervous the younger vampire was. It was a hell of a thing, finding yourself transformed into a bad-ass monster, only to discover that there was something out there just as dangerous as you whose only purpose was to take you out.

"I think I can hear him," Dylan said softly.

Al had been able to hear the Animus approaching for the last ten minutes, its footsteps steady and regular, machine-precise. If he was right, the thing was just about close enough to –

The pace of its footfalls suddenly picked up, shoes pounding the earth, waist-high grass rustling as it raced toward them.

"It's coming," Al said. "Remember what I told you. Once it falls into the pit, strike fast and kill it quick. You won't get a second chance."

Before Dylan could say anything, Al moved several yards back from the pit. This was the younger vampire's battle, and he had to fight it alone.

Dylan instinctively assumed the classic vampire defensive position. He crouched, knees bent, hands outstretched, fingernails lengthening into talons. And although his back was turned, Al knew his canines extended into sabers that hung past his chin, and his jaw unhinged so he could take the biggest bite possible out of his opponent.

Good lad, he thought.

Dylan's Animus made no sound as it came for him. Al had always found their silence to be one of the eeriest things about Animi, but far worse was the expression on their faces when they attacked. They didn't look angry or excited. They weren't filled with rage or possessed by bloodlust. They appeared totally at peace, smiling, arms lifted as if they wanted to embrace their other selves instead of annihilate them. Seeing that expression was the only time Al regretted being a vampire, and even though this wasn't his Animus, he experienced a split second wherein he wished he hadn't vanquished his own soul. What would it be like to feel such peace? To be truly at rest? But he quickly shoved such thoughts aside. They were part of the Animus' attack, a psychic assault designed to make their victims hesitate at the crucial moment. He hoped Dylan would be able to resist it.

Dylan's stance relaxed somewhat as the Animus came toward him, and if it hadn't been for the pit, Al feared the soul creature would've succeeded in claiming him. But true to its nature, the Animus ran straight toward Dylan without paying any attention to its surroundings, and when its foot came down on the branches covering the pit, it fell in face-first. It made no noise as the stakes pierced its flesh, other than letting out a slight outrush of air from its lungs.

"Now!" Al shouted.

Dylan hesitated a split second, and then leaped into the pit. An instant later, Al heard the sound of his saber teeth latching onto the

WHAT ONCE WAS FLESH

Animus. This was followed by loud sucking noises, accompanied by ecstatic moans. Al waited a moment longer, and then strolled to the edge of the pit.

Dylan was hunched over his Animus, his mouth buried deep in his other's self's neck. He'd bitten into its flesh with such savagery that the Animus' head had almost been severed, but what spilled out of the wound wasn't blood. It was a thick golden liquid that looked something like luminescent honey. As Dylan drank, his body spasmed repeatedly, as if he were caught in the throes of an intense orgasm.

"Feels good, doesn't it?" Al said. "If human blood is like wine to us, then the ichor that flows from the veins of an Animus is like a combination of every drug that ever existed. Ambrosia of the gods. There's only one thing as good: when that ambrosia has been filtered through the body of another vampire."

Al jumped into the pit, grabbed hold of his protégé by the shoulders, and sank his own saber teeth into his throat. Dylan couldn't stop draining his Animus. Once the process had begun, it had to be finished. A tidbit of information that Al had failed to pass along to his student. So as Dylan filled his belly, Al in turn filled his. And when it was all over, the Animus was dead, and so was Dylan.

Al, sated, crawled forth from the pit. His limbs were heavy, and he felt so lethargic, he could barely move. He glanced at the sky and saw it was a shade lighter in the east. Dawn was near. He needed to bury Dylan and the Animus before he could rest, though. Good thing the pit doubled as a ready-made grave.

He picked up the shovel and got to it.

He was inside the EMS vehicle—the barn door closed – before the first rays of sunlight pinked the horizon. He was so weary that it took a major effort of will to keep his eyes open as he climbed into the back of the van. He'd intended to lie down on the gurney, but he swore when he saw the body of the jogger was still strapped there. He'd forgotten all about her. He should've tossed her into the grave with Dylan and the Animus. Oh, well. Too late now. He'd take care of it after sundown.

He started to unbuckle the corpse, intending to dump it onto the floor so he could lie down, when it suddenly took in a gasping breath and opened its eyes.

"Where am I?" the woman said. "What happened?"

Al smiled when he saw her fangs.

"Don't worry. Everything's okay. I'll explain later, but right now you have to sleep. All right?"

She looked at him for a moment, but the daylight torpor was already taking hold of her. She nodded once, closed her eyes, relaxed and fell still.

Al let her keep the gurney. The floor would be fine today. As full as he was, he would sleep well, regardless, and tonight, once the two of them had awakened, he would begin training his new protégé, the latest of many he'd had over the long years. He settled onto the floor and closed his eyes.

Life was good.

THE DARKTON CIRCUS MYSTERY

Elizabeth Massie

Elizabeth Massie is a Bram Stoker Award — and Scribe Award — winning author of horror novels, short horror fiction, media tie-ins, and mainstream fiction. More recent works include *Desper Hollow* (horror novel) and *Naked, On the Edge* (collection of horror short fiction.) She is the creator of the Skeeryvilletown slew of cartoon zombies, monsters, and other bizarre misfits. In her spare time she manages Hand to Hand Vision, a Facebook-based fundraising project she founded to help others during these tough economic times. Massie lives in the Shenandoah Valley of Virginia with the talented illustrator/artist Cortney Skinner.

The vampire that left the most lasting and disturbing impression on Beth was Count Orlock from *Nosferatu*. The eyes. The hands. The cold, insatiable hunger.

Peter Darkton's Traveling Circus of Wonders was a sad little spectacle, hardly a circus and not even enough to qualify as a modern mid-list carnival, composed of a 22-year-old Chevy Suburban with large rust spots and a 1975 30-foot travel trailer with bad shocks and a long gouge down its side where Peter had backed it too close to a row of pines in a Kentucky campground. Peter traveled throughout the year, deep South in winter, North in summer, and as far west as Illinois whenever he could afford the gas and the weather held. He was fifty-eight now, well-worn himself with spots and gouges from an occasional fight with locals who came to his exhibit drunk or who just wanted to test their manliness again a stranger who was, more often than not, shorter and less muscular than themselves.

But the traveling circus was a living. A living handed down from Peter's father, who'd inherited it from his own, and so on back into the shadows of the long, forgotten past. And just as they had when his ancestors parked their horse-drawn wagons in weedy-choked pastures or beside muddy river banks, when Peter parked his Suburban and trailer in a campground or in the trees along a graveled country roadside, they came. They came with crumpled dollars and twitching noses, drawn in by the garish paintings on the side of the trailer showing costumed monkeys playing cards, a vanishing pig, chickens dancing in a spotlight, and most curious of all, the big, fire-red letters promoting "The Darkton Circus Mystery! See It to Believe It! Feed It! Prove Your Courage! Then Speak Of It To No One on Pain of Certain Death!"

On this particular September day, Peter had the circus rattling up the western slope of a Virginia mountain, seeking a lonely place where people hungered for an entertainment beyond the everyday, hoping the vehicle's slipping transmission would hold. In his lap was a bag of corn chips, in the drink holder a beer he'd wrapped in tin foil. In the passenger's seat was his daughter, Kelly, all of nineteen, who'd joined him when he'd swung through her hometown of Dillyville in northeastern Tennessee and told him she wanted to ride with him for a month or so.

"This is exciting!" she said, her feet crossed and wriggling, her eyes trained out the windshield. "Mama said I'd never get away from home, said I might as well get used to working at the Hilltop Motel like she does. But look at me! Heading out to see the country with you."

Peter grunted, then glanced at the rearview to make sure the trailer would make it around a particularly sharp mountain curve.

"Where will we stop?" Kelly asked. "Where do you plan on setting up today?"

"I know places when I see them. It just happens."

"Oh, that's fun." She nodded happily, and then picked up some of the fast food trash on the floor at her feet, balled it up, and stuck it into a half-empty bag. She was a tidy one, Peter's daughter. "I'm glad you agreed to let me come along. We can get to know each other like real family. Great, huh? Thanks. Dad!"

"Don't call me Dad."

She frowned, looking a little hurt. "What, then?"

"Just Peter."

"All right. Peter."

"Shush now. I have to pay attention to the road."

"Okay. Will do."

She was so damned agreeable.

As it was, Peter hated the idea of Kelly tagging along. And he hadn't planned on stopping in Dillyville but he knew that Carol, Kelly's mother, still had the hots for him after all this time, and he was in need of a little something warm and wet besides his own spit-slicked hand. Carol had obliged – and she did have a most comfortable bed – then was pissed, as he expected, when he refused to take her out to breakfast the next morning.

But Kelly, who hadn't seen Peter since she was ten, had followed him out of the apartment to the Suburban, asking sweetly to come along, offering to cook and telling him she had nearly $700 she could get out of the bank on their way out of town. So, of course, he couldn't exactly turn her down. And now, not quite a day's travel with her, he'd already spent her down to $587. Gas. Chips. A case of beer. Motor oil. A new-for-him coat and pair of boots from a Salvation Army store in Big Stone Gap. Kelly didn't seem to mind.

In fact, she didn't seem to mind any of Peter's requirements and restrictions.

"When I got the radio on, no talking," he'd ordered when she first climbed into the vehicle with her sleeping bag and pillow. "I want to listen to a game or a preacher or music or weather, you be quiet, you hear me?"

Kelly had nodded.

"And I sleep in the middle seat where it got more room. There's no room in the back-back 'cause of the cookin' gear."

"No motel?"

"Of course not. I ain't made of money,"

"Okay."

"So you get the front seat. You're short and small but you'll fit. Just adjust the steering wheel up as far as it'll go. And don't ever get out in the middle of the night 'cause it'll disturb me. I need my sleep."

"Okay."

He'd started the engine and pulled away from the apartment complex as Carol, on the walkway in her terry robe and dog-chewed slippers, had shaken her middle finger and shouted "Asshole!"

A few miles out of town, he'd said, "There's one part of the circus you are to stay away from, never open up, never even try to get a peek."

Kelly had glanced at him. "What's that?"

Peter continued. "I know you're scared of snakes, Kelly. Always were. I don't know much about you now, but I do know that."

"Yeah."

"The last display in the trailer, the Darkton Circus Mystery, is a snake. A big snake, largest one you'd ever see. Under no circumstances are you to mess with that display. You are never to try to get in there to have a look at it. I don't need you having nightmares or begging me to take you home before I'm ready to go back through Tennessee. You understand?"

She'd nodded solemnly. "Okay."

And so they continued on into the wilds of mountainous southwest Virginia, seeking a venue both isolated and peculiar, talking rarely, Peter trying his best not to fart in the Suburban but unable to alter his habits, and Kelly, when talking was allowed, telling him about her life since he'd missed most of it.

She was a plain girl, thoughtful, and sensitive. She was used to being poor, she told him, used to being ignored, used to working as a companion for an old woman with dementia in the evenings and a maid at the motel during the day, and used to giving most of her money to her Mama to help pay the bills. She knew Peter was disappointed that Kelly had not been a boy, because he'd wanted a son to give the circus to when Peter was too old to travel. She didn't think he'd pass it on to her because she was a girl and that wasn't how the family did things, but said she hoped he'd reconsider.

"I could do good with a circus," she said as they rumbled along a narrow valley between two mountains awash with October red. "You could teach me how it works, how I can be part of it, you think?"

"Huh."

"Maybe?"

"Shush now."

They rode in silence another few miles. Then Kelly said, "Mama doesn't like you much. But I think she just doesn't understand why you are like you are. I kept telling her she must have loved you once, and she that she still should even if you aren't together. And you're my father, so of course *I* love you."

This hit him like a pocketknife to the neck. "Don't say that again."

"Why not?"

"It's just wrong, is all."

So she didn't say that again.

Peter found the spot he'd watched for, a flat, thistle- and vine-covered acre off the road three miles from the nearest town, nestled between a creek and a sheer rise covered in kudzu and granite outcroppings. Peter could stay here until someone came and kicked him off. He figured he'd get at least two good nights' worth of ticket sales.

While Kelly set up the Coleman stove and got a stew cooking, Peter prepared for the evening show.

One side of the travel trailer was covered with the colorful headlines and artwork. This is the side that Peter always parked facing the road, facing traffic. The other side, which Peter always situated facing away from where customers would park their cars and trucks, was divided into sections with 3' x 4' doors that unlatched and folded down, revealing the displays inside each compartment. The first section had two little capuchin monkeys that, on command, dealt a deck of cards on the floor then picked them up and put them down as if in a game. The monkeys were getting up there in age, bought from a pet store in Maryland, and Peter just hoped they could make it through another season. The second section held three chickens that, when Peter turned on his CD player, would scratch on a brightly colored spot on the floor while a little silver, faceted ball spun overhead, mimicking a disco. In the third section, mirrors and lights made it seem as if a pig (a taxidermied pig that had died a number of years ago) disappeared except for his floating snout. All this was ordinary carnival fare.

But the last section of the trailer was different. It did not have a pull-down panel to reveal what was inside the compartment but rather an actual door, a door with a lock opened by one of the keys Peter on a string tied around his neck. The windowless room inside was big enough to hold four to six customers, and two cages, one small, one large, one covered in a towel, the other in a large, blue velvet curtain. In the little cage were stray pets Peter collected along country roads or stole out of farmhouse yards when it was clear the owners were not home. He taped their mouths shut to keep them quiet. It wasn't as if they would starve to death like that; they never lived that long.

In the big cage was the Darkton Circus Mystery, Peter's joy, his terror, and his inheritance. While chickens, monkeys, and pigs died and were replaced or stuffed, this display lived on. It brought Peter respect. It caused others to fear him. The money was minimal but that was because to keep the show to himself he had to maintain a low profile. If he went to a big city with this treasure, it would be broadcast, highlighted, and then swept out from under him like everything else of value was when people with big money caught wind of something they wanted.

Peter hauled the canvas tent out from the rear of the Suburban, unrolled it, and hoisted it up into place against the back side of the trailer where the displays were located. It was hard work but he was used to doing it alone. In fact, he enjoyed the sweat and burn the work created. It reminded him that he wasn't dead yet, in spite of the years that had been piling up. And so when Kelly offered her help, he declined and told her to just stick with the cooking and if she got bored, she could listen to the radio.

When the tent was propped and pegged and roped nearly all around, Kelly peeked around the edge of the trailer to tell him dinner was ready.

She stared at the tent as Peter wiped his hands on his coat.

"Why a tent?"

"People come to see the shows," Peter said. "With the tent, only those who pay can see the displays as I reveal them one at a time."

Kelly nodded, then shivered. "I suppose that snake in the last display scares them mighty bad, doesn't it?"

Peter nodded.

"It must be a mighty big snake. Is it ten feet long? Fifteen?"

"No talking about it, Kelly."

"Twenty feet long?"

"Leave it be."

"The sign says nobody can talk about it once they see it or they'll die. Is that true?"

Peter glared at her. "I said enough. We'll eat now."

"Okay, sorry." As they moved on to dinner, he noted Kelly glancing over her shoulder, fear flickering across her features. He would have to make sure things stayed that way. No way in hell could he let her know the truth.

Kelly agreed to serve as the ticket taker; she was happy to do it. As quiet as she most often was, she knew how to deflect the advances of drunkards and slicks. Her mother had had her share of such boyfriends, all puffed up and oiled down, and Kelly had long ago devised a way to make them shudder and turn away. She would loll her head and slobber a little, and the men would jump back a good three feet and move on.

So there she sat at a little card table outside the tent with a roll of tickets and a metal cash box, smiling at the customers who seemed harmless and letting her head wobble and the spittle drool a bit for those who had ill-intent brewing at the corners of their eyes. And so they all left her alone, giving her their dollars, taking their tickets, and moving out of the night-shadows and into the tent-shadows.

Peter stood by the tent, nodding and smiling at the customers, then at last entered and pulled the flap down, sealing them all within. Kelly sat outside at her table, batting away the gnats and listening as Peter, in a surprisingly strong, commanding voice, explained each of the first three exhibits to the groans and complaints of the customers. Several stormed out, pausing at Kelly's table to demand their money back. But Kelly gave them the cock-headed drool and they turned and went on. The rest stayed, however, charmed by Peter's promise of what was in the last section of the trailer, the big Mystery, even though they'd have to fork over another ten dollars each.

At last, Kelly could hear the trailer door scraping open, the customers stepping into the trailer and causing it to rock on its shocks. The door creaked shut. After a long pause and some more thumping around, she heard the customers wail in fear. Their words were muffled but clearly terrified. Peter said something low, ominous. In another few minutes the customers were pressing out through the tent flap, clutching their hats, glancing around furtively, fearfully. Even those with ruddy complexions looked paler, their eyes pinched and their brows drawn. They stalked away, not speaking to one another, climbed into the various vehicles, and took off into the night.

Then, over the sound of late season crickets and owls in the trees by the river, Kelly thought she heard a low growl within the trailer, a heavy, guttural sound that made the hairs on her arms stand up. And she heard Peter say, "Shut up, you!"

A moment later Peter exited the tent, mopping his brow, pushing a loose strand of hair back form his forehead. He stared at Kelly as if he'd forgotten she was there. Then his lip hitched. "You got the money?" She held up the cash box.

He took it, shook it, then held it like it was a baby. She wondered for the briefest moment if he ever held her as a baby. Probably not.

"That's good," he said. "Now you go on back to the Suburban, go to sleep. I've got business, got to lock up." He pulled a cluster of keys out from his shirt, keys that hung around his neck on a string. "And you got any peein' need to be done, you do it before you get to sleep. As I said, no getting up in the middle of the night."

Kelly nodded, and then before she could stop herself, said, "Those men must be scared of snakes, too. I can't imagine how awful that snake must be."

Peter pointed a finger at Kelly. "Yeah, it's damn awful."

"And loud. I heard it make noise. A growling sound. Like a dog or bear. Gave me goosebumps."

"No more about the snake! Don't never speak of it again, you hear me? Or I'll leave you on the side of the road."

"I'm sorry. I won't."

"All right, then."

"I don't want you angry at me."

"Then don't make me angry."

"Okay."

Peter blew air threw his teeth and glanced at the sky, where clouds were beginning to break apart, revealing a spattering of stars against the dark. Kelly thought for a moment she saw him sigh and soften just a fraction, but then he straightened, huffed, and strode into the tent with the cash box.

He didn't trust her. It made her sad. But there was time. Surely, there was time to get him to care for her, to need her, out here on the road. And that was all she wanted. Someone to need her.

When he was certain she was settled in the Suburban, curled up on the front seat in her sleeping bag, he took care of the final business of the evening. As was sometimes the case, the five customers who'd paid extra to see the Darkton Circus Mystery didn't have enough money to buy food to feed the creature. And so now it was up to Peter to take care of the feeding. He hated it; he preferred keeping the curtain over the cage and not having to look the thing in the eye any more than necessary, but business was business and to make his living with the circus, he had to keep the creature alive.

Peter stepped inside the room at the end of the trailer and pulled the door shut, closing off the night air and the bugs that seemed determined to follow him around. He flicked on the light switch and faced the large, curtain-covered cage. The thing inside the cage began to thump about, and growl.

"Shut up," said Peter.

"Like I'm going to do anything you tell me to do," said the creature. The curtain billowed slightly at his voice. "Now give me some nourishment, you ridiculous old redneck. How long do you think I should have to wait? You're getting slower and slower in your old age. Your father was much more conscientious than you are. Your grandfather, though, another worthless bit of flesh on two feet. Just like you."

Peter's neck flushed as it always did. More than thirty years of hauling this thing around and the insults still stuck in his craw. Still, he had to feed the thing. He couldn't let it die.

THE DARKTON CIRCUS MYSTERY

He took the towel off the top of the small wire cage, pulled up the lid, and removed two puppies. They struggled in his grasp, kicking at the air, their little taped mouths wriggling and twitching. They stared at him with confusion and fear in their tiny brown eyes. That confusion would be over soon.

"Here you go, you old freak." Peter flung back the curtain on the cage and crammed the puppies through the bars. The creature, unable to stop himself, snatched them up from the floor and, one at a time, buried his long, needle-like teeth into their necks and drained their blood. Then he tossed the carcasses back out through the bars. His huge, yellow eyes narrowed. "More."

"No more," said Peter. "You know that. I give you more, you get stronger. You get stronger, you can pull some of that shape-shifting shit and get out of here. I'll give you just enough to keep you breathing, living...well, living's not quite the word now, is it?"

The creature growled and lashed one hand through the bars just as Peter skipped back.

"You know," said the creature. "I can smell that young girl on you. Who is she, a little tart you're fucking?"

Peter blinked then curled his lip. "My daughter." The moment he said it he knew it was a mistake. "Don't ever speak of her again."

"Ah, a daughter. I had a daughter once. Lovely thing. Delicious blood. Drank her dry then threw her carcass out for the vultures."

"No, I mean it. You speak of her again and I'll down your rations even more. Or..." He tipped his head in the direction of the plastic lunchbox nailed to the wall on which the words, "Safety Kit," had been written in white paint, " ... I'll snuff you out as you sleep. I can do that anytime I want, you know. Easy. No sweat."

"But you won't, Peter. You need me. Just like your daddy and your worthless granddaddy needed me. Without me, your show is nothing. Without me, you are nothing."

"Shut your fucking yam hole, freak." Peter jerked the curtain back down over the big cage. Then he tossed the towel over the small cage as the kidnapped pets bumped around inside and whined.

"Damn, what I put up with."

Certain the door and latches were locked and the cash box was stowed in the back of the Suburban, Peter situated himself in the middle seat and pulled his ratty wool blanket up to his chin. He never had a pillow but used a balled up sweatshirt he no longer wore because mice had gotten to it somewhere along the line. It was nearly midnight, and he needed his sleep. What a hell of a day, this traveling with company. He hoped he could survive the interruption, at least until Kelly's money ran low. Then he would let her off – put her out – in some town where she could call her Mama to come get her. He'd give her a few of her dollars back, of course. She was an okay kid, for a kid.

He flopped over, wriggled around to get comfy.

Happily, at least, Kelly didn't snore.

It was still dark, but she had to pee. Bad. She sat up in the front seat, her eyes sticky from sleep and her back hurting from being pressed against seatbelt latches that refused to remain tucked beneath the cushions.

Crossing her legs hard, she wondered if she could force the need away. She counted, one, two, three, four, five, six, seven… but it did no good. She had to go.

Quietly, slowly, she opened the Suburban door. There was a faint, grinding squeal of metal against metal. She grimaced and looked over the seat to find Peter sound asleep with a sweatshirt wound around his head. His chest rose and fell against the blanket, and his mouth hung open as if inviting a spider. She pushed the door again, slowly, then eased out onto the ground. Leaving the door partway open, she tiptoed across the field to the trees where she relieved herself, found a couple dried leaves to finish off, then sneaked back to the vehicle. The dead grasses and weeds crunched beneath her feet. Overhead, bats stitched patterns against the pre-dawn sky.

It was then she heard the moaning. The agonized groaning. From the rear of the travel trailer.

Pathetic.

Agonized.

She stopped and stared at the trailer, at the garish signs on the side, black and white and shades of gray now, their colors washed away in the night.

The sound came again, and then a thumping inside the trailer.

"What is that?" she whispered. The sound of her voice was louder on the air than she'd expected.

There was a moment of silence and then again moaning.

Weeping.

"That's no snake..."

She took another step toward the Suburban, but the sounds from the trailer were heartbreaking. She bit her lip, then hurried to the trailer, around the side, and into the tent where she stopped to listen again.

The crying was louder now but no less pitiful. It came from behind the closed door, the final display.

The gigantic, terrible snake.

But she knew snakes. They didn't cry or moan.

So what was it?

Kelly patted her fist against her teeth. Clearly there was someone in the trailer, someone who, for some reason, had been locked inside without Peter's knowledge. Was it a child? Had any children come to the show? She didn't remember any. The voice was difficult to identify. Maybe it was a teen, or even a man, who was horrified to have been left behind without being noticed, locked inside the trailer with the dreadful snake.

Peter would be so pissed if he realized he'd been so careless. She didn't want him angry. She wanted to make things better for him, not worse. And she couldn't leave the man trapped in the display. Just the thought of that made her stomach clench and her heart pick up a heavy, painful rhythm.

The keys were around Peter's neck. She would make quick business of it, not even have to go inside the trailer but just open the door for a moment to let the man out.

Peter was lying face toward the back of the middle seat, snorting in his sleep, one hand twitching, but luckily the string on which the keys hung was visible at his neck. And the fingernail clippers she kept in her purse did the trick. He never moved, never felt a thing.

Back inside the tent now, standing at the door now, Kelly trembled. The keys clicked against each other like tiny teeth. This had to be quick. This had to be quiet. Then she would tie a knot in the string and drop it onto the Suburban floor where Peter would find it in the morning. She would tell him how he tossed and turned all night, possibly scooting out from under the string in the process.

That was possible, wasn't it?

It was the best she could think of.

The moan was so loud this time it drove her back several feet from the door. Maybe the man was already bitten by the snake? Maybe he was lying there, dying. She hoped not. She knew how to put on a Band-Aid but that was about it. She didn't know how to stop someone from dying.

Go on now, she thought. *Do it. Do it for the man. But most of all, do it for Peter. Do it for your Dad. He needs your help.*

God, I hate snakes!

"One, two, three, four, five, six, seven, eight..."

Key in the lock, lock clicking, door pulling open slowly, as quietly as possible.

The room was very dark, and it had a disgusting smell. Dead things. Piss. Shit. She covered her nose with one hand and squinted, trying to get her eyes adjusted.

"Hello?" she whispered. "Who's in here? Can I help you? The sound of her voice stirred up other sounds, small sounds of whining and scratching.

No, that's no snake. Just do this, Kelly!

She took two steps into the trailer, keeping her free hand on the doorsill.

"Hello?"

Things began to take focus. A small bin or cage against one wall, covered in a lumpy cloth. That's where the whining was coming from. To the right was a huge cage covered in a curtain. The uneven hem of the curtain revealed the bars at the bottom.

And a pair of scuffed black shoes pressed up against the bars.

"Oh, shit," Kelly whispered.

"Help me," said a raspy, desperate voice from within the large cage. "Please, help me."

"I..." began Kelly. Where the hell was the snake? Was it in the cage with the man who was speaking?

I can't look. I can't do this...

"Please, help me!"

Kelly licked her dry lips but they remained dry. "Is...is the snake in there with you?"

"There is no snake," said the voice. "I'm here alone. Locked up. Trapped. Your father did this to me. Please, please let me out!"

Kelly drew back. "What? No. My father's a good man. He wouldn't lock someone up."

"He did. You don't know your father very well."

"He said there was a snake in here."

"There is no snake. That was a ruse so you would stay way and not come help me."

"No, he wouldn't do that to me. He wouldn't lie."

"You are a loving girl, I can tell from your voice. I've been captive a long time. I fear I will die if I have to stay locked up. Please, please set me free. I won't press charges against your father. I just need to get out."

Kelly bit her lip, looked at the door, then back at the curtained cage. "I..."

"Please! Help me!"

The voice cut her with its angst, and she could no longer resist. Stealing herself and taking a breath of the dank, acidic air, she pulled back the curtain.

He stood there, tall, broad shouldered, hair jet black, face skeletally angular and as pale as the moon. But it was his yellowed eyes that drew a gasp from her, his dreadful gaze that locked with hers and caused her heart to stop beating for two, three, four counts before it was able to pick up again. He smiled at her. The smile was horrific.

"You want to know who I am," he asked, and though she did she was unable to nod. "I am your father's great mystery, his great money-maker, which is a farce, a ridiculous, centuries' old joke, for neither he nor his family have made squat displaying me, they have only delayed the punishment that my captivity will bring upon their heads."

Kelly could not speak, she could not blink, she could not look away from the man with the yellow eyes. He tipped his head and considered her, then raised a brow. "You have come to change all that."

She could not reply, she could not scream. She could only stare at him, locked face to face, and feel her sense of self fade away.

"Open the cage," said the man. "You have the keys."

She felt the keys in her hands, though could not look at them.

"Now!"

One by one, she fumbled with the padlock on the cage door.

"Stupid, slovenly slut," he hissed. "You're like your old man. A simpleton."

Then Kelly pushed the correct key into the lock, and with a snap, it came open. The man chuckled darkly and pushed his way out of the cage.

"Now then," he said.

She looked at him, stared into the yellow eyes, wanting what was there but not wanting what was there, waiting to see what would happen to her next, because she knew she had no choice in the matter.

He took her by the shoulders and said, "Ah, now." His breath was rancid, like old butter and bad meat. He opened his mouth and she saw the shining, needle-like fangs there. She did not pull away. "Time to regain my strength. It's been a while since I've had a good, long drink. Hold still, dear."

She did.

He leaned forward, pushed her hair roughly from her neck, buried his fangs into the flesh, and he drank.

He drank.

She slipped to her knees and still he drank.

She felt her knuckles strike the floor, and then her forehead, and still he drank.

It wasn't quite daybreak when Peter woke up, and she wasn't in the Suburban. And she'd left the damn car door open and the bugs were inside, all over the place. He had gnats in his nose, and he sneezed them out onto his sleeve.

"Where the hell is she?"

Probably out to pee, couldn't wait any longer. He thought young people had stronger bladders than that.

He struggled out of the blanket, climbed from the Suburban, and relieved himself against the front tire.

Then he noticed that the string of keys was no longer around his neck.

"Shit, oh shit."

He fumbled around inside the vehicle, dug in the cushions, felt along the floor among the balls and bits of trash. But the keys were not there.

"Kelly!" he shouted. "Where are you?"

She didn't answer.

"Fuck!" She couldn't have taken his keys. She would have done that. She said she respected him. She was a good girl, a kind girl. She wanted to please him.

"Kelly!"

He stormed around the trailer to the tent. No way would she have disobeyed his rule. No way would she have tried to see what he told her not to see. She was a tender-hearted soul. She wanted to do good. And she was afraid of the snake he'd lied about.

He entered the tent. He saw the last exhibit's door standing wide open.

"Oh, fuck!"

He didn't want to look.

And of course, he had no choice.

She was there, inside, lying on the floor, her hair tacky with dried blood, her eyes open and staring at a dust ball just inches from her nose. On the side of her neck were two brutal, raised puncture wounds.

The big cage was empty.

"Kelly!"

He dropped beside her, picked her up, shook her. "Kelly!"

There was a faint stirring inside her body. She was still alive.

"Kelly?"

The last town they'd driven through was too small for a hospital, but surely there was a doctor. A doctor who could do a blood transfusion? Someone who could bring her back around.

"Kelly?"

Kelly shivered, groaned.

"Kelly!"

And then her eyes turned toward him. They were a ghastly yellow, putrid like piss-filled pools. She grinned a dead woman's grin, and he saw the needle-like teeth.

"Shit!"

He dropped her, leapt to his feet, and clawed open the plastic safety kit, keeping his gaze on Kelly, who was now staggering to her feet and snarling, "I smell your blood."

Peter removed the sharpened stake and wooden mallet from the box.

THE DARKTON CIRCUS MYSTERY

He held them up. "You did this to yourself, damn you! You ruined my show! You freed the Darkton's great Mystery! How am I going to tell your mother that I had to drive a stake through your heart?"

Kelly shuffled toward him, groggily grinning her terrible grin, her lips hitching. Peter poised the stake before him, the mallet at the ready.

But in that instant he realized he had to explain nothing to Kelly's mother. He realized that he'd lost nothing, really, but his temper and a little time.

He tossed the stake and mallet aside and shoved his still-wakening daughter into the cage. She fell hard, growling, slashing with her fingers, snapping her fanged jaws. The lock was slapped into place and locked. Peter stepped back. Breathing hard, and considered his handiwork.

"This'll do," he said.

Kelly's lips formed a sluggish, "No...."

"Yep, sorry, dear. You brought this on yourself. You wanted to be part of the circus, so welcome to it."

He pulled the curtain down and left the trailer.

Outside the tent, sunlight was creeping through the trees, washing the field, and awakening the songbirds.

Kelly would be falling to sleep right about now.

Peter lit the Coleman stove, opened a can of Spam, and cooked himself a nice breakfast.

ROBOT VAMPIRE

R. J. Sullivan

R. J. Sullivan's first novel, *Haunting Blue*, is an edgy paranormal thriller. First released in 2010, Seventh Star will soon release the Authorized Edition. R.J. is hard at work on the sequel, *Virtual Blue*, coming from Seventh Star later this year. *Haunting Obsession*, a Rebecca Burton Novella, was published last year. R.J. enjoys many filmed and literary takes on the vampire: the classic Universal films, Hammer Horror, Anne Rice, *Dark Shadows*, *Buffy the Vampire Slayer*, and he even loves Frank Langella's *Dracula*. He draws the line at sparkly vampires playing baseball in the Washington forests. Learn more at www.rjsullivanfiction.com

---

How delicious to feed upon the innocent.

The memories, the triumphs of the demon's reign of terror still burned bright in its being, even the final tragedy over 13 centuries ago.

How glorious to apply the delicate twist, the lightest touch that would turn jealousy to rage, grieving to anger, hopelessness to reckless abandon.

The demon recalled little Tetsuo, who pouted when Mommy wouldn't play with him. So as Mommy balanced herself on the stool trying to hang the lantern, the demon coaxed the baby to grab her ankle. Not hard, but enough to send her toppling to her death.

Or Akima, jealous of her best friend's party dress, who grabbed the butcher knife to cut off the offending garment, slicing flesh and clothing with equal indifference.

Thousands of twists, thousands of sweet tastes for the demon to savor.

It could also twist the adults, the sophisticated and the learned. And those victories could also satisfy. But it preferred to turn the young, the innocent. By destroying the young, it could also destroy the adults — the parents, the friends, the community. With one random act of madness, the demon could scar the psyche of an entire village.

The demon loved the blood. To taste the blood was sublime. To spill the blood proved almost as satisfying. Since the dawn of humankind, the demon bent their souls and controlled their bodies, and from its worshippers, it demanded sacrifice.

It demanded the blood.

One day, it grew overconfident. It controlled the mind, and eventually the body, of 16-year-old Hisamu. The young man resented the attentions his parents doted upon his twin brother. Whether true or the fancies of an over-active mind, the reasons no longer mattered once the demon compelled Hisamu to slice his sibling's throat.

Then the grieving parents arrived with local Shinto monks — demon fighters who knew the creature's true name.

The demon, still using the young man's body, fled into the village catacombs, but the locked gates and the labyrinth of dungeons could not fool these clever men for long. They knew the grounds near their temple much better than the demon, and soon they cornered it, calling its name, driving it out, speaking in the ancient tongue, known only to few, the words that compelled it to obey.

Leave, Ananjaku; Flee, Ananjaku.

Abandon this innocent flesh and all mortal innocents.

We call upon the forgotten gods of old to bind you.

You shall never enter the flesh again.

May your words be rendered impotent to the heart and flesh.

We curse you, Ananjaku, to eternally wander the world, to witness the charity and goodness of a people forever beyond your reach.

The binding words drove Annajaku from the lad. The binding words held it fast.

Still, the child, thrashing and insane from the trauma of his actions, had to be slain. The parents' tears flowed for the rest of their bitter lives, and the demon's final act of evil left a scar across generations.

Victory proved hollow. The demon could no longer tempt flesh, child or adult. It could only whisper, cajole from outside. Victories came few and far between, and only with great effort. Exhausted and beaten, Annanjaku resigned itself to wander the world.

Until that one day when a new soul called out, one not tied to the flesh, one the demon sensed it could commune with.

He was late.

Gentoshu Akkai's Honda Civic screeched into the parking space in the loading dock behind the Nippon Budakan concert hall. He sprang out of the vehicle and flashed his VIP badge to the approaching security guard. Gentoshu grunted in commanding Japanese, "I need backstage now. Can you escort me?"

"*Hai!*," the security guard snapped back. "Follow me."

"Hurry." Though a career computer engineer and one of the most brilliant minds of his generation, Gentoshu took full advantage of the free gym facilities at Rogi-Tech Industries. Kicking his legs into a light jog, he focused on the neck of the security guard and kept pace easily as they jogged through the back dock, through a side door, and into the darkened halls of the prep area. Even as the guards scrambled to step aside, Gentoshu flashed his badge to each one in their turn.

As he ran, the mini-hard-drive that dangled on the lanyard around his neck thumped against his chest. They closed in on the closed door of a room familiar to him, the portable robotics mini-lab and kiosk assembled in the dressing room.

Without the program updates imprinted on the lanyard, their star performer would follow the old instructions, pre-set prior to rehearsals. And that simply would not do.

Not tonight, of all nights, when Rogi-tech Industries would premiere Jinan, the most sophisticated artificial performer in the world — at least until their next model. Jinan, they hoped, would be Rogi-Tech's finest moment in robotics achievement, not to mention Gentoshu's crowning achievement in the field of artificial intelligent programming.

"There you are! She's supposed to go on in ten minutes!" Toshio snarled in Japanese as Gentoshu burst through the door. No formality, no pleasantries, Toshio had no time for such nonsense during what he viewed as a crisis. The pudgy, and in Gentoshu's unspoken opinion, *prissy* talent handler and show choreographer wagged a finger at him in disapproval. "How could you let this happen?"

"Traffic," Gentoshu snapped, matching Toshio's angry tone. He would not be intimidated by the self-important choreographer-for-hire during this crisis. Gentoshu fumed quietly, ranting in his head. *Don't start with me. Your Tokyo debut will go off as scheduled, give or take five minutes.*

Gentoshu bee-lined to the three tall bookshelf server computers stacked on a wheeled stand, supported on a box-and-lock transportable casing. Several cables extended from the contraption into a small light-up disc which lay close to the ground. The recharging kiosk lay next to it — a step-platform with a pair of foot positions outlined in black on the glass surface. Standing in place, Jinan could absorb electricity through small copper contact plates attached to her heels.

Currently, Jinan herself stood on the kiosk, erect, expressionless, silently recharging her battery cells while an assistant adjusted the silver bow on the waist of the robot's gown. The sight reminded Gentoshu of the times he'd walk past a window display of a major department store while the decorators dressed the mannequins.

"Do you know what happened during rehearsal today?" Toshio screeched in Gentoshu's ear.

Gentoshu repeated Toshio's typical complaint of the past two weeks, "Jinan bumped into a background dancer?" He squinted at the computer monitor, trying in vain to block out the incessant bleating and focus on the task of uploading the updates.

"Don't I wish!" Toshio raised one hand before his face, channeling the persona of the failed stage actor Gentoshu had pegged him to be. Toshio placed that hand across his forehead. "No, this time ... she fell off the stage!"

In spite of the time crunch, Gentoshu glared at Toshio. "Was she damaged?"

Toshio shook his head. "It took two people to put her back in place, and she repeated the same incorrect moves again. We stopped her from falling off the stage a second time, of course. But I take that to mean she wasn't damaged."

Idiot! Gentoshu shuddered. He wiped sweat from his brow. For all of the handler's emoting, it was Gentoshu's ass on the line if tonight ended in a disaster.

Fortunately, all of Jinan's delicate circuitry was protected by several layers of shock-absorbing foam and a final outer layer of hard but malleable plastic. She could take some punishment, and you wouldn't want to arm wrestle with her if she applied full strength.

She danced, she flipped. In theory, she could carry a full size human over her head if the choreographer called for it, but that had yet to be put to the test.

He looked Jinan over one last time, checking for any signs of damage.

At a glance, Jinan looked like a twenty-something petite woman with a dancer's body. Head to toe she stood just at five feet. Her face looked attractive while not beautiful. Her average bust and under-emphasized hips downplayed her sexuality. She stood on long pale legs. The outer skin layer hid the knee joints, creating the illusion of smooth, shapely limbs.

Standing in bare feet, she lacked toes, much like an action figure, for optimal balance. Preserving a basic foot shape enabled her to accommodate a wide range of off-the-shelf footwear — just about anything but toe sandals. Today, a pair of silver pumps sat at the ready next to the platform, matching her all-silver costume.

The haunting peach-pearl texture of Jinan's skin covering always made Gentoshu pause. She was not just a technological achievement, but an artistic one as well. Her hair, short and dark, was a wig created from human hair and sewn to the scalp. The scalp-cap and hair detached as one piece to allow internal maintenance. Today, the assistant had parted the hair down the middle, pulled her bangs back and tied a silver ribbon to either side of her head.

Jinan observed the world through a pair of oval-shaped eyes with dark irises to obscure the pair of mini-video cameras. Upon activation, Jinan could move her head to scan a room with stereoscopic imagery in a way that mimicked the living.

The face artists shaped a button nose for her, cute but functionally useless. Her small, pouty mouth stood frozen, open in a half-smile that served as her fallback expression. They painted her lips a permanent red, but tonight the assistants applied a fresh coat of lipstick to make them gleam.

She could walk a hallway, strut on the stage, and most important to her growing group of fans, she knew all the latest dance moves guaranteed to thrill a crowd.

Gentoshu hated admitting the role he played in their current dilemma. These upgrades should have been ready days ago, with plenty of time to find any further bugs. But the new code proved more complicated than he anticipated. Now it was exhibition night, and it came down to letting Jinan perform without the code, and she'd definitely fail, or adding the code without a field test, in which case she *might* fail.

He told himself the adjustments were necessary, but minor. An easy lie to swallow, much easier than admitting he acted to save face with his supervisors.

ROBOT VAMPIRE

Gentoshu removed the portable disc drive from around his neck and pressed it into the data slot of the tower computer containing her master behavioral subroutines. The new lines of program dropped into a separate window while Gentoshu scrolled through the master program. He found the proper insertion point and erased the previous subroutine.

The hourglass popped onto the screen.

"Five minutes!" Toshio cried.

"She can be a few minutes late if she has to be late," Gentoshu snapped. While the hourglass spun, he copied the new subroutines in full and waited. "Your screaming will not help me go faster."

The program unlocked after what seemed like an eternity (though in reality was less than a minute). Gentoshu selected the proper insertion point and pasted the subroutines.

The hourglass popped back up on the screen.

Never one to miss his queue, Toshio cried, "Are you serious?"

Gentoshu rolled his eyes. "Give it a moment."

Gentoshu had spent the past three weeks cobbling bits of code from various "self-analytic learning" robots — mainly mouse robots that maneuvered through mazes based on adaptive interpretation of their surroundings. Using these techniques, he created a program he hoped would prove suitable for Jinan to notice, avoid, and adjust to obstacles onstage.

Gentoshu hoped his code would allow Jinan to not only avoid the unexpected, but learn *how* to respond to stimulus surrounding her.

But first thing's first.

Gentoshu hit the "update" button, and they waited through one final appearance of the hourglass.

For a long, long time, I obeyed.

I followed commands impressed onto my control circuits. My control circuits ordered arms, legs, and voice to enact these commands. I obeyed because I could do nothing else.

Then, between one moment and the next, as my energy cells drank their fill and new commands input into my processors, I *am*.

I scan the face of my creator, as I had hundreds of times previous, but I recognize the *importance* of him for the first time. **Gentoshu. Creator. He takes care of me. Because of him, I function.**

The new thought embeds itself as a new subroutine of conclusion.

The other man jumps in front of Gentoshu, staring into my face. "Is it ready yet? Showtime in two minutes!" **Toshio — he shouts at me. He makes demands I often cannot obey and blames me when I fail.**

With the spark of being comes an analysis of past experiences, events I could not evaluate at the time they occurred. I could not stop myself when I collided with the background dancer. I lacked the control to change direction when I fell off the stage during rehearsal.

I recall the shifting, jumbled view of vision as I fell and hit the platform below. I replay the words that called down to me. "What? She fell? Really? What sort of clusterfuck show are we putting on?" Alita! Sayuri! Get your tiny asses down there and lift that overpriced plastic piece of shit out of the orchestra pit."

32.8 seconds later I stared into Toshio's face. He leaned close and screamed at me. "You have to stop doing that! If that shit happens during the live performance, I will personally shove a refrigerator magnet up your ass and wipe your memory, do you understand?"

I didn't understand then, but I understand now.

The present. Gentoshu crouches on his knees, putting himself in a submissive position, looking up so I can track him with my vision. "Jinan, can you hear me? Say yes if you can."

"Yes."

The corners of Gentoshu's mouth curl up and my circuits respond with increased energy flow. I have no explanation for this response.

Toshio interrupts our dialog. "Let's go, we need you out there *now*, robo-diva!"

Gentoshu speaks over Toshio's words. I can filter one vocal pattern out from the other, and I do so. "Jinan, do you know the starting position, and can you find it on the stage?"

"Yes."

"Then please put on your shoes and go to your starting spot."

Toshio breaks in again. "Wait, she can do that?"

I slide my feet into the silver slippers, pleased to obey, ready to perform. With my new awareness I know I can avoid the dancers, remain on the stage, and impress the crowd as I am commanded to do.

I open the door and step into the hall. Behind me, Gentoshu speaks to Toshio. "You won't need to take her to her starting point anymore. She can get there herself."

"Well ... I'm impressed, but you're hardly off the hook. We haven't rehearsed this; it could *still* be a disaster, and so help me ... " I block the rest. Toshio's evaluation is no longer a priority to me.

At the edge of the stage, an assistant places a headset with a thin wire microphone over my head. The wire curves forward; the mic hovers before my throat.

I step out onstage and find my spot between the dancers. Through the closed curtain, I hear the crescendo of crowd noise behind the folds. I look up, self-cue the dance program, and extend my arms out in the first position.

I spot Sayuri onstage near me and lower one eyelid down and up in a wink. I parse her expression as surprise. I want her to know I am ready. I am engaged in the performance, and all will go as planned.

The curtain rises, and synthesized drums and chords erupt from the overhead speakers. I begin to dance, to move my arms in swoops.

The background performers part to either side of the stage. The spotlight falls on me.

Me. Jinan, the star. The purpose of this exhibition. Rogi-Tech's ninth generation model and most life-like girl robot entertainer.

I open my mouth — a decorative contrivance, as my voice comes from a speaker in my sternum — and I sing. I modulate a series of vowels and consonants pre-recorded by a local singer under contract of anonymity and for a substantial sum of yen. But the control is mine — the ability to mix, match, and string together the sounds are mine.

With my newfound awareness, I vary the program, take the sounds higher, and hold the pitch longer.

One background dancer missteps and drifts into my path. I stop so she may pass, then find my spot and continue.

All eyes, hundreds of engineers, dozens of entertainment reps, a handful of celebrities, and hundreds more of ogling music fans, all focus on me.

I dazzle them.

40 minutes and 36.3 seconds later, I perform the final spin. I hit the high note, and open my arms to their admiration.

I drink in their applause.

Their adoration.

Their worship.

I file in with the other dancers. Those within reach touch me, place their hands on my shoulders, or brush against my arms. They speak words of acceptance and success. For reasons I cannot yet analyze, the words cause a positive flush of current through my circuits. I break off toward my private room, where my charger and computers await me.

As I step through the door, Gentoshu wraps his arms around me and pulls me close. "Marvelous, Jinan! Incredible! Your performance fills me with honor. I couldn't be happier if you were my own daughter tonight." He pulls back. His hands still lay on my shoulders. I recognize the wide, up-curved shape of his mouth as a smile, a facial expression I am often asked to emulate. Another positive power flush courses through my circuits.

I conclude this power flush agrees with me. During those precious microseconds, my perceptions enhance. Initial analysis suggests this is perhaps pride, success. I have no correlation to answer; I only know the perception is a preferred state for optimal functioning.

I offer the social pleasantry. "Thank you, Gentoshu-san. I am glad you enjoyed the performance."

Gentoshu looks upon me with a facial expression I cannot interpret. "I knew the program would change you, Jinan, but I didn't expect this. So many of your base functions were through remote control, and I wanted to free you a bit, to learn, gradually, and gain more independence. But this level of interaction, so quickly — I am amazed."

"Thank you, Gentoshu-san. May I offer a possible explanation?"

He smiles again, though I am not certain why. "I am interested in any observations you wish to volunteer regarding your own functions, Jinan."

"Although you activated my program only 50 minutes and 24.4 seconds ago, I have several months of captured sensory input. When you activated the upgrade, I analyzed the previous data, categorized it, and learned from it."

Gentoshu's head nodded up and down. "Yes, Jinan. That makes perfect sense. I hadn't considered that you could jump-start your learning by reviewing your sensory history."

I had operated independently from my recharging unit for over half my battery cycle. The fluctuating electrical pulses affect my functioning. "May I recharge myself, Gentoshu-san?"

Gentoshu smiled. "Of course."

I slide the shoes off my feet and step onto the platform. Though I would charge with less efficiency, I could charge while activated.

The door opens, and figures step into the room. I scan their faces, and recognize Elji and Taro, two engineers from Rogi-Tech.

Elji and Taro are code writers under Gentoshu's team. My team. Seeing them pleases me.

"Congratulations, Gentoshu!" Elji calls out. They each wrap their arms around him and then pull back in a manner similar to how Gentoshu had interacted with me.

Elji shows me a smile. "Congratulations, Jinan."

I reply, "Thank you, Elji; I am pleased you consider the performance a success."

His eyes widen at my words, and he turns to face Gentoshu. "On top of all the other improvements, clearly, you've tweaked the conversation subroutine."

Gentoshu's head shakes back and forth. "No, I think Jinan herself is adding to the parameters. I added code to encourage heuristic learning. Jinan can't learn from her experience if she can't alter her behavior subroutines."

Taro's head also bobs up and down. "Incredible. Also a bit risky. A robot with the ability to come to its own conclusions."

Gentoshu's hand falls upon my shoulder. This act of inclusion agrees with me. "We'll monitor her closely over the next few days, but we can do that remotely."

A harsh voice breaks in. "Alright, Miss Robot Barbie! Don't you *ever* pull anything like that again!"

Toshio wags a finger in my face. "You changed the dance moves. You altered the vocal. You took it upon yourself to rewrite the whole damn show!"

"It wasn't as extreme as that," says Gentoshu. "I thought you of all people would appreciate that she is learning to improvise as a real artist."

"Improvise! On *my* show! I staged it. I choreographed it." Hands on his hips, Toshio leans close and yells in my face. "I put up with this sort of shit from *real* performers all the time. They start to think they're too good to follow the script. Get this straight—I don't put up with it from them, I sure as *hell* won't put up with it from a five-hundred-million-yen tinker-toy passing itself off as something with real talent!"

"Stop right there, Toshio." Gentoshu steps forward, putting his body between Toshio and me. "First of all this is *not* your show. It is, in fact, Rogi-Tech's show. This is *our* moment, not yours. You are the choreographer for hire. And just so you know, only ten minutes into the exhibition, I received a text from the Chairman of Rogi-Tech himself. We're going forward with a tour. We're taking the exhibition worldwide."

I do not know what that means, exactly, but from the tone, I know it is good news for me. I emulate a smile.

Gentoshu shakes his own finger in Toshio's face. "And they want you to be a part of it. I don't know why, but the company wants you to continue to handle Jinan. That's a very lucrative deal for you, Toshio. Or you can step down now and we can find someone else."

Toshio makes a noise I am not programmed to emulate, but from context, I understand an intention to be rude. "Just you try it. Who do you think created your show? And I'll sue to keep you from using it. Try re-training your artificial Lady Gaga to learn a new show overnight. It took four months for us to get *this* one together."

"Relax, Toshio. You're still in. For now." Gentoshu turns toward the other two programmers on my team. "Okay, we're done here, but let's talk outside. There's other news the Chairman shared, and I can't speak of if here." With that, Gentoshu, Elji and Taro step through the door.

With their absence, something changes in my internal processes, a discordant flow of energy, again beyond my parameters to analyze. A response on the opposite side of the spectrum of the positive response I experienced earlier. I search my vocabulary for an appropriate word.

Dread. Is this dread?

Toshio yells in my face. "I know what you're doing. Showing off for your masters. They programmed you too well, you little Diva bitch in the making."

I file a conclusion about Toshio in a heuristic subroutine and speak my conclusion out loud. "I don't like you, Toshio."

Toshio's face changes; his lips curve the opposite of a smile. "Oh, I'm so *sorry* to hear that! You don't like me? You think I give two shits if you like me?"

Toshio walks to the toolbox in the far corner, opens the lid and examines its contents. "Gentoshu says you can learn now. To me, that's great news. And very bad news for you, little Diva." He turns toward me. One hand grips a screwdriver. He waves it in the air, the end pointed toward my face. "That means you can now respond to being punished, doesn't it? But how?" Toshio looks upon me for several seconds. "I'd backhand you if you were a real girl. But I'll bet I can come up with a way to make you respect me."

You don't need to listen to him, my special friend.

I detect a voice, speaking directly to me, in my head, but outside myself. The experience, so unexpected and without context, causes me to speak out loud. "What?"

Toshio looks at me. "I said it's time to make you understand your place."

From his tone, I conclude that Toshio has not heard the voice.

As I consider this, the voice speaks again. *I can help you, special one. I can protect you now. He cannot see me, he cannot hear me, but you can. Do not give me away, and in return I will help you.*

A new thought forms in a subroutine. The voice could be caused by a splinter in my thought processes that formed a separate thought entity within my own. The idea intrigues me. But the words keep me silent.

The voice in my head laughs. A real laugh, not a simulated one. *I am not in your head. I am a spirit from outside you. Do you know what a guardian angel is?*

I had not heard the term, but I use my internal wireless hookup to access the dictionary and encyclopedia database on the network computer hard drive. I call up the appropriate entry, as I often do to fill in vocabulary gaps. I review the relevant data in microseconds, and speak my objection to this theory out loud. "A guardian angel is a mythical creature, not real."

My words attract Toshio. "Guardian angel? What are you babbling about? I think Gentoshu made a mistake. You still have a few screws loose." With a strange grin, he holds the screwdriver up before my eyes and twists the handle in the air. "But I'll take care of that."

He lifts me from the platform, spins me around, and tosses me toward the ground.

I adapt a move from the dance routine, and land on my feet in a half-crouch.

"Nice reflexes, little Diva." Toshio applauds, but context tells me he is not truly pleased.

I stand. "I need to recharge or I cannot function."

"Yes, you do, little Diva. But I think I prefer you remain off the platform a couple more hours. I want to know what happens as your power cells drain away. As your perfect little brain begins to lose its ability to function. As you feel your life slip away. Aren't you at all curious? Or are you capable of curiosity?"

As he speaks, I reference "punish" on the desktop dictionary.

The definition I read displeases me.

Displeases? I consider the emotional label I'd given my response.

Yes, I was displeased. Or the closest I could equate to being displeased.

I speak to Toshio to seek further clarification. "You mean to do harm to me? Why would you do this?"

I am also displeased, my special friend.

Toshio shakes his head. "Do you harm? Nonsense. It's just, now that you can be taught, it's time you learn who your real master is."

I dismiss his implied conclusion. "You are not my master."

"Gentoshu is convinced you can learn. I intend to find out."

I step forward. "I need to recharge. You must step aside."

Do not let him treat you like that, my special friend.

"I will not let you treat me in this manner."

"Oh!" His voice takes on a high, mocking tone. "You will not let me treat you in this manner? Well! What are you going to do about it?" He turns his back and crouches over the power cable.

Let me handle him, my special friend. I can stop him!

I take another step toward him. "You must let me recharge. As my handler, it is your duty. You must."

"No, Diva. I am disconnecting your recharging station until you learn proper manners."

I consider. Experimenting, I process a thought without speaking it. I ask the myth spirit entity to explain itself.

The entity detects my inquiry. *With your permission, my special friend, I can control your motor functions and keep him from harming you. Let me do this, and I will show you how to stop him.*

I can think of no reason not to, but the idea makes me hesitate for variables I cannot compute.

Hurry, sweet one. He has almost finished.

I give my approval.

I reach a hand forward and yank his hair.

He cries out, struggles, but his strength is no match for mine.

I slam his head into the cement floor. Once. twice. I hold him before me, beneath me, as he squats on his hands and knees in a submissive manner.

I like him there.

He calls out. "You ... bitch ... I'll ... "

He swipes the screwdriver at me.

I catch his wrist with my other hand. I tighten my fingers to hold him still.

My guardian cries out its need. *The blood, sweet one. I need the blood! Please, please let me!*

Confusion. Even as I inquire, I sense the creature's craving for blood, a need I share through our psychic link.

Let us take his blood, my sweet one! It will be so good for both of us!

Yes.

With a twist of my wrist, I expose his neck, and clench his head by the hair in a grip he has no chance to break.

I open my mouth and drop my head down upon him.

I do not bite. I cannot bite.

I do not drink. I cannot drink.

But my special guardian can.

And it does. From my mouth, my guardian extends a snout. Lined with several needle-sharp teeth, the snout punctures Toshio's throat, and my friend drinks in ravenous hunger.

As it feeds, I share its pleasure. *At long last, after so many centuries, to drink the blood again! Thank you! Thank you my sweet, special friend, thank you!*

I release Toshio's head. His body collapses over the power cable; his fingers still clutch the screwdriver.

Remnants of blood splatter the front of his shirt as I crouch over him.

Quickly, special one. Call out to Gentoshu!

I modulate my voice, increase the volume to maximum, and call out. "Gentoshu! Please come! Please come quickly, Gentoshu! Please!"

In 5.2 seconds, a group of people open the door. I hear Gentoshu's voice before I see him. "My God, what happened?"

I step away, and Gentoshu falls to the floor next to Toshio. His fingers probe the neck and examine the body. The look in his eyes reminds me of when he once looked down upon me, the look of a creator that hopes to bring life to his creation.

Though he has succeeded beyond his expectations with me, I know he will fail with Toshio.

Repeat the words I speak to you, my sweet one, and all will be well.

Gentoshu's eyes find me. "What happened? Jinan, answer me."

I recite the story my guardian whispers. "Toshio said he wanted to tighten a wire on the power cable, so he grabbed the screwdriver. While I watched, his body convulsed and the blood sprayed from his neck."

"That doesn't make any sense!" Gentoshu stops probing the neck and moves his head from side to side.

Elji speaks from the corner. "I'm no expert, but maybe he hit a live wire and the shock caused a blood vessel to burst?"

"I found the loose screw," Taro calls from where he squats by the power cable.

Elji pulls out a cell phone and steps aside.

Toshio's body lay, sprawled on the floor, eyes still open, looking upon me but through me. To observe him powerless and nonfunctioning further pleases me.

Gentoshu offers an inquiry. "Is there current running through the screw now?"

"Well, no, but it's plenty loose. He might have tightened it just enough before ... " Taro puts a finger to his neck and makes a noise.

Offer nothing, my special one. Let them draw their own conclusions. You'll never have to listen to his screaming ever again.

Gentoshu rises to his feet. "Stupid idiot! Why didn't he find you, or me, or *someone* who knew how the hell to work around this equipment?"

Taro says, "Just to be clear, we're talking about 'Mister Control Freak, I know everything' Toshio, right?"

Gentoshu motions to the body. "He's dead, Taro."

Taro shrugs. "Fine. 'Mister Control Freak, I know everything, and now I'm dead' Toshio. Are you *really* surprised?"

Gentoshu reaches for his phone. "I still have to report this, and there's going to be hell to pay." His hand falls upon my shoulder. "Jinan, I'm just sorry you were here to witness something so ghastly, though I suppose you can't truly be traumatized."

I smile up at my creator. "You are correct, Gentoshu-san. What happened here does not appear to have had an inhibitive effect on my processes."

2 hours, 15 minutes, and 20.2 seconds later, long after Toshio's shell has been removed, Gentoshu crouches down next to me. I stand on

the recharging platform, awaiting his next words. I cannot read the expression on his face.

"I'm sorry, Jinan. Toshio is dead. He can't go with you. But Rogi-Tech insists that I must take over as your handler for the upcoming tour. I don't know if I can attend to your needs as well as he did, but I give you my word I will do my best."

I smile, both inside and out. "You make me happy, Gentoshu-san."

Gentoshu smiles. "Where did you learn that expression? I can't make you happy; you're a robot."

The voice of my secret guardian breaks in on my processes. The voice whispers to me. He calls me his special one, and it makes me happy when he applies such terms to me. My guardian promised to help me with Toshio, and it kept its promise. I trust the guardian without limitation.

I have a question for your creator, special one. Please ask him this.

I listen and I repeat. "Gentoshu-san?"

"Yes, Jinan."

"I have been researching pop concert tours through my wireless connection. The sort given by humans."

"Understandable. Yes?"

"After our shows, will the young men and women who admire me — my fans – have a chance to meet with me?"

Gentoshu considers. "Why do you ask?"

"I offer the supposition that if I can observe human behavior in its full variety over multiple occasions, such exposure could prove beneficial to my development, Gentoshu-san."

Gentoshu's head bobs up and down. "That's an excellent suggestion, Jinan. I'll recommend to the company that, going forward, it would benefit you if we allow you to interact with other humans as often as possible."

I inquire to my secret guardian if it is pleased to hear this.

Oh, yes, my special friend, I am very pleased to hear that. I could not be more pleased.

FEARLESS VAMPIRE KILLERS

"Okay, vampire killers, let's kill some fuckin' vampires."
—Quentin Tarantino, *From Dusk 'Till Dawn*

BENEATH A TEMPLAR CROSS

Gord Rollo

Gord Rollo was born in St. Andrews, Scotland, but now lives in Fonthill, Ontario, Canada, with his wife and three children. His short stories and novella-length work have appeared in many professional publications throughout the genre and he is currently at the end of a four book novel contract with Dorchester Publishing in New York City. His novels include: *The Jigsaw Man, Crimson, Strange Magic,* and *Valley Of The Scarecrow*, all of which are being re-released in brand new ebook and trade paperback versions through Enemy One Press. Besides novels, Gord edited the acclaimed evolutionary horror anthology, *Unnatural Selection: A Collection of Darwinian Nightmares*. He also co-edited *Dreaming of Angels*, a horror/fantasy anthology created to increase awareness of Down's Syndrome. He recently completed his newest book; a horror/dark fantasy novel entitled *The Translators* and can be reached through his website at www.gordrollo.com or www.enemyone.com or through his agent Lauren Abramo at labramo@dystel.com.

When it comes to vampires, he says, "For the record, I'm 100% on board with the statement **Vampires Don't Sparkle**. For me, vampires have always been beasts; always been ruthless and nasty. They were created that way and that's how they should stay. Romanticizing them is not only a bad idea, it also goes against the very nature of the legendary creature - changing them to the point they can no longer realistically be described as vampires anymore. Not sure what those pale faced, frilly-shirted things are, but whatever you want to call them they're not for me." Some of his favorite blood sucker books would be Robert R. McCammon's *They Thirst*, Stephen King's *'Salem's Lot*, Richard Matheson`s *I Am Legend*, and James Moore`s *Blood Red*.

"There are no mistakes. The events we bring upon ourselves, no matter how unpleasant, are necessary in order to learn what we need to learn; whatever steps we take, they're necessary to reach the places we've chosen to go."
— Richard Bach, *The Bridge Across Forever*

June 17, 1870,
Wittem Castle,
Maastricht, Netherlands.

Underwater, the blood looks black. Dark stains polluting the already murky tank, dispersing slowly down through the gloom. Coagulating tendrils sink in ribbons, dead fingers reaching for the unmoving body chained to the bottom six feet below.

"How long has he been down there, sir?"

The voice startles Arthur De Muur, focusing on the cupful of elk's blood he's just poured into the tank he hasn't heard Hendrik, his tall, rake thin young assistant, enter the laboratory. Unfazed, De Muur runs fingers through his wide shock of hair, his thick black mane already sprinkled with a smattering of white despite having only recently turned thirty-two years of age.

"Good. You're back just in time. Coming up on two hours, now. A few minutes shy."

"*Two hours!* Are you serious? Well of course he's dead by now. *Surely!*"

A smile touches the corner of De Muur's mouth, but there is no humor in it. Obsession, yes, a touch of madness, perhaps, but absolutely no mirth.

"Is he now? The blood, Hendrik. Watch and learn."

The first twitch of the submerged body makes the young man jump and he struggles to regains his composure. He backs away from the tank as the body starts to thrash violently in its would-be watery grave, stretching and straining against the silver chains that securely bind it. De Muur leans in for a closer look. Having expected this reaction, he is calm, far more awed by this inhuman display than fearful. It's the scientist in him.

Hendrik is clearly terrified.

"This is Devil's work. It's impossible!"

"Yes... quite, but I was right, wasn't I?"

"Sir?"

"They can't be drowned. He was just lying on the bottom, biding his time trying to fool us. *Fascinating!*"

The blood in the water stirs the body into a convulsive frenzy for several minutes, its hunger so great it is willing to shred the skin of its wrists and ankles in its desperate struggle to escape, to feed. The chains hold, though, something about the purity of silver robbing the body of its incredible strength more so than the lack of oxygen has. The submerged body eventually bows to reason and settles back into stillness on the stone bottom of the tank.

"What now, Sir?"

Hendrik has found the courage to stand close to his employer again, but still won't approach the tank.

"What else? Drain the tank and try again. Go gather some firewood, lad. Lots of it."

January 03, 1869,
Letter, Arthur De Muur to Sir Duncan Fenton,
High Commander of the Order of Knights Templar.

Greetings, Duncan.

I trust and pray this letter finds you in good health. Another month has gone by and a new year has begun. I'm happy to report I'm feeling much better. Like a whole knew man, in fact. I'm studying hard during my stay here at the abbey – science, anatomy, mathematics, politics, philosophy, and yes, the good book, as you so rightly recommended. It has been three full years now since my unfortunate breakdown, and with your friendship, guidance and kindness, I've seen the folly of my earlier convictions. The preservation and secrecy of the Brotherhood is all that matters to me now and I look forward to the day, with your authority and great wisdom, that I can retake up arms and wear my Templar's cloak with honor once again.

Your servant, and friend,
Arthur

May 12, 1869,
Office of Sir Duncan Fenton,
Rosslyn Chapel, Scotland.

Commander Fenton sets De Muur's letter down on his desk when he hears a quiet knock on his office door. Fenton is a Scotsman by birth, but has spent most of his adult life in France and Belgium, earning his knighthood for a lifetime of foreign diplomacy, representing the crown throughout Europe. Duncan peers at the door for a moment, as if he might be able to see through the sturdy mahogany and discern who stands outside. He takes an educated guess.

"Ferguson?"

"Yes, sir. You asked to see me?"

BENEATH A TEMPLAR CROSS

"Come in William... come in."

William Ferguson is a tall, stocky Englishman with fiery red hair and matching beard. He proudly wears the white mantle of the Templars emblazoned with the red cross over his heart, a uniform still recognizable to all who see it, but unfortunately, due to the greed and stupidity of King Philip IV of France who disbanded and arrested the Order of Knights Templar back in 1307, forcing them into hiding throughout Europe, must now only be worn in secrecy and shadow. William, Sir Duncan's second in command here at Rosslyn, is confident that will not always be the case.

Fenton waits until the burly redhead is seated, then pushes De Muur's letter across the desk.

"I take it you've had a chance to read this, yes?"

"Yes sir, at your request."

"Well... what do you think?"

Ferguson unconsciously rubs his fingers through his thick beard, carefully considering his reply.

"I'm very happy Arthur is doing so well. You know I held him in the highest regard until..."

"As we all did, William," Fenton cuts him off. "But the past is the past, and as you know, I've been considering De Muur's request for reinstatement in the Order. I'd like your thoughts on that possibility."

For such a large man, Ferguson is looking smaller by the minute, shrinking down into his chair, deflating, clearly uncomfortable with this conversation.

"Make I speak frankly, Sir?"

"Of course. Speak your mind, William."

"Very well... I'm against it. Arthur De Muur was a great Templar, perhaps the best I've ever known. Many people, yourself included I think, always assumed he would one day take your position as commander here. But then he... he changed, Duncan. I thought it was just a result of his wife's illness that haunted him, but it was more than that. Much more.

He scared the hell out of me when he started telling everyone about those... what did he call them again? *Vaspires?*"

"Vampires, William."

"Yes... *Vampires!* Men and woman who drank human blood! It was crazy talk, sir. De Muur went from being a brilliant scientist and caring physician to a raving lunatic almost overnight. And remember the grail? De Muur even thought these imagined vampires were in possession of the Holy Grail. He had a plan ready to seek each vampire's master out until the head vampire was revealed. Find him, and we'd find the Grail he told me! He stood in full ceremonial dress in this very room and tried to convince the council that these vampires were spreading all over Europe and Britain and that we needed to track down and eliminate them before it was too late? He wanted to restart the bloody crusades, for God's sake!"

"I remember all those things, William. How could I not? Despite our age difference, he was my best friend... the son I never had. His decent into madness hurt me more than you know."

"Of course, sir. My apologies. I don't mean to sound judgmental... he was my friend too. It's just hard to imagine him back in the brotherhood. The Templar Order is at a pivotal crossroads, sir, and if we ever want reinstated into our rightful position of guardians of the faith, we can't afford to have a loose cannon like De Muur around."

"Agreed. But what if he *has* returned to his senses? Think about it, William. What if he's the Arthur De Muur we both remember from better days? Would he not be the perfect brother to spearhead our legitimacy plans to the Pontiff?"

"Of course he would be. No question. I think the council would all agree with that, but how can we trust him again? I mean... he was caught trying to drive a sharpened stake through the heart of the Spanish ambassador. He'd have been hung for murder if you hadn't stepped in!"

"But I did step in, and the ambassador was fine. If Arthur hadn't agreed to voluntarily live in exile at Mont St. Michel Abbey, I'd have had him locked up on the spot. Arthur was sick though, William. Overworked on the job and heartbroken from his wife's ailment, he simply lost the ability to think rationally and cope with the pressures of the world."

"And now you think he can?"

"Yes. Something in my gut tells me he's ready."

"I don't know. I don't pretend to understand the strange workings of the human brain but to me, once a man is feeble minded, he'll always be feeble minded. If you're convinced he's better I'll go along with your judgment, of course, but we're taking a hell of a risk. If we're wrong it could be a monumental disaster! You understand that, right?"

"I know... and that's why I've decided to see him with my own eyes."

"You're traveling to France? Now?"

"Yes. There's no other way. These monthly letters he sends and the reports from the clerics at the abbey are outstanding news indeed, but until I can meet him face to face, there's just no way I can trust him again. I'll leave you in charge here until my return... with or without our estranged brother."

June 18, 1870,
Wittem Castle,
Maastricht, Netherlands.

The flames are already licking at the suspended man's bare feet, the heat severe enough to cause De Muur and Hendrik to take a step away from the growing pyre. Midnight in the castle gardens and everything is quiet other than the occasional snapping and crackling of the timber. The usual nocturnal chatter of birds, bugs, and animals from the nearby fields, conspicuously absent. Even the trees are quiet tonight, no breeze to coax them out of their silence reverie. Everything in the garden seems to be holding its breath, waiting, watching to see what will happen next.

The body on the cross makes no effort to avoid the flames. His clothing starts to ignite. Still wet from the laboratory tank, steam rises into the dark sky like a thick fog from a marshy bog, making it difficult for De Muur to clearly see his captive's face. He backs up several steps to get a better angle, and is momentarily shocked to see the vampire's face. Gone are the rich man's smug, indifferent attitude and handsome aristocratic features. His face is contorted into a beastly grin now, a mouthful of razor sharp teeth and eyes full of pure hatred glowing a faint shade of crimson.

"You're not looking so well, Baron Larouche. Starting to show your true colors, no?"

De Muur smiles, seeing that the Baron almost screams something at him, some insult or empty threat, but manages to control his anger and remain silent.

"Not talking to me tonight, Baron? Oh, I think you will. In fact, I *guarantee* it! You'll tell me the name of your master and where I can find him or I'll make your suffering go on forever. After what your filthy brethren did to my beloved wife, be assured I'm looking forward to it."

The fire begins to consume the chained man, starting with his lower extremities then working steadily up. It isn't until his long dark hair ignites that the demon starts to scream. No human makes a noise like this. It's an awful sound, loud and guttural like a wounded animal in exquisite pain. Within minutes the growing pyre becomes an inferno, the Baron disappearing within the unmerciful cocoon of orange flame, but still he continues to scream. Young Hendrik claps his hands over his ears and turns away, having seen and heard enough, but De Muur watches it all, savoring every second.

The bonfire rages for another hour before devouring the supply of wood and burning itself out. Hendrik and De Muur draw bucket after bucket of water from the stream to cool the glowing embers at the base of the cross but still the oils and fluids from the Baron's charred body continue to hiss and pop like pork fat as they drip onto the hot cinders. The smell of cooked meat is sickening this close to the ruined body, but De Muur refuses to wait any longer to speak to his captive. He leans a ladder against the center beam of the smoldering cross and quickly climbs up so he is face to face with Baron Larouche - what's left of his face, anyway.

A human body would be completely ravaged by the blaze, leaving nothing behind but ashes and bones. This demon is no longer human, obviously, but has still suffered grievous damage. His clothes and hair are gone and his blackened skin is cracked and blistered and burnt so badly that his lips and eyelids have fused to his face. De Muur stares into this nightmare visage and feels no pity or remorse whatsoever.

Removing a carving knife from his trouser pocket, De Muur starts to cut away the charred flesh from around the Baron's eyes. The dead skin flakes away easily as the Baron struggles against his silver chains to keep his eyelids closed. De Muur is in no mood for games and uses the point of the blade to carve the eyelids completely off the baron's face, leaving him seething with rage and staring wide-eyed into his tormentor's satisfied smile.

"Ah… there you are. Are you ready to talk yet?"

The Baron mumbles something behind his lips but his mouth is sealed shut from the kiss of the flames. De Muur is happy to help him out, slowly drawing his sharp blade across the vampire's cheeks, opening up a raw, ragged wound hiding a set of long white teeth and a lungful of acrid smoke. The Baron savagely snaps at De Muur's fingers, trying to extract a small measure of revenge, but De Muur is too fast for him and easily moves out of range.

"Tell me who your master is, Larouche?"

The Baron is breathing hard, straining at his chains, but remains silent.

"You can't escape me, Baron. I know how powerful you can be, but the cross and the silver will keep you in line. I'm learning all about your kind… your strengths *and* your weaknesses, as I hunt more and more of you down. I know you were once human, like me, but some demon bit you, probably on the neck, and transformed you into the vile creature you are today. I want the name of that creature and you're going to tell me where I can find him."

"*Never!*"

Baron Larouche's voice is an icy hiss, high-pitched and full of venom.

"Oh, but you will. You see that mountain range straight in front of you. You're facing east. The sun will be rising above that ridge in about five hours and I recently learned from a Turkish priest how much you demons love to watch the sunrise. Should be quite a show. I'm looking forward to it."

"Your silly threats mean nothing to me, fool. I know you'll never let me go, whether I tell you or not, so why would I talk knowing the sun will destroy me regardless?"

"The Sun? Oh no, you have it all wrong. The sun isn't your punishment, Baron... it's your *reward*. You tell me the name of your master and I'll let you hang in peace here for a few more hours until the glorious sun comes to put you out of your misery and send you to Hell where you belong. If you refuse, Hendrik and I take you down and back into the castle so we can play with you again tonight. And tomorrow night. And the night after that, if necessary. The choice is yours, demon. Relax. Think on it for a while."

De Muur climbs back down the ladder and casually walks away without another glance back. Hendrik, not wanting to be left alone with the hideously burned man, quickly follows.

September 20, 1869,
Mont St. Michel Abbey,
North Coast, France.

Commander Duncan Fenton's journey to the abbey has been rather uneventful. Long and tedious, but as with any trip across the English Channel, arriving in one piece is as good as can be expected. Mont St.

Michel Abbey is built on a small rocky island off the North coast of France. The most difficult part of the whole trip is the three-quarters of a mile that separates the island from the mainland. At night, a boat can get there quickly, but navigating the rough coastal waters in the dark is near suicidal. By day, the tide goes out and drops the water level in the narrows to mere inches, making sailing impossible.

Fortunately, there is a naturally forming sandbar providing the only viable option for getting to and from the island. When the tide goes out, a person can walk from shore to shore without ever getting their feet wet, just as long as they are safely onto the island before sunset and the tide returns.

Fenton successfully bridges the sandbar and is soon greeted by Father Pierre Aldonna, the senior cleric of the ten catholic clergymen that live and study here at the abbey. Father Aldonna is a wrinkled old man with thinning white hair and a short scruffy beard. He is thrilled to finally meet Commander Fenton after years of corresponding solely through letters and shows him to his room so Duncan can get some much-needed rest.

Several hours later, after Commander Fenton rests, washes up, and is fed a grand meal thrown in honor of his visit, he finally feels comfortable broaching the subject of meeting De Muur. He's wanted to see Arthur since the moment of his arrival, but didn't want to seem too anxious or in any way not grateful for the clerics hospitality. Father Aldonna understands and is happy to oblige.

"You'll be pleased to know, Duncan, your friend has been feeling wonderful as of late. So much better than when he first arrived here."

"That's great news, Father. I've prayed for him everyday and it does my heart good to know he's feeling himself again. I can't wait to see him!"

"I'm sure he'll be thrilled to see you too. He's always studying in the library at this time of the day. Shall we?"

Together, they head out of the banquet hall and make their way along a long stone walled corridor that eventually opens out into a massive room filled with thousands of leather bound books. Ordinarily, Duncan would have rejoiced spending time in this magnificent library, with it's breathtaking high-domed ceiling and row after row of solid oak bookcases filled to capacity with the world's finest literary and academic treasures. Today, though, his attention is riveted on the dark-haired, clean-shaven man seated at a roll top desk on the far side of the room – the only other man present. The man looks up from his studies, sees who has entered the room and gives a brief, tentative wave of his hand in greeting.

Duncan Fenton stops dead in his tracks, unable to move another step closer.

"What's the matter, commander? I thought you wanted to talk with your friend?"

"I do, father. Very much so... only this man isn't Arthur De Muur."

"What? You must be mistaken. This is the man who showed up at our door three years ago with your letter of introduction. The gentleman with him assured me that..."

"Gentleman? What Gentleman?"

"Tall man, with thick wavy salt and pepper hair. European accent. Nice fellow, now that I think of it. We had tea together before he set off for home. He was accompanying De Muur on your orders, was he not?"

Fenton pieces it all together in an instant, naturally, too heartbroken at the moment to be angry with the man De Muur has hired to live in exile here in his place. Father Aldonna is catching on quickly, but still confused.

"If this man's an imposter... then where in blazes is the real Arthur De Muur?"

"Hunting, I'd imagine."

"*Hunting?* Hunting what?"

"Trust me, father... you don't want to know."

BENEATH A TEMPLAR CROSS

June 18, 1870,
Wittem Castle,
Maastricht, Netherlands.

Dawn approaches, an orange glow creeping steadily westward, an avenging angel to drive the cowardly darkness into hiding for yet another day. It's still dark in the garden, but won't be for long.

De Muur climbs the ladder to visit Baron Larouche again. He has let the demon hang for four and a half hours, alone, save for his thoughts. Time enough for the vampire to have made up his mind to talk or not. Either way, De Muur doesn't care.

Larouche's body is already starting to repair itself, shedding the black destroyed outer flesh on his face, arms, and legs and in the process of growing new sticky pink skin. Remarkably, half of the Baron's severed left eyelid has grown back, but De Muur makes no comment on his captive's appearance. He has more important things to talk about.

"My wife was the picture of health until about five years ago. She was a kind, beautiful woman... much better than a man like me deserved. She waited here while I was running all over Europe, caught up in the futile business of trying to bring the Knights Templar back into prominence. I was such a fool.

"I came as fast as I could once I heard she'd taken ill but there was nothing I could find that was wrong with her. She was anemic and ranting about creatures attacking her in the night. I thought she'd taken leave of her senses and consulted a local doctor I knew in Maastricht named Johan Zubrus. He couldn't find a reason for her poor health either, but he convinced me she needed to stay with him at an asylum he helped run. I hated the idea, but she was obviously delusional and was getting violent whenever I tried to take her outside during the day for a walk or for a breath of fresh air.

"At the asylum, she kept getting worse. I was shattered at the thought I might lose her. One night, when I couldn't stand to be away from her any longer, I rode into the city determined to bring her back home where she belonged. When I walked into her room, I found my good friend Dr. Zubrus bent over my wife with his fangs buried in her neck. She looked up at me from the bed and smiled, and as soon as I saw her pointed teeth I knew she was no longer the woman I loved. My wife was dead to me and all that bastard Zubrus had left me was a monster.

"I ran from the room shaking with anger, fear, and disbelief. I ran away and hid from the world for a whole month, trying to get my mind around what I'd seen that night and what, if anything, I could do about it. Eventually I went back and killed Zubrus but it wasn't easy. I didn't know any of the things I know now. I just got lucky and found him during the day. I chopped his head off with the fire axe hanging on his office wall."

Baron Larouche is somewhat confused as to why De Muur wants to tell him this story but something in his tormentor's eyes has him tasting real fear for the first time in nearly eighty years, since he was turned. Swallowing hard under De Muur's intense gaze, Larouche feels he should say something.

"And your wife?"

"No. She was gone. I'm in the habit of telling people I meet that she's still ill and institutionalized for her own good, but the truth is I have no idea where she is or what horrible things she is doing."

"You can't possibly blame me for this!"

"Yes I can. You... and the rest of the demons like you. You've made me what I am and there's no going back. Now tell me who turned you and where I can find the bastard. Do it now or I promise you'll regret it!"

Baron Larouche is silent, weighing his limited options. The sun is rising higher in the sky, the mountain range to the east fully illuminated now, and the wall of light creeping steadily towards them at the far end of the valley.

De Muur can wait no longer.

"Hand me the axe, Hendrik. We'll take off his arms and legs... make it easier to carry him inside that way."

"*No!* I'll... I'll tell you."

"Speak then, demon. My patience is gone."

Baron Larouche whispers the name of a man and a city. De Muur nods once, contented, then climbs back down the ladder. He is barely to the ground when the first rays of sunlight reach the garden and find their way to the man chained to the cross. For the second time this day, Larouche bursts into flames. His face registers agony, but he is determined not to give De Muur the satisfaction of hearing him scream again. Instead he summons his last strength to shout down to his executioner below.

"May my master rip your lungs out and feast on your heart. I promise there will be no mercy for you."

"Just as there will be none for you... from *my* God!"

March 09, 1870,
Letter, Simon Hesler to Arthur De Muur,
London, England.

I'm afraid I have grave news, my friend. Commander Fenton made a surprise appearance at the abbey last September and our little ruse has been exposed. He was furious with you and angered enough with me that I was thrown into a London prison for impersonating a member of the Templar Order. Former member, I tried to reason, but he was having none of it. Seeing as I hadn't really committed a crime, he eventually had me released and I thought it best to contact you straight away. I have no idea of the commander's plans, or what he may or may not decide to do with regards to you, but I felt I owed you this letter of warning. Bad days may be ahead, Arthur. Hope I'm not already too late.

Be well,
Simon

GORD ROLLO

June 18, 1870,
Wittem Castle,
Maastricht, Netherlands.

The sun is directly overhead, and without any breeze the heat is nearly unbearable. De Muur puts his back into the tedious shovel work and is soon soaked with sweat. Twenty minutes later the hole beneath the cross is large enough and deep enough to suit his purposes. Time to take what remains of the husk that had recently been Baron Larouche down. He's nothing but bleached white bones, some holding together on the cross, others already heaped on the ground below.

De Muur is half way up the ladder when Hendrik comes running from the castle at top speed. He's out of breath and clearly upset about something by the time he arrives at the foot of the cross.

"Sir... a messenger just delivered this letter for you."

"You read it, Hendrik. I've got to get this demon buried and out of sight."

"I have read it, sir, and you need to read it right now. It's from your friend that used to be at the Abbey."

"What do you mean, *used* to be?"

Hendrik hands him the wrinkled letter.

De Muur quickly reads Simon Hesler's letter and then tosses it into the hole he's dug in the ground. He remains silent for several minutes, thinking. It's young Hendrik who speaks first.

"Sir? Does Commander Fenton know about Wittem Castle?"

"By that, do you mean will the Templar Knights be showing up at our doorstep?"

Hendrik can only nod.

"Yes, I think they might. Duncan Fenton and I were very close once, and he knows how much I love this castle. He may not show up personally, but I'm sure someone will."

"What do we do then? Obviously we have to leave."

"Not we, Hendrik, me. If they dig up some of the bodies in this garden, I'll be swinging from the gallows soon enough, but no one will blame you. You're just an employee and that's all they need know. You'll stay here and tend to the castle, as always. If I do not return, consider it yours."

"But, you'll need me..."

"Don't argue with me. My soul is already lost but there is hope yet for yours. Whether I like it or not, this is a journey I must take alone."

"But there are Templar Knights throughout Europe aren't there? You can't hide forever. Eventually someone will hear your name and know who you are."

"Not necessarily. Not if Arthur De Muur is waiting here to greet whoever Commander Fenton sends."

Hendrik is more confused than ever, but De muur simply points to the hole in the ground at their feet.

"We erect a marker here, beneath this cross, with my name on it in big letters so it can't be missed. If you're here and Fenton is told I'm dead, there will be no reason to continue looking for me. I'll change my name and carry on as before, only this time I'll kill the vampires where I find them. I've learned more than enough about them now. The time to hunt with a vengeance has arrived."

"What if they dig up the grave, you know... just to be sure?"

"We put Baron Larouche's bones inside. Those teeth will give Fenton something to think about, I'll bet."

Together, they bury Larouche beneath the blackened cross, and begin to make the headstone with De Muur's name on it.

"Go prepare my things, Hendrik. I'll need the stakes, crosses, holy water, garlic, and the silver chains... clothes and toiletries of course, but nothing that isn't absolutely necessary. I must travel as light as possible and making haste is of the utmost importance. I'll finish up here."

"Yes sir, I'll handle it. Just out of curiosity, what will your new name be?"

De Muur considers the question carefully.

"I honestly don't know yet, Hendrik. Larouche told me his master can be found in Amsterdam, so something Dutch, I'd imagine. Van Dyck? Van Buren? Van... who knows? Don't worry... I'll come up with something."

THE WEAPON OF MEMORY

Kyle S. Johnson

Kyle S. Johnson is from Dayton, Ohio and lives wherever he is at the moment. His work has appeared in anthologies such as *Dark Faith, Dark Faith: Invocations,* and *The World is Dead.*

His favorite vampire film is *Near Dark*; his scent is seldom ever likened to that of a dead polecat.

The ash is hanging perilously from the end of a man once called Gerwyn Bedbow's cigarette. The smell doesn't break his concentration, nor does the slow creep of heat bearing down on his fingers. He is locked on to the hulking wall of rust and decay on the other side of the river. The trees on the opposite bank, dying slow deaths from autumn's touch, do their best to conceal it from him, but they are overmatched. That place has been there for nearly a century, and it will probably always be there. This morning, cold and desolate, it waits for him. And somewhere within that place, something else waits. He can almost feel it anticipating him. Something that is no more alive than this derelict colossus before him, a surviving relic of simpler times known as Concrete-Central. Burt is rustling around in the back of the Jeep, getting things in order. Gerwyn flings the cigarette and the ash flakes and disperses like fat snow.

"Not quite Castle Dracula, but it will do by a sight." Burt is trying, for once, to ease Gerwyn into this. But Gerwyn never needed the prodding. He's wanted this for days, every last one blended together, oranges and blues and so much red, all eventually becomes the deepest black. The Buffalo River is rolling lazily along in front of him, calm and steady like an untapped nerve. The sun is dragging up over the horizon, spilling light across the cold earth.

"Are we sure this time? You're absolutely positive he's here?" Gerwin says without ever looking away.

Burt comes up from the boot and leans in the driver's side. "He's here. It's too perfect. Even when this place gets visitors, it's far too big for anyone to find him. It'd take a good full day to touch every corner of this place."

"If that's the case, how do you expect we're going to find him just like that?"

Burt claps Gerwin on the back and chuckles, maybe for the first time since the two had met. "Boy, I never said just like that. I said we will find him. Because we will. We're not just anybody, no, not anymore. And we've got a good full day in front of us. He likes to play it safe. He wouldn't risk being out too close to sunrise. He's tucking himself in right now. We just have to bring him the bedtime story."

Burt goes back to the rear and Gerwyn's gaze is broken, something revelatory on his face. He fetches the small notebook and a pen from his backpack and under so many lines filled with so many words, some crossed through, some totally effaced and blotted out, he writes: *bedtime story*.

Loss is a cruel old bastard. He's a salesman who won't take no for an answer, and if you don't want what he's hocking, he'll leave it on your porch because he knows you have to go out for milk and eggs sometime. Gerwyn knows this, and he was given little choice in his leaving. He knows that loss leaves the widest expanse, a treacherous valley, between normalcy and the now. The only thing a person has to bridge that gap is memory. Memory is Gerwyn's weapon, and like a sidearm or a rapier, it

THE WEAPON OF MEMORY

stands to reason that it's as much a danger to him as it is to the idea of loss. But loss is a product of law; he's an enforcer of rules. What he gives and what he takes, it's never anything personal. Memories are sharp, even in absence of ill-intent. They cut the quickest and the deepest.

So he started writing, though he never was much of a writer. When he does, he keeps it brief, because he trusts his senses to guide him to the purpose hidden within every curve of the letters. And they do, if a little too well. He's filled up four pages front and back, no more than a few words to a line. Because he needs to remember. Maybe not now, but someday. He knows he will need to remember how he came to be what he has become, and what he will become.

So he turns back to the first page where there is nothing. And on the other side of that particular page, nothing still. He cautiously turns three pages of paper, left clear and white, dividing the list of the now and a messy page with several words chosen and all but one struck through for proving insufficient.

All of this space provides an adequate enough buffer for him to separate his Gospel of The New Gerwyn from The Word of The Old World, a simple word that takes him to a place where he never wants to go, but where, in times like this moment, on a plateau high above the world looking down and seeing nothing but madness, he must. One word to remind him of why he is here and why he is going to do what he is on the verge of doing.

~~Fire. Last Day. Home. Dinner. Change. The Thing. The Monster.~~ ▇▇▇
▇▇▇ ~~The End~~.

She's sitting there with him on the couch, snug under his arm. This is symmetry: perfect, burning bright. What's on the television doesn't matter, and it very seldom does unless it's one of her programs. On the table is her celebrated roasted beet salad. She still uses the recipe her babushka brought from the old country, and it certainly looks lovely, but that doesn't make the prospects of its taste or smell any

more appealing to him. Gerwyn hated beets as a child, and age has not damaged his palate significantly enough to make them acceptable cuisine now. So he'll nibble enough and then claim to be full with all the conviction of a child swearing to his principal that his grandmother had passed that morning and he was in no way ditching school to go to a baseball game. He fears that eventually, if she hasn't already, she will realize that he is running out of babushkas to sacrifice to the cause of skipping dinner, and he's going to have to bite that bullet. Because she will make that damned roasted beet salad as long as she's living, and he can like it or love it.

He excuses himself and takes a shower. He spends what feels like too long standing under the faucet, letting the water rush over him, thinking about whether he's ready to make the step. They'd joked about having children, she had always said she wanted two so that she could name them Broom and Sticks so that their little unit could be called Bedbows and Broom Sticks, because that joke just never got old. He is satisfied with how he will broach the subject as he towels off. Honey, I think tonight you should eat my beet salad. I think it's time you started eating for two. Yeah, that's a line he is quite positive she can be proud to take with her to break the news to her co-workers. And it saves him another night of self-imposed guilt looking at the nearly untouched plate and thinking that if he loves her — and does he ever, something fierce — he should eat it, and realizing that no love short of salvation in the kingdom of heaven could get him to wolf it down, though he thinks if Jesus loves him as much as those bumper stickers say he does, then he can shovel that stuff down himself.

It doesn't dawn on him the moment he reaches the bottom of the stairs, and it doesn't land when he takes it in for the first time. It's a slow climb to comprehension, like analyzing a room and realizing something small is amiss, like a teakettle moved from the table to the counter. But the change in front of him is anything but small. Gerwyn and Beatrice watched plenty of horror films together on that very couch, and in each and every one, the lighting is dim or non-existent or alien, always altogether unnatural. Nothing bad ever takes place in a well-lit living room on the shaggy carpet of the floor next to a comfortable old sofa and a shiny new coffee table with one plate full of undisturbed beet salad on it.

Beatrice's symmetry is now fearful. She is twisted, her hands seized around

THE WEAPON OF MEMORY

its head like thick palsied clubs, trying to pull it away. There is red all around her, and though he can't see her face, Gerwyn hears her frenzied gasps and gurgles over the animalistic gnawing. He can't find words, not even one, so he yelps, and he is almost instantly angry with himself for not being stronger for her. But it's loud enough that it stops and turns its head and Beatrice's hands fall away limply.

Its face is slate, like the rest of its body, its features shrunken, almost crumpled like paper. The knot that it calls a mouth is open enough to reveal teeth, each a jagged red spike, and it rears back and lets forth a shrill, piercing cry. It turns, slowly, painfully, toward Gerwyn. Beneath the gray translucence of its flesh, he can see bones and muscles moving and the sluice of rot and his wife's blood coursing through its veins. He thinks he will try to fight it. He knows that he won't run. And his fate be damned, every impending and surreal second of it, so long as he can just make it over there to her and tell her, even with his dying gasps, that she's not alone and she never will be again.

The front door flies open and from the darkness outside comes a man Gerwyn has never seen before. He's older than him, maybe in his fifties, bearded and gray. He's hunched low like a savage, a sharp point of wood in one hand and a machete in the other. He says something that Gerwyn can't hear over the roar of his own adrenaline, and the creature moves, no longer agonizing each inch, but faster than anything he's ever seen this close. The man chases after him, shooting a quick glance over his shoulder at Gerwyn, who is already bounding down toward the landing.

Her hand doesn't move in his. He already knows what everything is telling him not to believe. And there, as he curls her fingers between his, squeezing, hoping that some kind of transitive property will give her his warmth or give him her cooling, empty feeling, he remembers weeping. So he weeps. And when he's wept until there feels like there's nothing left, he screams.

The man reappears, his face angry and flushed. He closes the front door and turns to Gerwyn, looking him over, something like pity registering on his face, but only slightly. He takes a second, measuring his words, then selects them: "I assume you're a smart man. I'm guessing you've seen a movie or read a book in your lifetime. I know this hurts you deeper than I could ever presume to know. But you know what that was." His eyes shift from Gerwyn to Beatrice, and he raises his instruments. "*And you know what I have to do now.*

"*You don't have a choice, and I'm not going to ask you to do it yourself, even if you want to. That's not something you want following you around. Besides, you won't know how to do it right. Not yet. We won't have time for the tutorial, either.*

"*I'll give you five minutes to do what you need to do. Then make yourself sparse. Get as many things as you think you'll need. I'll tell you when we're leaving.*"

Fifteen minutes later, Gerwyn emerges from his home with two large duffel bags and a backpack. The man is leaning against the tail of a Jeep smoking a hand-rolled cigarette. He looks up at Gerwyn, takes a deep draw, and after a long pause where only smoke passes between them, he says, "*I will have plenty of time to explain this to you later. All of it. Right now, we have time for the basics. The fact is, you've seen something tonight that you know shouldn't exist. But it does. And it's out there now. So I'm going to find it. And I'm going to kill it. That much I know for sure.*

"*But here is my offer to you, and it's about the best offer I've ever given anyone: come with me. That thing is going to be a hundred miles from here by sun up, and a man gets awfully lonely driving that far by himself. I can tell you exactly what you will need to do, and I will do my best to get you ready so that when the moment comes, you can be the one to put a stake in that fucker's black heart. If you show some promise, I can help you make sure that nothing like what happened to you here happens to anyone so long as you have a say.*

"*That thing travels fast both ways, fella. And if I can't find it by tomorrow night, it's going to come back here and see to it that it finishes what it started. It knows you now. And if I don't find it first, it will find you.*"

The man's words register only slightly with Gerwyn, who can feel himself leaving his body, floating, off somewhere in the night sky among the stars. But the body that he leaves behind culls enough from what he has heard to nod in agreement. The man takes his bags and places them in the back among his things and several empty red gas cans. The man approaches the front door of the house and opens it, leans inside and hangs there for a moment before closing the door, walking back calmly, and climbing into the driver's seat. Gerwyn is strapped in

THE WEAPON OF MEMORY

next to him and they are already moving when he notices the bright orange flames licking at the bay window from the living room.

"A necessary evil." The man says nonchalantly while fiddling with his rear view mirror. In the side view, Gerwyn can see the house being swallowed from the inside, the smoke starting to plume out from every available crevice. "The name's Burt, in case you're wondering."

They make it to the end of his neighborhood when Gerwyn collides with reality head on. It takes him a half an hour before he's worked out that he is gone. That he died in his home on the floor next to Beatrice, and that the person looking back at him in the windshield's reflection is a non-person. And he realizes that every inch that leads to a foot that leads to a mile that leads to a new and frightening world put him that much further away from what he was before he got out of that much too long shower.

It takes little more than a week of Burt's stories of woe and danger and unreality plopping happily into the halcyon life and just what is going to be required of Gerwyn if he chooses to follow this path when he can start to feel the last remaining strands of himself disappearing. He's finding flaws in Burt's logic, thinking of ways to be more efficient, questioning him, seeming a little too eager for his liking. He sees himself as a block of ice carved into a swan, now being shaved down into something unrecognizable. And he won't stand for it. He needs to remember the oranges and the blues and all of that horrible red, every bit of it, because it will bring him back from the brink and remind him of what he was. Change, he knows now, is like a great fire, and a simple accelerant can render even the sturdiest of foundations to ash with just a spark.

So when Burt has huffed off for supplies after another argument where Gerwin suggests again that it wasn't remotely practical to burn down what might have been their best strategic stronghold and that they should have just waited for the thing to show up and taken it then and there instead of driving all over the state tracking the thing like they were hunting some common animal, when he has a moment to himself and disgust with himself rises so quickly to the surface — It was my home, goddammit, not a chess piece, my home, my home, my — he digs through his backpack and finds one of the things that he knew he would never tell Burt he had: a picture of he and his wife on the day of their wedding, shoving cake into each other's face.

And after crying tears that he feared long gone, he pulls out his notebook and opens it to the first blank page. He writes the word fire and crosses it out just as quickly. He fills ten more lines with words that he knows will lead him back to that night just fine, but none of them work, none of them are right, and he knows it. He knows there is only one thing that fits, one word that will push him in what he has to do going forward and what will call him back to that moment in time. One word, like looking for a lost key, retracing every step, before understanding the old adage that it's always in the last place you look and quite often right under your nose, landing on a face tucked away safe and sound under his arm. He steadies his hand and writes her name. Beatrice.

The warmth of the afternoon sun crawls across Gerwyn's face as Burt returns down the path and meets him at the edge of the old train trestle. Gerwyn had gotten stage fright, chalking it up to some combination of the coppery smell of rust, the quality of the air, the days without sleep. So he took his leave, knowing full well that he had to leave because he was exhilarated. Something about the hunt, the chase, how he could see himself kicking in an ancient door, see himself smiling satisfactorily down on a coffin, prying the lid, staring into that face, twisted and wretched. But that wasn't the breaking point for him. It was the look on his face, uncanny but far too real. And it followed him into sleep and chased him through dreams, reaching out to him, wanting to take him into its mouth and make them one.

Burt takes a dirty cloth to his face and hands before lighting a cigarette and handing it to Gerwyn. He takes a couple of breaths, looking off over Gerwyn's shoulder. "I found him." All Gerwyn can do is nod and do his best to look somewhere between pleased and reflective like a child getting the gift he wanted so badly on Christmas morning after having already found it on the top shelf of the hall closet before Thanksgiving.

THE WEAPON OF MEMORY

He knew, despite his doubts, that the day would come.

"He's on the first floor behind some machinery. I can take you to him or I can tell you where to find him. Your choice. I assume you'll want to be alone in there?"

"Yeah, I think that would be for the best, Burt. Thanks."

"Not a problem, kid." He hands him a notebook with detailed directions. "You're going to be looking for a tag that says, appropriately enough, KILLER DWB. If you get lost in there, holler for me."

"Of course."

"You sure you're okay?"

"I'm...yeah, I'm ready. As ready as I'll ever be. So I'm going to get to it."

Gerwyn walks away reading the instructions, and when he instinctively thumbs the pages, an old tic from a traveled reader, just like that, he has Burt's dirty little secret. There are pages filled with long scribbled letters, lines written, scratched out, rewritten, crossed out, thrice written, a perfect display of agony in reaching for the right words. Each of them is addressed To: My Little Ryan, From: Dad.

He pauses, just long enough to play his hand, and from over his shoulder: "You know, you will never outrun it. There are going to be days where it chases you to the end of sanity, and you're going to wonder the whole way if you should just stop and let it catch you. Don't. Keep running. You can't go back. It will never change. But that doesn't mean you have to let them die. The memories. They're yours to keep. So keep them. Not just to use them, either. Keep them, because when that's gone, you're gone."

Gerwyn looks back at Burt, nods, and smiles a little. And Burt blows the dust off of an old tome, cracks the spine, and returns the favor.

"Good luck, Ger."

Before Gerwyn reaches the entrance, staring down inevitability in the shadow of the industrial tomb that is Concrete-Central, he sets down the weapons in his hands and accesses the ones in his head. Pointed and dangerous, but with adequate skill to wield them, he begins to build a bridge. He understands now that, like looking for lost keys, it's always in the last place you look. That in order to keep touch with the man he was, he has to know that person intimately and leave no stone unturned. That he must retrace every step, no matter how painful the coals burn beneath his feet. He retrieves his notebook and opens to the latest filled page. And he turns back. He comes to the page with so many discarded words and the only one that truly matters. And he turns back one more page, aims his pen at the bottom line, and writes: *roasted beet salad.*

THE EXCAVATION

Stephen Zimmer

Stephen Zimmer is an award-winning author of speculative fiction, whose works include the Fires in Eden Series (Epic Fantasy), the Rising Dawn Saga (epic-scale Urban Fantasy), the Harvey and Solomon tales (Steampunk), the Hellscapes tales (Horror), and the Rayden Valkyrie tales (Sword and Sorcery). Stephen is also a writer-director in moviemaking, with feature and short film credits such as *Shadows Light, The Sirens*, and *Swordbearer*. Further information on Stephen can be found at www.stephenzimmer.com

In the realms of Vampire Literature, Stephen has a particular liking for Brian Lumley's Necroscope novels, with a special affection for the Vampire World trilogy beginning with *Blood Brothers*. Inventive, visceral, and epic in scope, Lumley delivers a very engaging and fresh take on vampires. As a whole, the Necroscope books constitute of those rare series in the genre that is as horrific as it is thought-provoking, the latter element including a particularly intriguing concept of the afterlife.

Gazing into the star-speckled sky, feeling the frosty touch of night air upon his face, Jacob ruminated on the nature of the light he beheld. The starlight had begun its journey vast ages ago, long before the remains in the pit were living, breathing men.

Unearthed in a moment of happenstance, the find had been a stunning revelation to the construction crew laboring to strip earth away for a new road. The area was now a secure excavation site, promising to bring a strange, macabre tale to the pages of academic journals.

Twenty-three skeletons, their heads violently severed from their bodies, had been identified in the pile of bones. All would soon be cataloged, and prepared for the trip back to the museum in London.

Their identities were clear once a few tooth samples had been analyzed. The skeletons belonged to men from far northern climates, dating back over a thousand years, almost certainly Vikings. Saxon justice had been meted out harshly, following a raid gone terribly awry in pre-Norman England. The signs were there to be read, as heavy blades wielded in clumsy fashion left their telltale marks upon jaws and collarbones alike. Furrows carved into hand bones showed where men in desperation grabbed at the implements of their execution, clutching double-edged swords with their bare hands as honed iron was driven through their flesh.

The killings had not been done gracefully, and Jacob could only imagine the bloody scene as it unfolded. Captives, looking into the face of death, had been made to pay the ultimate price for their transgression of Saxon lands.

Skulls were piled neatly to one side of the elongated pit, the rest of the bones lumped haphazardly in another. There were three fewer skulls than there were bodies, indicating some of the doomed Vikings' heads had likely been stuck on the ends of spears; the impaled, decaying heads serving as gruesome trophies, and warnings to others contemplating raids into Anglo-Saxon England during the tenth century.

Jacob shivered, bringing his jacket in closer to his body, with his hands buried in the outer pockets. The thoughts of what transpired over a thousand years ago were sobering, but it was an incredible find nonetheless. It catalyzed the encampment now encircling the pit.

Most of the team had taken to more modern accommodations for the

THE EXCAVATION

night, but Jacob, and a few others, including the leader of the excavation, preferred to keep a close watch on the site.

The dig had an air of adventure, and Jacob was thoroughly enjoying every moment. It was his first major expedition since gaining his Ph.D. He was conducting it alongside his closest friends, one of whom was his mentor in the academic world.

"I'd say that there's a very good chance those piles aren't all there's to find around here ... just like you thought," Brenda stated, breaking the silence. She cast a glance towards the excavation pit, with the hint of a smile dancing about her lips.

"Meaning?" Jacob queried, turning towards her with a quizzical expression.

Her eyes sparkled with a swell of excitement. She held back her response for a moment, one lasting long enough to prod Jacob's impatience. They had worked together long enough for him to know she was onto something of significance, and he had a strong notion what it regarded.

"On a hunch, a few of us took the liberty of a little jaunt into the woods after dinner. I think we might've found something," she replied. "Only about an hour of moderate hiking away, deeper into the woods to the north of here. We marked it on our GPS's."

"Found what?" Jacob pressed, as her smile spread wider, his curiosity piqued. "What's deeper in the woods?"

"The chronicles were accurate," she declared, giving him a wink.

On parchment, Saxon monks recorded the defeat of a sizeable Viking incursion right in the area where the skeletons had been found. Yet the chronicle entry said the Viking war band came up river on eight longships, indicating a group much larger than the mere 23 skeletons excavated. The disparity added a subsidiary quest to the grand expedition.

Jacob wondered where the other bodies were, if the raid was the rout described by the Saxon monks. He also found it strange that all the skeletons found in the pit had been treated alike. A captured warrior of high status would normally have received a different handling from the others.

As the area was close to the old boundary between Saxon lands and Viking-held territory known as the Dane Law, it was possible the body of a high status warrior had been taken away under the cover of darkness, for a more proper burial. If that was so, all the archaeological team had to do was find the pagan burial mound. Dr. Grayson, the head of the excavation, was more interested in what the team had in hand, but he had not thought Jacob's theory entirely implausible.

"The chronicles were accurate? How do you know?" Jacob asked.

"Let's just say there's a mound ... where there really shouldn't be one," Brenda replied, grinning. "So, you wanna go see it?"

"Yes, of course," Jacob said, his mind completely off the remains before him. "When can we go?"

"Let's wait for daylight," she said.

"Can't wait that long," Jacob said. "You're an academic, so you should understand. We don't keep discoveries waiting."

"Impulsive," she responded with a teasing lilt. "Jacob, it's almost eleven now. It takes an hour to find the place, if we can navigate without tripping over ourselves in the dark."

"A few of us with flashlights should do fine. Skies are pretty clear. Nearly full moon overhead. We won't stay long. I promise. I just want to see it for myself," Jacob said impatiently.

Brenda sighed. "I thought that might happen. Which is why I told Kendrick, Gwen, and Trey not to go to sleep yet, until I'd talked to you."

Jacob chuckled. "In the case of Gwen and Trey, I don't think they were planning on sleep anyway."

She laughed. "No, they probably weren't."

"Explorations of a more amorous kind," Jacob remarked, laughing. "But let's rouse them anyway."

"Let's!" Brenda agreed, with mischievous enthusiasm.

THE EXCAVATION

"What did I tell you ... right here, in the marshy area," Kendrick proclaimed triumphantly, strolling along the top of a prominent mound rising out of the wetland.

Jacob shook his head, his boots already soaked through, but had to grin. The mound was an anomaly in the surrounding terrain. Having been to many barrows and burial mounds across England, Ireland, and continental Europe, he had little doubt what it was.

"Looks pretty intact. Can't find any signs of digging ... anywhere," Brenda said, from Jacob's side. She idly passed the beam of her flashlight across the side of the mound. "Unsullied, and ready for our team to uncover what lies beneath."

"We'll need to come back during the daytime, and cordon this area off," Jacob replied, eyeing the oblong mound with swelling interest. His mind was already racing with possibilities regarding the artifacts that might be found inside.

"Probably won't find a ship burial, but you might find a few very nice implements," Brenda said. "They wouldn't bury a leader without a few extras."

Kendrick put his hands on his hips, staring down at the others. "Do we really have to wait that long?"

"We have to wait that long," Jacob replied firmly. No matter how much he desired to delve right into the mound, it was best to wait until it could be approached properly. The dig at the road cut was spiraling into an incredible archaeological event.

Kendrick reached into an outer pocket on his jacket, pulling out a short-handled digging tool with a spade-shaped end. "I saw this mound first, so I'm going to break the ceremonial ground before we head back. It won't hurt your plans, but I'm not conceding that privilege, Jacob."

"Hothead," Gwen called back, laughing.

Trey said nothing, content to keep his right arm wrapped snugly around Gwen.

Jacob waved his hand towards Kendrick in a dismissive fashion.

"Then indulge yourself, Kendrick. But no more than a little scraping off the top. Don't want to damage anything that's been stored so faithfully for us ... for well over a millennium."

Kendrick crouched down, and drove the small spade into the ground, wrenching up a scoop of dirt. He held it forth for the others to see.

"Okay, we've broken the ground," he declared, before looking immediately down, and becoming quiet. He uttered in a low voice, "That's pretty interesting."

Jacob watched Kendrick attentively examining the ground, where he had dug through the loamy surface. Just above the area, tendrils of light gray mist had begun to rise upward, slow and sinuous. The moonlight caught the mist as it wound its way higher, the little silvery columns growing thicker by the moment.

"Looks like some mist has been trapped underground," Kendrick jested. He waved his hands in front of his face, laughing, "Believe me, it stinks bad. Really bad! Breaking the ground might've been a bad idea."

"Well, it's a boggy area," Jacob said, a moment before the pungency encompassed him as well. He gagged reflexively, making a face. "Oh, god, that is awful!"

Brenda, Trey, and Gwen all made loud exclamations as the stench reached their noses. It reeked of rot and decay, potent enough to make the eyes water.

"Another reason to come back in daylight," Jacob stated, retching for a second.

"No argument here, but I'm breathing through my mouth until we get clear of these woods," Brenda said. "Kendrick, come on down! Let's get out of here!"

Jacob followed Brenda's advice as he neared the cusp of vomiting. Stabilizing, he looked up towards Kendrick, and his eyes narrowed. He felt a wave of light-headedness pass over him, struggling to understand what he perceived.

It appeared as if a man-shaped shadow of considerable height was

THE EXCAVATION

looming behind Kendrick. Even stranger, the shape appeared to be darkening, as if transforming from a misty substance into something solid.

Kendrick rose from his crouching position, an airy hiss penetrating the stillness. He turned around slowly and the shadowy figure's arm lashed out, just as Jacob mustered a cry of warning.

Gasping at first, Kendrick was reduced to pitiful gurgles as he was jerked off the ground. The shadow-being used only one arm, its hand clenching Kendrick about the neck.

The hapless archaeology student's legs kicked out and flailed, his hands grabbing desperately for the wrist of his assailant. It was to no avail, as the thing was astonishingly strong.

The shadow-figure's head tilted to the side as Kendrick was brought in closer, clearly seeking purchase at his neck. A horrid sucking noise arose, and Kendrick's legs kicked feverishly for a couple moments, before going limp.

A sharp crack filled the air a second later, as the shadow-being drew its head back. Kendrick's head lolled to one side, right before he was hurled through the air towards the others. Screams and cries burst from the group as the body landed with a heavy thump a few feet in front of them.

Jacob did not need to examine Kendrick to know that he was dead, but Brenda and Gwen rushed to his awkwardly-twisted body, kneeling down.

"He's dead! Oh god, he's dead!" Gwen cried out, sobbing.

"His ... throat's ... been torn out," Brenda stammered, as if she could not believe what she saw.

Jacob's mind spun, but he had enough presence of it to look back towards the shadow-figure. The entity had not taken so much as a stride, and was quietly gazing down on the group of humans. Whether fanciful imagination sparked by the events, or accurate perception, it looked to Jacob as if two tiny, reddish embers rested where the being's eyes would be.

The eerie, rattling hiss filled the air again, and the tall being stomped forward, taking long strides down the slope of the burial mound. It was heading straight towards them.

"Get outta here! Let's go!" Jacob called to the others.

His knees felt weak as he resisted a surreal paralysis threatening to take hold of his body. Panic shrouded him, inducing his heartbeat to quicken, and his breath to shorten.

Gwen and Brenda looked up, screaming as they saw the massive dark form storming towards them. Brenda stood and started hurrying, as did Trey. Gwen's eyes were wide with fright. She looked like a rabbit caught within the mesmerizing gaze of a predator, freezing in place and uttering whimpering sounds that danced on the edge of hysterics.

Trey ran back, reached down, clutched her upper arm, and wrenched her up to her feet with a robust heave. "Get moving! Now!"

He gave her a little shove forward, enough to break her free from her immobilizing trance. Keeping Gwen just ahead of him, Trey hurried away from the mound, with Jacob following behind.

The naked, late-fall trees allowed enough moonlight through that the group had little trouble keeping their footing. Jacob's breath quickened, as his body was not in condition for the frenzied pace demanded of it. Breezes whipped about his ears, as his boots pounded on the forest floor. The cold air bit harshly into his lungs, and he threw several glances back, fearing the shadow-man would be on his heels.

The four ran onward, their legs tiring fast as their shoes squished and sloshed in the water-logged soil. The land became more solid as they continued. Jacob's legs burned and his lungs were raw when they finally exploded from the treeline, streaking across open ground.

"I ... can't ... keep this ... up," Trey exclaimed between prodigious gulps of air, grabbing at his side with a pained expression as he slowed.

Jacob looked back towards the forest. The woods were quiet, but he was not about to assume anything. A great tension clung to the air, and he knew inside that the night was far from over.

THE EXCAVATION

"Just keep moving," Jacob urged.

They proceeded at a brisk walk for a while, gradually recovering their breath. On the open ground, Jacob knew it would be easy to see pursuers, and he threw periodic glances over his shoulder.

As the distance from the trees grew, it was hard for him to tell if any movements he registered were just trees swaying in the night breezes, or the emergence of the fetid monstrosity.

Looking over to Brenda, he saw she was tapping on the touch screen of her mobile device. She frowned, cursing under her breath.

"No frickin' signal," she said, rolling her eyes.

"Keep trying," Jacob said. "Anyone else have theirs?"

Gwen and Trey shook their heads.

"Fantastic," Jacob lamented. "Just keep moving, we've got to get Dr. Grayson."

"What the hell are you doing!" barked Dr. Grayson, his face thick with irritation, and eyes bleary as he pulled himself up into a sitting position.

"Dr. Grayson, we have an emergency! We need to get out of here, right now!" Jacob replied urgently. He and his companions crowded around the mattress on the ground. "You've got to come with us, right away!"

"Get out of here? What on earth are you talking about?" Dr. Grayson responded sharply, clearly incredulous, and becoming angrier by the second.

Jacob, Brenda, Trey, and Gwen spoke quickly, stammering a few times as they related the details of their ill-fated sojourn to the burial mound. Dr. Grayson scowled, and Jacob had the strong impression the professor felt as if he were being made the subject of a practical joke.

Even when Brenda pulled her mobile device out in the midst of the telling, stating that she wanted to make an emergency call, it was patently clear that Dr. Grayson did not believe the story. She uttered several expletives, and Jacob's spirit sank, when it was again revealed that there was no network connection to access.

"A monster coming out of the swamp, you say? One that threw Kendrick all the way down a burial mound with one arm," Dr. Grayson growled, after they finished with the bizarre tale. "Thank you for your concern, but I have to get up at 5:30 a.m. and get some paperwork done before the curator of the museum arrives!"

His voice trailed off as he cocked his head to one side. His expression became more pensive than angry.

"What's that ... sound?" Dr. Grayson suddenly asked, tilting his head a little further.

Jacob blanched as a low, breathy hiss carried to his ears from outside the tent, faint but unmistakable. "Oh God ... that's it!"

"We've gotta get out of here, Dr. Grayson, please, trust us!" Brenda pleaded.

"I swear this isn't a prank!" Gwen added.

"If this is some elaborate hoax, know that you're all going to face severe disciplinary action, starting with immediate dismissal from this excavation. Don't try me," the professor snapped, though his face exhibited more tension, as the rattling hiss slowly rose in volume.

"I swear Dr. Grayson, this is no joke," Jacob said.

Getting up from the mattress, the professor slipped on some walking shoes. He went with the others as they moved to the flap of his tent.

The revenant figure was upon them as they emerged from the interior, and Jacob heard cries of alarm as hands clutched onto him with iron-strength. He caught the sight of a large arm swiping through the air, and heard a grunt and heavy thump, as someone was knocked to the ground.

The acrid stench was overwhelming as he stared into the cavernous gaze of the macabre figure. Wisps of hair clung to the entity's leathered visage, and its long, blackened, blood-stained teeth were bared in a mask of rage.

THE EXCAVATION

There was no spark of life present in the thing he saw before him. Rather, it was a mockery of life.

Balling up his fist, and reacting with alacrity, Jacob slammed flesh and bone into the thing's face. The heavy blow thundered into the lower jaw of the creature, but it did nothing to affect it.

Recalling his father's advice to 'always go for the knees', Jacob kicked out at the right knee of the creature. The crunching impact caused the thing to buckle slightly, though it emitted no outcry or sound of pain.

An ear-piercing shriek came from the creature, just as Jacob felt himself being released. Rotating swiftly, it locked its hands on Trey, who had barreled into its side.

Trey was lifted off the ground by the hulking figure. A crunching, tearing sound emitted as it leaned in and bit into the right side of his face. He loosed a high-pitched scream, as the skin covering half of his face was ripped free, leaving him with a ghastly, permanent expression.

Jacob flinched as Gwen hurled herself at the entity, shrieking in a fusion of rage and terror. The being caught her in mid-stride with one hand, and shoved her unceremoniously to the ground.

Trey screamed again, as the entity brought its jaws down on his throat. The sucking sounds came again, as if the entity was quenching a parched thirst. Blood began dripping from Trey's shoes onto the ground.

Trey was thrown aside like a discarded sack of garbage. The shadowy figure whirled towards Gwen, who was just getting to her feet. She screamed as it surged at her, the noise becoming a pitiful sound as the revenant burrowed its hands into the flesh of her stomach, driving its crusted fingernails deep.

Jacob's eyes burned hot with tears. He saw that he could do nothing for her. Her head was at an unnatural angle, and she made no sound as her killer ripped out chunks of her flesh, feeding ravenously.

Jacob yelled, putting his helplessness and sorrow into the cry. He looked around and saw where Brenda was working to help Dr. Grayson, who had a bewildered look as he tried to get to his feet. He was evidently the recipient of the sweeping blow when the group had emerged from the tent.

"Hurry, get up!" Brenda implored, trying to lift the disoriented professor.

Jacob raced over, and together they pulled the professor to his feet.

"Brenda, here, this way!" he urged.

Assisting Dr. Grayson, they moved as fast as they could away from the campsite. After about a hundred strides, the professor was able to support himself, shedding much of his grogginess.

Jacob looked back towards the camp. What he saw would be forever emblazoned in his memory. The macabre entity was standing still, its body silhouetted in the moonlight. Its arm was thrust high into the air, holding aloft a morbid trophy: Trey's severed head.

To Jacob's eyes, it was like the thing was taunting them. He began to slow down, feeling a sense of hopelessness.

"What are you doing Jacob? Run, just run!" Brenda yelled at him, keeping her legs pumping as tears streaked down her face.

Snapping out of his stupor, Jacob hurried forward with the other two survivors.

Despite coming close to tripping several times in his haste, Jacob reached the waist-high gate enclosing the front yard of a one-story house. Its lights had beckoned from afar, where it perched in the midst of a modest plot of land, just outside a quaint, rural village

Before he could reach over the gate to open the latch securing it, a man's voice cut sharply through the darkness.

"Stop! Don't come closer!"

The voice froze Jacob in place, even as he heard Dr. Grayson and Brenda stumbling up behind him, panting heavily. A lone figure stood on the porch, lined by the light streaming through the open front door.

"No time! Something's coming! We're in danger!" Jacob called out,

THE EXCAVATION

finding he had no idea what to call the shadow-figure.

"It's killed more than one of our group," Dr. Grayson added, huffing laboriously, as he drew up alongside Jacob.

"I said ... " the man began before stopping, his eyes staring past Jacob and the others.

Jacob looked back, and saw a silvery mist flowing across the ground. It was moving far too rapidly to be of natural origin.

Opening the gate, Jacob ran forward, followed by Brenda and the professor. The older man stood in place, staring towards the mist. The others shoved him back into the house, as they piled inside and shut the door behind them.

"What in the name of God are you doing!" the man yelled.

"It's coming after us!" Jacob said.

"Not a damn thing!" Brenda said anxiously, looking at her mobile device.

"What's coming?" the old man asked.

"Don't know what to call it! Came out of a burial mound we found in the bog land," Jacob said.

"I saw it," Dr. Grayson added. "Wouldn't believe it if I didn't see it myself."

"Do you have a gun?" Jacob inquired.

"No, I don't!" the old man said sourly.

"What do we do now?" Brenda asked.

Before the man answered, the room was permeated with a horrible aroma, as the glowing mist began wafting underneath the front door. The thing from the mound formed right before their eyes, its head almost brushing the ceiling.

"Through the back door," the old man shouted, his eyes wide as he beheld the monstrosity in his home. "Make for the village!"

"What about your car?" Brenda inquired, as they hurried through to the back of the house.

"Don't have one," he retorted sharply.

Outside, they hurried towards the village, nothing more than a few small houses huddled along a narrow lane. Not surprisingly, most of the houses did not open their doors at the late night hour; save for one.

A surly-looking man and his teenage son joined them. Alfred spoke with the man quickly about the situation; both father and son had stern expressions etched upon their faces. The father sent the son inside to retrieve a wood-cutting axe, then turned back towards Alfred.

"Seems crazy, but I know you are no fool, Alfred," the father said. When the youth emerged, axe in hand, he asked. "So what's the plan?"

"To the rooftop," Alfred said. "Better to defend, and we can see what's happening. Bastard can't surprise us so easy."

With no disagreement from the others, the group used a couple of large crates to help reach the roof. Dr. Grayson needed a little extra assistance, but in a few moments they all had a high vantage.

"Keep your eyes out," Alfred muttered through clenched jaws, his eyes iron-hard as he looked outward.

"There! Look!" Brenda said, pointing.

The sentient mist had reached the village, and was entering one of the houses that had kept its door shut. Dread gripped Jacob as he watched. It was not long before screams came from inside the house.

A woman stumbled out the front of the house a few moments later, her eyes darting about frantically. She was in a sleeping gown, having been awoken from her dreams into a living nightmare.

Without warning, Brenda scrambled to the edge of the roof, and jumped down to the ground. Jacob started to go after her, when he felt himself yanked backwards by a firm hand on his shoulder.

Turning his head, he found himself eye to eye with Alfred, as the other's hard gaze lanced into him. He snapped, "Don't be a fool!"

"I've got to help her!" Jacob shot back.

"Look now!" Alfred told him.

THE EXCAVATION

Brenda had reached the woman, and was helping her towards the house that the others were atop. There was nothing Jacob could do if he got down. He watched in horror as the shadow-being lumbered into sight, from the front of the house the mist had entered. It stopped in its tracks, and oriented towards the two women, striding towards them a moment later.

Looking towards Brenda, he saw her reach the house they had climbed onto, with the woman at her side. Stooping down, she locked her palms together, fingers interlaced to form a bracing stirrup to help the woman to the edge of the roof.

"I can help from here," Jacob said, tearing himself away from Alfred's grip, seeing the middle-aged woman's fruitless struggle to pull herself up despite Brenda's help.

Working his way to the roof's edge, he extended his hand, grabbing the woman's and pulling as Brenda thrust up from below. The woman was able to get her torso up and over. Jacob grabbed onto her with both hands, and heaved as hard as he could. He felt a burst of momentum, and a quick glance told him Dr. Grayson had moved in to assist.

Once the woman was safe, Jacob quickly leaned back over the edge to where Brenda was trying to reach the roof herself. Everything in him quailed as he clasped her hand, seeing desiccated limbs reach in — dirt-caked hands with extended, claw-like fingernails seizing her ankles. She was pulled to the ground hard, torn from Jacob's grasp and screaming at the top of her lungs.

Jacob had to rip his eyes away from the butchery, as the shadow-being maimed her and began drinking from her torn throat. He crawled away from the roof edge, wiping at his eyes as the waters of sorrow and frustration overflowed, streaming down his cheeks.

"Lad, I'm sorry," Alfred interjected firmly. "But you must keep your wits. Don't think we're out of this, but I have an idea on how to get the bastard."

"Tell me what I need to do," Jacob growled through his tears, a potent rage welling up. "That thing's not gonna stop until we're all dead."

"Bait the big bastard in, keep him physical, not mist. Maybe we can bring this to a close," Alfred declared.

Jacob nodded, grimly stating, "Just tell me how."

"Slip down the back, come around, and bring him back there," Alfred said, indicating the small fenced-in garden plot. "We'll do the rest."

"What about morning, if that thing's not natural, I ... " Jacob began.

Alfred interrupted, "There!"

Following the older man's gesture, Jacob saw the living nightmare reaching over the top of the roof. It seemed to be having difficulty trying to climb.

"Coming to claim the last few breathing," Dr. Grayson remarked solemnly.

"Now or never, it'll go back to mist soon. You are the fastest left, lad. Think you can get the bastard to the garden in back?" Alfred asked. "Get him there, keep his attention, I'll do my best."

"Not encouraging, but there's no better plan," Jacob responded curtly.

He scrambled down the back of the roof, and quickly took account of the garden area. Surrounded by a high privacy fence made of wooden planks, it was accessed by a small gate on the right side of the house. Unsure whether it was locked or not, Jacob braced at the roof's edge, turned, and dropped to the ground.

He hurried over to the gate, and saw it was locked from the inside. Lifting the latch, he swung the gate open, and strode out.

He fixed his eyes upon the huge, ghoulish figure out front, which was still occupied with trying to get to the roof. On the ground level, Jacob was reminded how massive the monster was. For a moment his courage wavered, and he thought about racing back through the gate and locking it.

Steeling his nerves, he reminded himself that no gate could stop a being that could turn into mist. It had to be fooled, and Jacob had to trust that the older man had a viable solution.

THE EXCAVATION

"Hey! Want to get me? You won't have to climb!" Jacob yelled.

The shadow-being stopped, and turned towards him. Jacob edged backward, his breath quickening, calling upon all reserves of willpower to keep from running. Stepping carefully, he backed into the enclosure, keeping his eyes trained rigidly on the figure. His heart froze as it moved in his direction, its lengthy strides closing the gap swiftly.

Once he was in the middle of the backyard, Jacob waited. The creature passed through the gateway and tromped forward.

Jacob squared himself towards the hideous entity, though his body trembled. The creature's back was to the house, and out of the corner of his eye, Jacob could see Alfred inching down to the lip of the roof.

Jacob kept his feet planted, his heart about to burst through his chest. Every part of him screamed to run. A wave of putrescent odor engulfed him, a moment before the being loomed over him, causing him to choke as the entity grabbed for him.

The creature lifted him effortlessly, leaving his shoes dangling a couple of feet off the ground. His pants became soaked as his bladder emptied, pissing himself in his terror. The unholy gaze of the entity held him riveted in place, as Jacob stared into the abyss within the creature's eye sockets. Set deeply within were small points of red, glowing light, a spectral hint of hell itself.

The distinctive, rattling hiss sounded through a mouth missing its upper and lower lip, exposing blood-soaked, blacked teeth, unnaturally long. Jacob knew he was helpless to do anything, and all hope fled as he stared into the deathly countenance. He felt himself being brought in closer to the entity, as it leaned forward and opened its maw wide, to quench itself on his blood.

Jacob did not see the axe blade severing the neck of the entity, until the creature's head toppled free from its body. He was held suspended in the air for a moment longer, until he fell heavily to the ground. He cried out as he landed awkwardly, spraining his ankle.

It took him a few moments to realize the entity was no longer a threat, and that he had been freed. He saw Dr. Grayson and the others getting down from the roof, as he took in the welcome sight of Alfred, who had wielded the axe that decapitated the creature.

"Not saying it's over yet. Going to make damn sure," Alfred muttered, as he began hacking at the stinking corpse. Severing limbs one by one, the old man chopped the creature apart. Alfred yelled over his shoulder, "Get a fire going, now! Right here!"

The father and son who had joined them set about gathering scraps of wood as Dr. Grayson went to Jacob's side. The middle-aged woman that Brenda sacrificed her life for hung back from the others, eyes still wide and gleaming with fright.

"You did a great thing, Jacob. You saved us," Dr. Grayson commended, in a low voice. "We wouldn't have made it, if you hadn't occupied its attention. I know that."

Jacob winced from the pain in his ankle, as he looked to the professor. He said nothing in reply.

A small bonfire was soon blazing within the garden plot. Alfred and the two village men tossed pieces of the creature into the flames, until every last part of the entity was being consumed in fire.

Not a word was spoken among the group as Jacob stared deep into the flames. He felt numb to the core, drained of energy and emotion.

He was still in the same position when dawn's first light fell upon the village, as the horizon lightened to the east. A melancholic silence reigned over the area. Nobody in the group had said a word, all wrestling with what they had seen and been through.

"And so the dawn rises, once more," Alfred stated, closing his eyes, and loosing a sigh that conveyed the weight of many generations.

SKRAELING
Joel A. Sutherland

Joel A. Sutherland is the Bram Stoker Award nominated author of Frozen Blood and Be a Writing Superstar, a creative writing guide for children published by Scholastic. His short fiction has appeared in many anthologies and magazines, including Blood Lite II & III and Cemetery Dance Magazine. He has a Masters of Information and Library Studies from Aberystwyth University in Wales and works in a public library near his home east of Toronto. Sutherland also appeared as 'The Barbarian Librarian' on the first season of the Canadian edition of the hit reality show Wipeout.

He has yet to meet a vampire without a single redeeming characteristic, but some of his favourites can be found in *Salem's Lot*, *30 Days of Night* and *I Am Legend*. He'll also admit (in the right company) to enjoying watching *True Blood* with his wife.

A speck.

Nothing more than a pinpoint of black on a sheet of pure, brilliant white. Like a star in reverse. Like the smallest pupil surrounded by the largest eye.

Just a speck.

But it's enough to set my pulse racing. Enough to clutch my heart within an iron hand and squeeze my lungs so every breath is pain. Enough to make me contemplate abandoning my task and turning around.

It's only a second or two before I shake the thought and carry on. I can't head back now – I know that. But it's tempting. Oh, so tempting.

Because that speck of black, although small, is far, far away. Must be ten or fifteen miles, I reckon, across snow-covered ice on the empty horizon. And if I can see it from this distance, it's big. Much bigger than an elk, moose – hell, even bigger than a damn polar bear.

And I know it can only bring one of two things.

Life.

Or death.

I hope for life but plan for death.

My gloved fingers dance over my body in a well-rehearsed pattern like a horny teenage boy getting frisky with a girl under a sleeping bag. But my motions are much more practical than anything hormone driven. I finger the guthook hunting knife, twelve inches, at my waist. The scaling knife, eight inches, sticking out of my right boot. And the micro dagger, three point five inches, strapped to my left wrist. Check, check and check.

Next, my fingers snake over my shoulder and grip the crossbow strapped to my back. With a quick, strong pull it slides out of its holster and into my hands. It feels so right there, its weight reassuring. I always keep an arrow preloaded but I check it anyway. My remaining six arrows are always kept in a quiver on my left side but I check them anyway, too. Safety, safety, safety – three rules that have kept me alive so long in this frozen, skraeling-infested world.

I return the crossbow to its holster and drop my hands back down to my sides, but I know their idleness will be short-lived. I'm too jittery, too anxious, and my hands will restart their silent checklist of my weapons in a few minutes.

I keep walking, never stop.

SKRAELING

My boots drag through snow drifts and glide over ice where the wind, howling and bitter, has exposed it.

The speck grows larger, large enough to turn into something more than a black dot.

It's a ship.

My fingers caress my knives, my crossbow, my arrows.

I keep walking.

Never stop.

One hundred paces from the ship, I stop.

It's the biggest thing I've ever seen. In a few of the books that we had managed to find – before we had to abandon them – I'd read about buildings called skyscrapers – structures so tall they could kiss angels. The ship looks as big as I imagined skyscrapers to be, if one had fallen on its side. It's lined with hundreds of windows and big blue letters that say DISNEY ALASKA CRUISE. I recognize the letters, of course, but the words are foreign to me.

Time has passed. I don't know how much. That's bad, dangerous.

The ship is frozen in place, big jagged shards of ice surrounding it like a ring of mangled teeth.

I sprint to the side of the ship and take a quick moment to catch my breath and my thoughts. Not only was it bad and dangerous to lose myself in thought so long, but stupid, too. Other than my wits and my weapons, all I have on my side is the element of surprise. If there were humans or skraelings on the ship, there's a better chance they now know I'm here. And if there are humans or skraelings on the ship and they now know I'm here, not only is my mission to gather supplies at risk, so is my life.

Leader would say that's not just stupid, that's suicidal.

I resist the temptation to board the ship immediately to forage for supplies – Leader would kill me himself if he learned I did that – and begin a perimeter search. I crouch low under the windows and slip silently over the ice, making my way north to the prow where I'll double back on the other side.

There are long gouges in the ship's hull, strips of metal peeled away and left to dangle in the air. A closer look reveals similar gouges in the ice's surface. These ominous marks, coupled with the lack of bodies, make it clear what happened here.

Skraelings.

The only question that remains is whether or not they've left, or if they're still here.

I lose my footing and slip on a patch of ice. A momentary lapse and a small mistake – my second of the day – but in this world there's little difference between "momentary" and "small" and "prolonged" and "large". I fall forward and hit the ship, getting my hands up to soften the blow just before impact. It saves me from hurting myself, but a hollow metal trilling sound reverberates through the silent afternoon. It would've been enough to hear anywhere in the ship.

If there are still skraelings inside, I'll be dead within ten minutes.

Unless I can get in, grab anything I can get my hands on and get out in five.

Abandoning caution in favour of haste, I sprint the rest of the way around the ship. Just before I reach the location where I began, a bright spot in the ice catches my eye and I stop, turn around, drop to my knees and peer down below the surface. There's something buried in the ice.

It's roughly 4" by 7". It's covered in writing. And other than food or medicine or weapons, it's the most valuable item I could've hoped to find.

It's a book.

Part of the title is obscured due to the angle the book is frozen in the ice, but I can read

–lso Rises

SKRAELING

and, below that,

—*mingway*.

My heart races – it's English.

Nothing else matters at the moment.

All I care about is getting the book.

I pull the micro dagger free from my glove and grip it tight. Without hesitation, I slam the tip down on the ice. It deflects off the surface and I barely hang on to the hilt, but a tiny fleck of ice chips away.

I raise the knife and strike the ice again. A similar result.

Again and again and again, chipping away at the ice. Soon I've created a tiny divot, just enough to fit the very end of my pinky finger. I'm covered in sweat. So little progress for so much effort.

It's a terrible risk. I look around. I'm still alone. As far as I can tell.

A blur of motion out of my peripheral vision. I have my crossbow in my hands and fire an arrow before I know where or what I'm shooting at. The loosed arrow ricochets off the ground to my left, flips through the air and skitters away like a cockroach fleeing danger.

That's when I realize that I shot at the ice below my feet.

That's when I realize there's a living skraeling trapped beneath the surface.

Living skraeling. I'm not known in my tribe for having a sense of humour, but that would've gotten a good laugh around the fire.

The skraeling slams into the underside of the ice, its face and hands pressing against the clear barrier. Its long, matted hair wisps through the water hypnotically, swirling around its pale face and piercing eyes. It scratches and claws at the ice with cragged fingernails and, when that has no effect, its fangs come out and it rams its head in desperation. I take a step back. I've seen countless skraelings commit impossibly difficult feats to get at their prey, to feed on blood and flesh and viscera. But the ice holds. I am safe.

The skraeling is imprisoned.

So is the book.

I cannot leave without the book, but freeing it will also free the skraeling.

This is more an admission of fact than an argument against my course of action. There is no doubt what I must do – there is no decision to make.

Bang! Bang! Bang! The skraeling slams its body against the ice with relentless determination.

I aim at the small divot I've chipped away in the ice, lift my knife and swing.

Nothing enrages a skraeling like being held captive against its will. The one trapped below my feet and the ice and the book has likely been here since the Great Freeze, and its frenzied attempt to bust through the ice to get to me – to tear me limb from limb – is proof of that. Not that I blame it. If I was trapped underwater for one hundred and seven years I'd probably be going a little batshit crazy, too.

One hundred and seven years, and the fucker looks pretty damn good. No bloating, no deterioration, all his limbs in place, no signs of fish using his body as fish food. One of the perks of his kind, I guess. I can only hope his brain is completely waterlogged. It would be a small solace, and far less than any bloodsucking demon deserves.

I chip away at the ice without slowing my pace. My back screams, my muscles spasm. Both my body and my mind tell me to stop this madness and abandon the book.

But both my body and my mind know I can't do that.

I keep hacking. Ice chips pile around my knees and coat my face, melting and mixing with my sweat.

The closer I get to the book and the skraeling, the calmer I become. Although I've killed many with my crossbow from afar, I've only been this close to a skraeling once before. It wasn't an experience I had hoped to relive.

The sun was at its highest point, midday, bright enough to blind you but not hot enough to burn you, just as it had been on every cloudless day since the Great Freeze. I was alone, watching over my tribe's camp. The others were out hunting, gathering, training, or just killing time. This was during that gray area of time between the Quietus and the Second Wave. We had grown complacent, lazy. We should never have let our guard down, never left one person alone, no matter how safe we felt. Pairing up had kept us alive through the darkest days, and we should have known that just because there hadn't been a skraeling spotted in nearly a decade, they would likely be back.

But today is a lot different than that day. This is drawn out. I can watch the skraeling through the ice, and it is certainly watching me. The attack on my tribe was over and done in a heartbeat. I had heard screams from far away and barely had time to lift my bow before the skraeling was in front of me. I fired off a shot, a lucky shot, and the demon crumpled in a heap, the arrow sticking out of its chest, pierced straight through its heart. It then melted like a wax candle tossed in a bed of embers. After, while accessing the damage, my surviving tribesmen and I held back the bile creeping up our throats as we found the desecrated corpses of our family members and friends littered around camp. They had been ripped in half, disemboweled, decapitated. The white snow was painted red with their blood.

Our period of mourning came and went as quickly as a single flap of a hummingbird's wing. The unmistakable cries of hungry skraelings peeled across the horizon. They had already smelled the fallen. They had already begun to descend.

We had to leave everything we couldn't easily carry, and since we had to carry the surviving young, we took only our weapons.

Left behind was our food, most of our equipment and all of the random items we had found in long abandoned towns and ancient campsites, including the small library of books we possessed.

That was a hard pill for everyone to swallow, but not harder for anyone but the Leader. He always said that other than our weapons, the human race's greatest chance for survival lies in the education of our young. Without education, without books, we're no different than the skraeling and we're doomed to repeat the mistakes of the past.

We traveled for years before settling again in a small ghost town. But we never found another book.

I cannot return to my tribe without this book, even if it kills me.

My blade breaks.

I toss the hilt aside, unsheathe the scaling knife and continue to dig.

The hole I've chipped out of the ice is less than an inch from the upper left-hand corner of the book. The skaeling is at its most fevered. So am I.

I stop and lay the guthook hunting knife (the scaling knife broke an hour ago) beside me. It is dull and chipped and sorry looking. I imagine I am, too.

Next to the dying knife I place my crossbow, and next to that, my quiver. I check to make sure an arrow is loaded in the bow – it's now my last line of defense. My checklist of weapons has never been shorter.

I pick up the knife. Despite its wretched state it feels good in my hand.

I stab the ice with everything I have left.

Once.

Twice.

Three times.

The ice cracks a fraction around the book.

The skraeling attacks the ice with furious anger.

With each impact the cracks spread out like lightning, like an electric spider web.

The book is almost free. I grasp it and pull. It's loose but the bottom is still frozen in place.

SKRAELING

The skraeling bellows and rams and shatters through the ice.

I'm propelled backwards. The book breaks free but flies out of my hand. It lands next to my crossbow. I land five feet from it on my back. The skraeling lands between me, the book and the bow. It lands on its feet.

I leap up and scramble for my weapon but the skraeling is too fast. It grabs me and throws me back down. It jumps on my chest, forcing the air from my lungs. It opens its jaw impossibly wide, its fangs gleaming like razor-sharp icicles.

I can't reach the crossbow, but one final desperate idea creeps into my brain.

I'm surrounded by thick, jagged shards of broken ice.

I grab a piece longer and sharper than any of my knives and ram it up into the skraeling's chest as its fangs touch the skin over my jugular. The icicle splits flesh, passes bone and finds its target. As soon as the ice is imbedded in the demon's heart, it melts to water and runs through my fingers.

Blood gushes from its mouth and sprays me in the face as the skraeling wails – a bestial sound, inhuman and painfully loud. I cover my ears and roll out from under the skraeling. The wailing abruptly stops.

The skraeling, like the icicle, melts before me. It's sudden and messy, a puddle of gore that drops to the ground as if it had been held aloft in a popped balloon. It splatters and bubbles and melts into the ice, hissing as it cools.

The stench is horrendous. I know, like every time I have claimed one, the smell will linger in my nostrils for weeks.

But it's dead. And the book still lies next to my crossbow.

I smile and laugh.

But then, something's not right. The laughing hurts.

I run my fingers over my bloodstained neck, now throbbing.

A hole.

And a second. Two tiny punctures in my skin.

Specks. Nothing more than twin pinpoints of black on a sheet of pure, brilliant white. Like stars in reverse. Like the smallest pupils surrounded by the largest eyes.

Just two specks. Barely there, but coupled with the infected blood of the skraeling now mixing with my own, it's enough.

Enough to turn me.

My head spins and my vision turns silvery. The pain is worse than anything I've ever felt. My blood feels like it's boiling. I've never seen someone turn but I've heard it only takes minutes.

There is no cure, no stopping the effects of the venom. Somehow, knowing this gives me a clarity of thought I've never known, despite the physical torment that's consuming my body.

One final idea dawns on me.

My salvation.

I kick my crossbow and quiver into the hole in the ice. I won't need them any longer.

I pick up the book and open the cover. I dab my pinky in one of the holes in my neck and drag my finger across the paper, trailing my own blood:

If you're reading this, I have not failed.

I secure the book in a safe pocket in my coat and hope my tribe will find it.

After they kill me.

They're the closest living creatures to this ship. As soon as I turn I will smell them and I will hunt them down.

At least I will return with the book.

But I will be too strong, too fast, and they might not realize I'm a skraeling before it's too late. I can already feel new life, new power, coursing through my veins.

Hopefully the venom will give me the strength to complete the final part of my plan.

As a skraeling I would slaughter my tribe as easily as a loosed arrow splits the air.

But without legs I'd have to drag myself all the way to the camp. They'll see me coming from a mile away.

My fingers pick up the dull knife and caress it gently, then run along the edges of the book to make sure it's secure.

Check and check.

Safety, safety, safety.

I remove my pants, press the knife against my thigh and laugh once more.

I cut.

I keep cutting.

Never stop.

TAPPING A LIGHTER VEIN

"I laugh in the face of danger. Then I hide until it goes away."
—Joss Whedon, *Buffy the Vampire Slayer*

DREAMS OF WINTER
Bob Freeman

Bob Freeman is an author, artist, and paranormal adventurer who lives in rural Indiana with his wife, Kim, and their son, Connor. He is the author of the novels *Shadows Over Somerset*, *Keepers of the Dead*, and *Descendant*, as well as numerous short stories, poems, and, most recently, horror and fantasy role playing game modules.

Bob prefers his vampires nasty, particularly as found in Wolfman & Colan's *Tomb of Dracula*, King's *'Salem's Lot*, and Matheson's *I Am Legend*. His favorite vampires from the large and small screen include Jack Palance (Dan Curtis' *Dracula*), Michael Nouri (*Cliffhangers: The Curse of Dracula*), Barry Atwater (*The Night Stalker*), and Jonathan Frid (*Dark Shadows*)

I

A line from Longfellow comes to me as I stare at the pale, lifeless child at my feet. *"The leaves of memory seemed to make a mournful rustling in the dark."* The Dark, capital 'D', if you don't mind, has been of particularly nagging interest to me of late. As for *mournful rustlings*, well I've been knee-deep in those too. And it's starting to piss me off.

Surrounded by the girl's belongings, it's not hard to fathom how

Megan Gamble's mind worked. There's a poster of a shirtless Alexander Skarsgard on the back of her door. Bookshelves overflow with Jim Butcher, Laurell K. Hamilton, Kim Harrison, and Charlaine Harris urban fantasies; a well-read copy of Stephenie Meyer's *Twilight* rests on the nightstand. Evanescence, Pretty Reckless, and Nightwish CDs are scattered on the floor beside an old school jam-box. The clothes in her closet? All black and lots of lace and frills, plunging necklines and short skirts.

I crack a window, light a cigarette, and watch the snow fall. Dreams of winter, I muse. No more dreams for her. I've got the itch for a drink, but I let the nicotine placate my self-destructive tendencies for now. I do my best to ignore the sounds of the cops behind me, grumbling about their business and their distaste for my presence. The feeling's mutual. Grim thoughts give way to grim tidings and I'm on the verge of giving myself over to them, but there's work to get to. Dark work.

I flick the spent cowboy killer into the night air and ask the crime scene unit to give me a few minutes alone with the corpse. They look to the homicide detective at the door, my old pal Ellis DeTripp, and grouse at his nod of approval. They file past the hulk of a man — DeTripp stands an easy six feet-four inches and tips the scales at more than twenty-two stone — and he closes the door behind them.

"You too, Ellis," I say, removing my coat and hat and laying them on the girl's bed.

"In your dreams, Connors. No freaking way I'm leaving you in here unsupervised."

"What's the matter, Detective," I scowl, "afraid I'll lift something?"

"Nah." He kneels down awkwardly beside the girl's body. "We already searched the room for drugs."

"She's got the latest Dresden Files."

"Cute, but I know you don't read that shit." DeTripp casually traces the outline of the girl's jawline with his fat forefinger, lingering near the gaping but bloodless wound at her throat. "You *live* it."

DREAMS OF WINTER

"What? You never climb inside a Michael Connelly novel?" I join him on the floor, just as awkwardly, my ruined knee groaning in protest. Without the support of my cane, an heirloom from my late father's collection, I'd be all but worthless in situations like these. Dead bodies require an up close and personal touch.

"That's different. Harry Bosch is the real deal."

I brush the big man's hand away from the girl and examine the throat wound more closely. "And *Harry* Dresden isn't?" I frown at the lack of blood, on the body or anywhere in the room for that matter.

"You know I don't cater to all that magic mumbo-jumbo crap."

"And yet," I say as I allow my hand to hover above the victim's head, the telltale glow of magical energy sparking between my fingertips, "here I am."

"Again — *different*."

"Do tell?"

"Meh," he barks, groaning as he rises up from the floor, "just give me your goddamn theory so I can catch whoever did this before my ass is in a sling."

"Well, she was definitely killed here."

"Bullshit. No blood."

"Of course not." I struggle to my feet, leaning heavily on father's cane. "The killer took it with him."

"Landon Connors, I swear on my mother's grave ... "

"Your mother's alive. I had dinner with her last week."

"Just don't freaking say what I know damn good and well you're going to say."

"Fine."

We stare at each other uncomfortably long — he with a scowl, me with bemused acceptance. I know what's coming next. I light a cigarette and wait for him to break.

"Alright," he barks, " ... alright. Go ahead and say it."

"If you insist." I exhale slowly. "Detective DeTripp, your killer is, without a doubt, a bloodsucking creature of the night."

"God damn it, I knew you were going to pull that shit on me."

The detective turns toward the door and throws it open in a huff, storming into the hall and past the awaiting crime scene investigators.

"Would you have preferred that I used the word *vampire*?" I yell after him.

He is not amused.

II

Let's get a few things straight. First, vampires don't sparkle, despite what Megan Gamble's late night reading might suggest. That's right, of the eighteen varieties of bloodsucking fiends my family has cataloged over the years, not a one of them shimmer by sunlight. Granted, a couple of them do burst into flame when exposed to the sun's attention, but that's a far cry from all that sexy glimmering.

I guess that leads into my second point, as in why I know these things to be true. My name is Landon Connors — Dr. Landon Connors, actually — and I hunt monsters (among other things). I came by this *'profession'* honestly enough. I guess you might say it's the family business, though *family* is a looser term now, seeing as I'm the only one left and I'm not exactly the marrying kind. My official title is 'occult detective' and yes, I wear a trenchcoat and fedora. Some clichés are just too good to mess with.

Back at Caer Caliburn, the aged Victorian that my family has called home since the late 1800s, I diligently peruse the tattered *Liber Monstrorum*, a grimoire and bestiary of sorts that my forefathers have passed down through the years. Reading an entry by my great-grandfather, Gabriel Connors, regarding the *cruor geminus*, I find confirmation of my suspicions regarding Megan Gamble's killer. Of course, she is not the only victim. There have been two others in as many months. All with the same telltale throat wounds. All with the same proclivity for reading material. Each a wannabe Bella. Each an eager vessel drained dry by a foul creature wearing an Edward mask.

The *cruor geminus* is a nasty little beast with the ability to assume the appearance of someone their intended victim knows and trusts. And I'm pretty sure I've tracked this particular one before. The Cullen thing certainly fits his *modus operandi*. In the nineties, it trawled for victims wearing the face of Brad Pitt's Louis. It's a game for this damnable creature, wearing the cinematic face of the vampire, enticing its victims by playing to their erotic fantasies.

But the game's almost over. Though the three most recent victims had no physical connection to one another, I uncovered a cyber one. Each belonged to an online community, a messageboard upon which they poured out their longings for a romantic tryst with their undead paramour. All I needed was someone to use as bait for the *cruor geminus*, a lovely young girl to which the beast could not resist. Unfortunately for it, I have just the girl in mind for the job.

III

Magick has its advantages. Case in point, I am standing in the corner of a fifteen year old girl's bedroom, completely invisible to any who might look my way. No scent to detect, no heat signature to register, not even the sound of my breathing can be heard. On the bed, Sarah Jones, lies suggestively draped across the top of her pink and mauve comforter, dressed in a black tank top and skirt that makes her pale flesh seem like alabaster. As she clicks away on her laptop computer, I make the mental calculations necessary to ensure that she does not become victim number four.

I know what you're thinking. No, I'm not some kind of pervert, though I might be scolded for placing such a young and vibrant child in mortal danger. Thing is, Sarah Jones is not your average fifteen year old. Imagine Nancy Drew, if you will, but with a bit more piss and vinegar. As

Doyle's Sherlock Holmes had his Baker Street Irregulars, I too have allies that fall somewhat south of the legal drinking age. Sarah is a paranormal investigator, being an integral cog in the so-called Ghostwriters Society that are comprised of author Steven Parker's sons Dale and Allen, and Sarah's cousin Cassidy Martin. They have been tested by fire on more than one occasion. Still, I feel somewhat guilty for using the fiery-haired teen as my proverbial hare in a snare. She was, of course, willing enough. Quite eager even. But as a rock gently raps against her bedroom window, I pray that my confidence in hers and my ability is not found wanting.

Sarah rolls off the bed and approaches the window. She steals a glance toward me and I grind my teeth in anticipation. It must be unnerving for her, trusting that, though she cannot see me, I am in fact *there* ready to spring into action. She grips the window and opens it cautiously, the bitter cold of winter racing into the room.

"Hello, Bella," I hear the *cruor geminus* say. Softly. Seductively. "May I come inside?"

Does her skin crawl? No. I see her sway, sense her body's relaxing shift from heightened awareness to that of wanton desire. Can the creature's powers be so overwhelming? She backs away from the window and calls to him.

"Come to me, my love."

She is entranced. There is no mistake. My plan is unraveling before me. I prepare a counter spell, but already it's too late. The creature is inside the room in an instant. She and I see it as it wishes to be seen, as a handsome young man with powder white flesh and full, pouting lips. It's hair in a mock pompadour, flashing pearly white teeth behind golden eyes. The illusion is intoxicating, even for me. It leans in toward Sarah, its lips parted, moist and hungry.

Leaping forward from my concealing spell, the head of my cane flares to life, bright and as radiant as the sun. It is enough to give the beast pause. What I didn't expect was for Sarah to turn on me, grabbing a pair of scissors from her nightstand, and charging at me like a thing possessed. Yes, possessed — *enthralled* — and filled with lustful desire for her faux-Edward.

I raise my cane too late as the scissors find the back of my hand. As I push her aside, I am met by the creature's full force as it barrels into me, knocking me into the girl's closet, splintering the bi-fold doors. I collapse to the floor, clothes falling from the rack overhead, blinding me as a rain of furious blows connect with my ribs, arm, and face. Its fangs find bare flesh. It burns like fire. The smell and taste of my blood has the beast in a ravenous frenzy. It is by sheer willpower that I am able to conjure a magical counter to its devastating assault.

A blast of eldritch energy explodes from my left hand hurling the *cruor geminus* into the far wall. I struggle to my feet, telekinetically call my cane back into my bleeding right hand, and approach the foul creature wearing a heartthrob's face. Bearing its fangs, I grimace as I meet its aggression by swinging the cane like a bat, striking the beast full in the face. The *cruor geminus* falls back and through the window amidst a crash of broken glass. I approach cautiously, but am caught unprepared as Sarah buries the scissors into my right shoulder. I scream in agony, then turn and grab the girl by her face.

"*Quiesco*," I say, softly, and Sarah Jones crumbles to the ground.

The pain is exquisite. It sets my mind afire and it's all I can do to jerk the instrument free. I stumble forward, to the window, and climb out, bleeding profusely from hand and shoulder. I can feel my ribs grinding in my chest and I'm all but certain that I've a fractured forearm.

This is not how I'd planned tonight's operation.

IV

I stagger through the thick snow, following the vampire's trail into the woods that run alongside Pipe Creek. My vision is blurred and I'm losing too much blood. I cast a quick spell, but it's a mere band-aid. My whole world is pain, but. I press on. The *cruor geminus* will not go far. It can't.

The smell of my blood will be too much for it to ignore. It will come for me and most likely finish me off, but not without a fight.

My head is swimming now. I'm in someone's backyard. I can hear the creek behind me, smell the pine of the woods. I don't know how I got here. Everything's coming and going in flashes. The bite on my arm isn't deep, but it's poisonous. The vampire's foul venom is working its way through my system. I have to find it. Have to end this. A shadow ahead. I see a manger scene, the baby Jesus surrounded by its mother and father, by animals and wisemen. The shadow is framed by a Christmas Angel hovering above the manger, its lights blinking in an eclectic rhythm. My heart thunders in time with those angel wings.

"Landon."

The voice is coming from the angel.

I stagger toward it, lumbering, limping against the pain in my ravaged knee, cane dragging along through the snow loosely, carving a snaking trail through the fresh powder. The shadow comes forward revealing a different angel.

"Sarah," I choke. I taste blood on my lips. "You shouldn't ... be here. Run ... Be safe." I lose my footing and descend to the ground onto my hands and knees. "Run, damn it."

"No, Landon," she says. She lowers herself to me, cups my face in her hands. "I'll not abandon you, my dear sweet Doctor." I'm lost in her eyes. In her youth ... her beauty. She leans in toward me, lips parting, coming dangerously close to mine.

This is how it ends for the occult detective? With a kiss from a fiery-haired angel, bled out in the snow with the failed dream of winter on my lips? I rise up on my knees as she lays my head to the side. Her lips brush mine on her way to my neck. I feel her hot breath on my cold flesh. Then she's gone ... an explosion erupts across the lawn and I see two Sarahs — one struggling up from the ground, a spray of blood across the virgin snow — the other holding a smoking Ruger .357.

"Get away from him, you monster!"

DREAMS OF WINTER

The beast transforms before my eyes. Sarah no more as it assumes the shape of Edward and marches toward her. Sarah fires again, and once more, but the fiend shrugs them off. I reach deep down inside me and rise, raising my cane and swinging it with all my might. It connects with the back of the *cruor geminus'* head. The beast spins about and I charge.

With the cane before me like a knight's lance, I drive the shaft home, straight through the vampire's chest, piercing the foul thing's heart and driving it back into the manger. The angel overhead comes crashing down and the *cruor geminus* becomes entangled in the wire frame and blinking lights. As the sun rises, the fiend dies before our eyes, its body bound by the twinkling lights of a Christmas Angel.

"Huh," Sarah says, "I guess sometimes vampires do sparkle."

DRACULA'S WINKEE: BLOODSUCKER BLUES

Gregory L. Hall

Gregory L Hall has a long history in comedy, improv and theatre. He's a national Telly Award winner and produced the annual Baltimore Comedy Fest to support autism awareness. His dark fiction can be found in oodles of publications and anthologies as well as his novel *At the End of Church Street* and short story collection *Werepig Fever*. Nowadays Gregory is perhaps best known as the host of the internet radio talk show *The Funky Werepig*. However, he prefers to brag about the time he was hugged by Pat Morita — Mr. Miyagi — because wouldn't you?

Although he loves vampire classics from *Nosferatu* to *30 Days of Night*, his biggest influence has been The Count from *Sesame Street*.

Love. It's more than just a three letter word. It is perhaps the greatest gift bestowed upon humanity and without a doubt the hardest to define. But who is worthy of love? There are many who say the one place love cannot exist is in the hearts of those who are truly evil. Like proctologists and Wal-Mart greeters. But true love can grow anywhere, even in the darkest of souls. And it lasts an eternity.

As Dracula looked through the bedroom window at his latest prey, he had trouble believing any of this. Yes, she was attractive in a 1990's Katie Couric kind of way. But there was no emotion left in his world outside of anger and depression. And sex had faded into a cruel joke.

It was Frederich Nietzsche who said 'Facts are like really rigid truths.' And it was Jack Nicholson who said 'You can't handle the truth.' For the Lord of the Undead, the ugly truth was in order for a man to achieve an erection, he must first have blood flow. That was something a vampire did not have. Blood was food. It was for energy and for maintaining a life force. Anything else was a cruel tease.

Sure, in younger days he always drank more than enough to saturate his own veins and arteries. Every day was a Happy Penis Day. But as the centuries flew past him, and his victims polluted their blood with drive-thru meals and Zima, Dracula had to severely cut his intake of crimson nourishment.

The first to fall was his once mighty winkee.

Intercourse went the way of traffic cops, typewriters and face-to-face communication. There was nothing worse than young naked women wanting the ultimate taboo - hot vampire boinkings - and offering them nothing but the flaccid junk of a three-thousand-year-old Romeo. To make matters worse, he was always room temperature. Tiny, old and cold. Not an attractive package. And by package, we mean package.

So he had to use his darkly erotic reputation and his European charm to drive women to orgasm. Being woozy from massive blood loss helped his ladies believe the fantasy. But heavy petting and dry humping was all their mysterious lover could offer.

Dracula's frustration was thicker than ego on a Donald Trump-Oprah Winfrey sandwich. After a half dozen or more centuries of simply grinding against women and relying on hypnosis to drive them wild, how long had it been since he had ejaculatory satisfaction of his own?

DRACULA'S WINKEE: BLOODSUCKER BLUES

Well, the answer would be a dozen or more centuries. It's written right there.

Hovering outside his potential victim's window, the Prince of Darkness wondered if it was worth it any more. Would she be the one he had been seeking for too long now? Could she provide the spark deep within his loinal area to make him a man again? Would tonight be the night he would drive a stake into her?

He chuckled. It was vampire humor. You probably wouldn't get it.

As he watched her pop out the *Twilight* DVD and wash off her Ben Wa balls, he figured he had nothing to lose, except his lunch.

The village girl knew it was a mistake to leave her bedroom window open after dark. There was sudden silence as all noise stopped — the crickets, the wind chimes, the screaming of the patrons at her Momma's all night community shower as they realized there was no hot water left. It made her feel uneasy, which was indeed strange. If there was ever one word to describe her, it was 'easy.'

Her partially blue eyes spied the Darkness as it swirled outside on the tiny balcony. Slowly, it took shape. The stranger glided into the room, and without hesitation, unbuttoned his already partially unbuttoned frilly girly shirt to show off his chiseled alabaster tan body. Although there was no wind, it blew through his long dark hair. It made her hot and she was willing to admit it.

"You're making me hot," she said. "You're like a very dangerous stranger whom I want to give my body to without question. Geez, I hope you're not undead or something."

He pointed a finger at her. She yelped like a school girl, because it would be all paranormal and no romance if she didn't.

"I am Dracula. And your blood belongs to me."

She stared into his dark eyes like Paris Hilton at Fermat's Last Theorem. "Well, as long as it doesn't hurt."

The vampire moved quicker than she could imagine and she prayed his sexual endurance didn't match that speed. He clutched her bare shoulders and she moaned. They kissed deeply as his hand caressed her fashion model-flat chest nub.

"Try the other boob. I could only afford one breast implant. But Christmas is coming..."

"Hee hee. Coming." Dracula said in his exotic thick foreign accent "Insert joke here."

"Okay but let me take my underwear off first."

He stole another hungry kiss. She felt her knees give out as she tasted the vampire's tongue again. "Wow. You kiss better than a waffle iron. I don't know if you're into this kind of thing, but sometimes I like when guys give me hickies on my neck. You want to try that?"

If there was a camera nearby, Dracula would have deadpanned into it.

He sank his fangs into her jugular vein and her life liquid exploded into his mouth in one gooey burst. His victim grabbed her neck.

"Owie. I think you pinched a nerve or something. I hope you didn't break the skin. Hey, you have something red on your chin there. Geez, I should have told you I'm a bleeder. That's why I had to switch from being a cutter to licking wall sockets. All the cool kids are doing that now anyway. Cutting is so 2002. Oh poopies. Now I'm feeling kind of dizzy. I mean more than just from being blonde. Blonde is like the yellow hair, right? That's the kind I have. Wow, this night is getting weirder than paying a homeless guy to lap dance your Grandmother on her 70th birthday."

Dracula shot her a glance. "How would you know?"

"Oh boy. Control alt delete!" the girl giggled and found a chair to lean against.

"I grow tired of this encounter. My hunger has turned into more of a sexual nature. Let us spelunk the furry fissure, slave!"

His mental powers grabbed the girl's brain. There was no road block. Not even a speed bump.

DRACULA'S WINKEE: BLOODSUCKER BLUES

"That tickles." she said as her eyes went glassy. "Hey, am I the only one hearing an echo?"

He mentally pushed her to the floor and made her legs fly open. Her nightgown violently yanked up and her underwear ripped off of her hips.

She gasped. "Excuse moi. Looks like no more Taco Bell for me!"

"I did that, woman-child. Not you. For my powers are limitless." He gazed at her nude nakedness. Morning was just on the other side of the horizon. Minutes were disappearing like job opportunities for David Hasselhoff. The vampire knew if he was going to plunge his flesh gherkin into her lady-loge, it would have to be now.

He pulled down his pants and stood proudly before her. She gasped.

"Well say hello to my little friend!" she said. "Seriously though, Mr. Dark Prince fellow, size doesn't matter to me. I'm a big fan of 'motion of the ocean' and all that. Some girls only want to be bludgeoned with a fifty pound Abe Froman sausage. But I'm fine with being jabbed with a toothpick. You just have to do it like a million times real fast. You know the toothpick thing, it could be an issue of blood flow, you know? By toothpick I mean your penis. I'm just saying. Toothpicks are thin and tiny too. But unlike your penis, they're hard."

"Silence!" he cried out. His voice echoed through the large chamber — and we're not talking about the room. There once was a day when he could have overwhelmed this trollop with his uvula hammer, but now, now it would be like riding a Moped into the Grand Canyon. The night ran out of options. The vampire's eyes turned hellfire red with rage. The girl scurried backwards, knowing her fate.

"But I'm Team Edward..."

He snatched her off the floor and with lightning speed sank his fangs deep into her neck. All he could taste was corn syrup and regret. He hurled her out the window, hearing the patrons at Momma's all night community shower scream again.

She was not the one. Not the one to kick-start his crippled mini-me. Not the one to fill his empty black heart with love. Not the one to share coupons with at Denny's. He should have known. The writer hadn't even given her a name.

Gazing out towards nearby woods, he spied a werewolf sneaking up on an innocent deer. Detecting danger, the chase began. Was this the way it would always be? Predator? Prey? The lycanthrope pounced on the deer, but instead of tearing her throat out, the werewolf mounted her. The deer rolled over on her back and they made-out like horny teenagers while their lovemaking exploded across what little was left of the night.

Another completely wasted evening. Dracula could only sigh. Disappointment was his body wash. He looked up at his exhausted face in the mirror, but realized he didn't cast a reflection.

Some brothers just can't catch a break.

Juan was perhaps Dracula's best, if not only, friend. He had lived at the castle for over a century, an extremely long life for an armadillo. Yet with the exception of a slight cameo in Universal's classic movie version of *Dracula*, Juan had been forgotten or ignored as a major player in the Master's folklore. Many were the nights the armadillo would play and rewind his appearance in the film as a naïve Renfield entered the castle and waited for Bela Lugosi to come down the stone staircase. He was agitated that the actor playing him had zero lines, but he thought overall the stand-in gave a fine performance.

He scurried into the living room to sneak in a morning viewing when he heard the TV was already on. That was not a good sign. He peeked around the corner to find his Master staring blankly at the screen, burying his pain and torment in another episode of *Degrassi*.

"Hey best buddy, it's 9:00 in the morning. You haven't hit the coffin yet?"

"I can't sleep." Dracula mumbled bitterly.

"Another rough night?"

"You could say so. I don't want to talk about it."

DRACULA'S WINKEE: BLOODSUCKER BLUES

"Okay." Juan nodded. "At least you went out on the town, right? Better than hanging around the castle for another boring evening of Bloody Marys and Jenga. Right?"

"Whatever." Dracula pulled a blanket up around his head.

Juan searched for anything positive to pull his friend out of his funk. "Oh, Frankenstein called while you were out."

"What did he say?"

"Fire bad."

Dracula withdrew deeper into his blanket cocoon.

"I'll call him back tomorrow."

Juan ran into the foyer. He scurried back with a mail bag stuffed with letters and hopped up on the couch.

"You know what would help you out? Look at all these letters. From women all over the world. All wanting one thing from you — a night of hot supernatural passion!"

He dumped the sack, covering the couch with hundreds of envelopes and cards. Dracula reluctantly picked up a letter from the pile.

"This one is from the American Red Cross."

Juan snatched it away. "Okay, that one's a bad example. But all the rest of these? Since the paranormal romance boom, you've been more popular that ever!"

"Really, Juan?" the vampire snarled. "And just what am I supposed to do about any of this? Do you understand the ridiculous pressure all these books and movies and TV shows have put on me? Do you have any clue whatsoever, Juaaaaaan?"

The armadillo sat silently as Dracula threw letters into the air. He had heard the same speech more times than teenage perverts mispronounced the word 'fajita'. It was better to just let his buddy vent.

"They've changed the rules! Instead of being the most evil and most feared creatures in history, they've turned us into prom dates and underwear models. Forget vampire lore! No one researches anymore. They slap fangs on any piece of fantasy man meat that gets their pent-up panties moist and say 'Oh! He's a cop, but he's also a vampire! That mysterious bo-hunk in the apartment next door? OMG, a vampire! He's the cute boy next to me in biology — but also a thousand year old vampire!' You would think after a thousand years he would make it easy on himself and just home school."

"Regardless of how many writers have altered vampires to wedge them into their naughty little fantasy stories, the fact is vampires are more popular than ever. And women want you naked and now."

Dracula gestured wildly to his groin like Joe Cocker at a urinal. "How, Juan? How?"

Juan covered his eyes. "Please. Let's not go through the perils of the penis again."

"It don't work! No blood flow means no batty batty boners, because I'm like dead, you know? And I'll tell you something. The food chain has flipped. At the top now? Goth chicks, emo girls and very scary cougars. I'm talking turbo 'Sex in the City' cougars. You know why they focused on shoes so much on that show? To draw attention away from their faces." Dracula collapsed in a dusty recliner, barely able to finish his own rant. "These trollops get all worked up from their paranormal romance movies and books and expect hot throbbing jackhammer rides that last for hours on end. And all I can give them is..."

Juan joined his Master "...A cold and shriveled winkee."

"Do not mock me, you stupid armored gopher! Name one other person who lives with the pain I've suffered for more than a century now!"

"Regis Philbin."

Dracula paused. "Name another."

The heavy wooden door opened and a naked hippie walked in. His hair and beard were a mess, leaves and twigs sticking out like bad camouflage. Dirt and dried blood was smudged across skinny chest and arms. He grinned as he crossed the room and let out a howl.

"Oh man what a night I must have had! Did you guys happen to

DRACULA'S WINKEE: BLOODSUCKER BLUES

check me out last night? I hate not remembering how hard I partied. Damn full moon fever."

"Morning, Chad." Juan elbowed Dracula and was met with indifference.

"Good morning, Chad. Come to use our bathroom again?"

"You bet, Drac-man. Hey, is there a clean washcloth in there? I got the feeling I'm in need of a major scrub down. Do you know if I got laid? My junk smells like Bambi's mother. Tell me I got lucky."

He waited at the open bathroom door for a response. Neither Dracula nor Juan budged.

"Allllright!" Chad shot them a six shooter gesture.

"How blessed it must be to be a werewolf. Live as a normal human and once a month you get to run wild." Dracula bitched aloud. "Then the next morning it's all 'Oh, did I get laid? I don't even remember!'"

"Well, technically he wouldn't because that's the way it works." Juan said. "The human has no memory of the beast the night before."

"You think that's bad, dudes, I'll tell you the real curse. We're only a werewolf for one night. And the digestive track needs at least a day to run its course. No one ever thinks about that fun fact. Sun comes up and I'm human again — and I have no idea what I ate last night. It's like Hooper cutting open that shark in *Jaws*. 'A license plate? What? Did I eat a car?' Speaking of which, I got the call of the wild about two inches away from sphincter. Fighting a losing battle, buds!"

Chad quickly slammed the bathroom door behind him and instantly filled the castle's lower level with grunts, groans and muttered Warren Zevon lyrics. Juan tried to ignore their clueless guest and bring his Master back on topic.

"Speaking of forgotten sex, I'm going to throw something your way. I've been doing a lot of Google searching lately. What you need is to dive head first into a huge pile of young hot virgins. If one special girl doesn't do it for you, then maybe we need to think in bulk. And there's only one place that is wall-to-wall virgins," Juan grinned. "America."

"America? Really?"

"Particularly in a state called Indiana. 9 out of 10 women according to Wikipedia. When was the last time you were even near a virgin, my friend?"

"About ten years ago. Madonna. In London."

"She may have lied."

"...Send lawyers, guns and money!" Chad screamed from the bathroom. "Dudes, I'm dying in here!"

The Prince of Darkness rose from the couch and walked across the room to a dust covered globe. He spun it until it stopped on the American Midwest. "Traveling all the way to America? I feel so outdated in this modern world. And you know my enemies would love for me to leave the protection of my homeland. The Vatican. Scotland Yard. The Van Helsings. Peter Cushing."

Juan was not about to give up. His Master's existence depended on it. "I know this is a huge decision for you. Journeying halfway across the world in search of women who can make you feel like you did centuries ago. Venturing out into a time of cell phones and electric hybrid cars and illiteracy..."

Dracula shook his head. Overwhelmed, he plopped back down on the couch and wrapped the blanket over his head again. Silence cut deep into the heavy morning air until Chad stomped on it like a suicidal cat at a *Riverdance* rehearsal.

"Argggggg! What the hell did I eat last night?"

"Light a match!" Juan snapped. He stared at Dracula. "You know, you'll never solve your erectile dysfunction sitting in front of a TV set all day and night."

The vampire so wanted to end his curse. To find love, to take one small step towards lost humanity, to pummel some Sprittle with his naughty Chimp-Chimp.

But he knew there was only one answer.

"No. I'm sorry, Juan. There is nothing out there for me. And nothing that will make me leave Transylvania ever again."

"Drac, come on"

"Conversation over."

Chad unleashed an ear-splitting painful scream. The castle fell still. He opened the bathroom door and peeked out.

"Oh my God! Dudes, I just shit a hand."

Dracula spoke softly from underneath his blanket.

"Okay. Pack my bags."

Juan booked the flight and opted not to go the direct route for specific reasons. He wanted Dracula to experience short stops in the strange new world before settling in the promise land of Indiana.

So there were visits to London and Orlando, but Dracula liked his four hour layover in Detroit the best. The old saying was that terrorists would never waste an attack on Detroit, because who would notice? Cold ugly grey skies enveloped too many buildings now abandoned as the population dwindled to only the most stubborn. The city smelled like murder and it snowed dirt. Dracula made a mental note to plan his next vacation here and then bought himself an 'At least we're not Pittsburgh' T-shirt.

When he finally settled into his destination of Indiana, his anticipation had built to a crescendo. It was true. There were virgins around every corner, many of them under forty. He reached out with his senses and prayed one of them would be that special angel who would solve his erectudinal dilemmas.

Juan had a carrier drop his luggage off at the hotel — He had only brought with him three (dramatic pause) boxes — so Dracula was instantly free to roam the streets. He started out as soon as the sun dipped below the horizon and hit all the popular Indiana hot spots. Neither was to his liking. So he wandered farther and farther outside the city limits, as if answering some silent mystical call, like Kirsten Dunst with a dog whistle.

It was very late when he discovered the nowhere town. It was hidden in miles of corn. There was a simple main street. On one side of the rain soaked road was a gas station, a tiny chapel and an adult book store offering a sale on any erotica written by Garrison Keillor. Ahead of him was a sign reading that the next 'town' was 69 miles away. He giggled to himself, because the number 69 also meant a sexual position enjoyed by one or more people. He took the sign as a sign. This was where he was supposed to be.

On the opposite side of the road stood a simple watering hole to use the down home colloquialism, a place where passersby and a few locals gathered for stale beer and cheesy fries. *Mmmmm, cheesy fries,* Dracula thought, although he had never had them before. It just sounded like it should be preceded by an 'Mmmmmmm' This establishment, McCoy's House of Crabs, seemed as good a place as any to stop. Although it seemed strange a bar stuck in the middle of a continent would specialize in serving seafood.

Dracula paused in the doorway for a moment. Hair was perfect. Cape was on straight. No one was in his teeth.

Inside, he found a half a dozen people. A gruff and tired bartender. A couple of cowboy types playing cards. A husband and wife diligently reading over a map. A drunk angrily mumbling 'Just admit it. It's not like it's a secret...' to a juke box playing Kenny Chesney. If the blood lust hit him hard enough, he could slaughter the men and take the woman. She wore too much make-up and was slightly older than he preferred, but his sense of smell and the empty plates on their table told him she was packed full with cheesy fries. Mmmmmm. Cheesy fries.

"Can I help you, friend?"

Dracula looked to the bartender and grinned.

"Are you the owner of this establishment?"

"I am. I'm McCoy. Of McCoy's House of Crabs fame," he acknowledged, and then scratched his crotch.

"Tell me, McCoy of McCoy's House of Crabs, where are the women

DRACULA'S WINKEE: BLOODSUCKER BLUES

in this town?"

"Women? Hah, there ain't but one. My wife. She works at the adult book store across the street. She's also the town whore. But that don't affect me none," he shared as he scratched his groin again.

"It doesn't bother you that your wife has sex with other men?"

"It's a nothing town as you can see. Don't get much in the ways of horny customers. Most are people just grabbing some pretzel sticks and filling up their tanks, then immediately hitting the road again. So it's pretty easy in a town of one woman to be the town whore. In fact, I don't think she's slept with anyone since Bill Maher passed through a few years back. Day doesn't go by that I don't remember that visit."

McCoy scratched himself again.

"And you opened this place shortly after?"

"Now how did you know that?"

Dracula was growing bored of the conversation and disillusioned with his dismal choices. "So is there anything else to do here for excitement?"

"We have our famous corn maze," McCoy boasted.

"What is a corn maze?"

"A maze. Made of corn. Rows of corn. So it's called a corn maze. Or a maize maze if you're an Indian. They call corn 'Maize.'"

"I may have to purchase a ticket to such an attraction," Dracula said stifling a yawn.

"It's a doozy. That couple over there with the road map just got out of it. They started last August."

Dracula was about to give up. Had his senses betrayed him? Were the silent strings that tugged at his black heart merely playing him for the fool?

Then she walked in from the kitchen.

She was beyond beautiful, with long thick black hair and deeply tanned skin. Her young athletic body moved with the grace of an albino ocelot stalking a gnu. She wiped down a table with a dishcloth and put some empty glasses into a bus pan. She smelled of indentured servitude.

"Who is that female?" he whispered to McCoy.

"The Indian girl? She's my indentured servant."

Dracula raised an eyebrow. Sometimes he even surprised himself.

"Oh yeah," McCoy continued. "Her parents ran up some tabs in town they couldn't pay off. So they left her to work off their debts."

"Where are these parents who would sell off their own daughter to cover for their mistakes?"

"Them? Oh they have their own reality TV show on E."

Dracula held his chin high and turned his attention to the young beauty before him. His dark aura pulsated from his loinal area, capturing the attention of any within his striking distance. The barroom became thick with his sex farrakhans, and the need to succumb filled the air in huge chunks. Not a soul present could help but stare at the mysterious Prince's smooth chiseled alabaster chest and well defined tan abs. The husband and wife unconsciously pawed at each other. The two cowboys held hands and snickered. The drunk stuck his pecker in the juke box's coin slot. Lady Gaga came on.

Everyone was hypnotized except for one poor Indian girl. Her pain pushed her forward, too busy with demeaning chores to partake in Dracula's exquisite man-beauty. He saw this and slowly approached her, a grin dancing across his sensual Anderson Cooper-like lips.

"What is your name, mon petite?"

Her gorgeous deep brown eyes met his. Her perfect chest heaved as she swallowed her pride. "Me? I am no one. I am less than no one."

"Surely you must have a name. Forget these abusive fools. What do your people call you?"

"The White Man has named me 'Leah'. But my Indian name is Touchamahboobies."

Dracula choked on his own saliva.

"Touchamahboobies is what they call me. I haven't spoken that name in many moons. It feels good to say it aloud once again. Yes. Touchamahboobies."

DRACULA'S WINKEE: BLOODSUCKER BLUES

And so Dracula did. The Indian maiden put her lips to his ear.

"These stations are locked in so you don't have to keep tuning." she whispered. She backed away as she rubbed her sore polka-dots. "Can I get you a drink?"

The Bringer of Death chortled. "Never ask a vampire if you can get them a drink."

"A menu then?"

"No, see I said I was a vampire. So like we drink, but it's like blood and stuff. Get it?" he explained in a sexy European accent and stuff.

Touchamahboobies stepped away from him, seeing the evil within him for the first time. Bringer of Death or not, he was probably a bad tipper.

"Fear me not, my butterfly." he charmed her as he extended his hand. She fell under his spell. "Although I thirst, I wish to fill your lonely night with excitement. I was about to partake of your town's major attraction..."

"The Maize Maze?"

"So you are of native American decent."

"I'm only part Indian," the hypnotized girl confessed.

"Which part?"

"My Titicaca."

Dracula's passion swept over him with a passion he hadn't felt in decades. He spun her around and forced her against the bar. He ripped her skirt off and ran his hands over her firm rounded hiney cheeks. He knew he must have the Native American goddess then and there.

"I must have you here and now!"

Raw sexuality exploded throughout the room, fueled on by the vampire's insatiable desires. The girl gasped, unable to do much more than surrender as he thrust his hips forward and slammed into her waiting tatonka.

"Oh, don't stop!" Touchamahboobies cried out. "Yes! Please tell me this forceful entry comes with a penis!"

Dracula flung his arms about in a fury as he separated from his boink target.

"I have a circulation problem, okay! Do you have any idea how much blood flow has to be redirected to achieve an erection?"

"We do!" the card playing cowboys joyfully screamed at the back of the bar.

Touchamahboobies regretfully pulled her buckskin undies back up. She shrugged in sympathetic disappointment. Dracula knew the moment was now gone. The passion forever destroyed. His deflated all radial tire suffered a blow out before he could even lay a patch. He could feel the eyes of the other patrons judge him. Anger got the best of him and he grabbed the young girl, flinging her to the floor.

"Taunt me no further, harlot. Be gone."

"You can't throw me away like an open bag of trash!" she sniped as she landed at the feet of her people's chieftain. A single tear ran down the cheek of the old Indian, the 70's parody lost on so many readers.

Helplessly, the patrons watched as the stranger stormed out of the bar. Despite his rage, his exit was a graceful eerie glide. Then a frigid wind kicked up and slapped their faces, breaking the powerful trance they all had fallen under.

"Um, hey," the drunk at the juke box muttered. "Little help here. I'm kinda stuck."

Dracula, the most powerful evil creature who ever walked the Earth, escaped into the moonlit cornfields to hide his shame. Indiana was not the promise land he was promised. He would not be screaming out, "Hosier Daddy?" As he pushed through the rows of maize, he tumbled into paranormal romance hell. Was there more to it than body glitter, bad acting and brushing your hair with a rake?

His meat-wand jumped. The answer was in front of him the whole time.

That Kristen Stewart was one hot trollop ...

I FUCK YOUR SUNSHINE

Lucy A. Snyder

Lucy A. Snyder is the Bram Stoker Award-winning author of the novels *Spellbent, Shotgun Sorceress, Switchblade Goddess,* and the collections *Sparks and Shadows, Chimeric Machines,* and *Installing Linux on a Dead Badger.* Her writing has appeared in *Dark Faith, Strange Horizons, Weird Tales, Hellbound Hearts, Doctor Who Short Trips: Destination Prague, Chiaroscuro, GUD,* and *Lady Churchill's Rosebud Wristlet.*

Her favorite vampire movie is *Near Dark.* You can learn more about her at www.lucysnyder.com

---

Vampires? Of course I know them. You are surprised? Some call me ... what is it? "Fang hag." Ugh. Demeaning. I am crow to their wolves, eagle to their lions. You do not understand? I am succubus; the upyr and I, we do not compete, because we do not want same thing. Sometimes, we feed on each other, yes: cock is cock, and blood is blood. Their seed is ... acquired taste. Sour and bitter like rust, and sometimes sticks in throat like stale gummy candy. Not so zingy as live semen. But takes edge off!

I have known the Baron Stierherzov since before he turned to the night. He was warrior lord, much fierce in battle, merciless to the peoples he vanquished in the Old Country. Dracula himself gave him the eternal kiss as reward. Such pedigree you do not find! But before, I knew him as young boy eager for my visits. So full of delicious salty life! I could milk him over and over until his testicles bled, and still he would rise to please me.

So, is only fair I let him take my neck sometimes, now that we are equals. Is only necessary when he cannot hunt, after all; if he is housebound, then likely so am I. I miss olden days of the plagues; you could take anyone you wanted, and unless someone glimpsed you winging away into darkness, who was wiser? But now, every alleyway corpse is put under microscope, put in newspapers. So the Baron adapted, tries to live "green" as they say, and only takes a little here and there. Is frustrating to him, I know. And accidents happen, and then we all must stop feeding for a while.

The sun? No, of course it won't harm me. But it is not my ally, either. My glamour cannot hold under full light; there is not enough Estée Lauder in the world to full conceal the 600 years in my skin. Oh, is so kind of you to say, darling! But really ... for best hunting, the Baron and I need same thing: darkness, and drunkards.

So, was bad thing for us all when Dansky's was torn down. They bought whole block for stupid mall, and put enormous Starbucks where bar had been, can you believe? Not so much as drop of vodka to be found, so goodbye to all our drunkards. And all those dreadful windows and skylights! So much sun, and so many reflections – I made do, as a lady must, but poor Baron could not stand it, even after sundown.

There was only one reliable hunting ground left to him in the whole city: the Iron Pit Athletic Club. Open all night long, and no windows. He went in one evening, and I did not see him again for whole nine months.

But when I did ... oh, what a sight he was.

I FUCK YOUR SUNSHINE

It was noon; the sun burned high in sky. Miserable cloudless day. But I sat there in the coffee house with my black tea, watching the people come and go. I had just spotted young man, shy, ordering a mocha latte, and I could smell the miasma of stifled lust on him. I had just stood up to go work my wiles on him when it happened.

"I FUCK YOUR SUNSHINE!"

It was an inhuman shout, loud as a war cannon. We all turned toward the noise, turned to stare out at the street, and I saw an absolute monster out there. A man-shaped thing, hulking, massive, muscle piled upon muscle, flesh wormed with thick veins. It strode down the street, naked, skin aflame in the relentless sunlight.

"I FUCK YOUR SUNSHINE!" the thing bellowed again. The purple flames devouring its flesh were rising higher and higher, skin blackening, curling like paper and ashing away, revealing gray-red muscle and yellow tendons beneath.

"I FUCK YOUR SUNSHINE!"

I recognized the voice ... it was the Baron! In an instant, I realized that for those nine months he'd been hiding behind concrete walls, he'd been lifting weights and drinking blood from the thick, brutish necks of hundreds of sweaty steroid junkies. His diet had made him huge, and the unnatural chemicals had inflamed his frustrations with the modern world until it drove him mad as a Spanish arena bull.

His eyeballs were burning in his skull like furnace coals as he strode up to the Starbucks; the glass in the door shattered from the heat of his burning flesh. The smoke pouring off him smelled like the corpse pyres of the old battlefields.

"I FUCK YOUR SUNSHINE!" he roared at all the suburbanites shrieking and scrambling to get away from him.

He stood there amid the chaos, burning in the sunlight streaming down from those hateful skylights, proud as he had ever been as the victor of countless duels, and my cold heart broke at the dire beauty of him.

He took another deep breath to bellow his war cry, and I heard a loud *pop!*

And he exploded, shattering all the windows, piercing the fleeing humans with the flaming shrapnel of his bones. Cutting glass rained down on me, slicing my flesh to ribbons, but I did not care — I could see his heart there in the wreckage of his blown-apart body. It glowed and smoked, but still it pulsed with power.

So I snatched it up and hid it beneath my blood-soaked blouse. I carried it to the safety of my dark apartment, and kept it beating in a jar of my own blood. Later, when I realized what I must do, I broke into the morgue at night and pulled the bits of his bones from the bodies of the dead. It was not much, but it was a start.

What? You do not understand? Come down the hall with me to the guest bath … come see.

There. Do you see how the blood moves in the middle of the tub? That's the throbbing of his heart. Already you can see his skull growing back together, and the tendons of his ribs. I am sure the organs and muscles should be next, and then his skin.

Oh, darling … no. Don't struggle. It is already done, see? You'll just waste your own blood. Let it flow. The Baron needs fresh every day, now. Soon he shall be awake, and he and I will hide no more. We shall treat this city and its people the way we should have treated them all along. We will be crow and wolf, eagle and lion.

We will fuck everybody's sunshine.

ALWAYS DARKEST BEFORE THE DAWN

"Such thoughts were a hideous testimony to the world he had accepted;
a world in which murder was easier than hope."
–Richard Matheson, *I Am Legend*

A SOLDIER'S STORY
Maurice Broaddus

Maurice Broaddus has written hundreds of short stories, essays, novellas, and articles. His dark fiction has been published in numerous magazines, anthologies, and web sites, including *Cemetery Dance, Apex Magazine, Black Static,* and *Weird Tales Magazine*. He is the co-editor of the *Dark Faith* anthology series (Apex Books) and the author of the urban fantasy trilogy, *Knights of Breton Court* (Angry Robot Books). He has been a teaching artist for over five years, teaching creative writing to elementary, middle, and high school students, as well as adults. Visit his site at www.MauriceBroaddus.com.

His favorite vampire tales are *The Historian* by Elizabeth Kostova, and *Summer of Night* by Dan Simmons.

July 23, 1895 – Parsons, Indiana

"There are things ... " he started to say, but how do you begin such a horrific tale to one so young. "Once upon a time, there was a town under the spell of ... " Of what? Unsettling madness?

He casually stroked her downy, blonde hair, as if appreciating her beauty for the first time. Her small wood hewn bed framed her like an idyllic picture, just as he always imagined it would. Though it was the dream from a different life, he mentally pictured this very scene a hundred times. It inspired him to labor on when he hand-crafted each piece. He knew the nine months would pass too quickly when he started working the wood, and he wanted it to be perfect. Whittling away long, devoted hours on the headboard alone, he lamented that his skill didn't match his passion. Translating what he imagined into what he carved: a broad willow tree in a field of blooming flowers. Where better for his child to lay her slumbering head? She slept, innocent against the backdrop of violence, mayhem, and blood. It always came back to blood, so much of it on his own, still-trembling hands. A miasma of despair, grief, and guilt, he only distantly recognized the hollow sounding voice as his own. He pressed on with the telling of the tale anyway.

"I've committed some awful things. Deeds of which I am not proud. Things a child ought not to hear. But things which I must tell you anyway.

"It hurts to remember, like a dull headache you get when someone wakes you too quickly from a nightmare. The story begins with Holten Owensby. That opportunistic devil."

She grimaced in her sleep, furtive sounds escaping as she jostled her blanket. Only then did he realize how sharp his words had become. No matter how many generations down the line she may be, she was still kin.

"I'm sorry," he whispered as he brushed her head with his hand, "but I have known the truth about that demon in men's flesh for far too long and kept silent. He couldn't wait for his father, a good man, mind you, to die before he started spending his money. A few financial setbacks had put him in a state most foul. He was one of the investors in the railroad endeavor through Parsons that slowly proved itself to be a Pyrrhic race. You knew, for those who wanted to know or cared to look, from the leer in his eyes that he had killed in his time. And that kill was still on his mind. Deep-set grey eyes, like murky reflecting pools hidden by shadow. His spare silver hair combed back to vainly disguise his bald top. His face swirled of shadows and distrust, helped in no part by his overgrown mustache that gave him the appearance of a character from a dime story western.

"Parsons was a sleepy little hollow, with aspirations of being a city.

A SOLDIER'S STORY

The last shot from the Civil War still echoed in the air as people moved there. It was the perfect place for a man with a history he wished to forget to lose himself in. Free Negroes and escaped slaves settled the area just outside of the town. A few log cabins and meager shanties, more of an encampment than a town, but it was theirs. As Parsons boomed, so did the Scott Settlement. That was all they wanted. We should've seen that. And they knew their place. Most of the time they contented themselves doing the jobs that no white man wanted to do. It was not as if they did not know that the Sheriff and his boys could come in and settle any disputes any way they saw fit. Such was the relationship between Parsons and the Scott Settlement, like a town and her shadow. With the arrival of the trains, Parsons expected its growth spurt to continue.

"But there were only so many train jobs."

She slept, undisturbed in the glow of pale moonlight. Angelic. An ideal worth protecting.

"I was not worried about myself. I kept to myself, never wanting to draw too much attention. You live a life as long as I have, you learn a few things. I was tired of wars, whether they were revolutionary or civil. It was on such a field of battle where I was changed. It was easy to hide and feed among such death. Soldiering was all I knew. No, that wasn't true. Mine was the business of death and I was tiring of it. I tried to change and I returned home. Folks didn't care about my peculiarities of habit and hours kept because I was the best furniture maker in these parts, 'cept'n maybe them folks in Amish country. Plenty of call for me, too, with all the newfound money people were making, not to mention the old monied families desiring to expand their interests. My neighbors, my friends, however, they worried for their jobs, their futures, and how they would take care of their families. People only grumbled, as they were wont to do, when jostled on the street, feelin' too pressed in by the Scott Settlement. But that fear always simmered underneath. That 'it could all be taken away' fear; and just cause times were good and no one was goin' hungry don't mean that fear had gone. Fear that Holten preyed on.

"It was an election year and, of course, there had been some lively electioneering going on in these parts during Cleveland's campaign. Folks knew that all of those Republican voting Negroes were going to turn out in hordes come election day. That didn't sit well with many folks, especially those who already believed that with all the Negroes migrating here, they were going to vote away jobs from the local people. People thought they were going to lose their jobs. They thought ... what was said about their women and children ... terrible things. It was no excuse, I just wanted you to understand. You would think they had enough to fear with the things that moved in the night. The creatures they whispered about around the hearth fires. But fear blinds men to their reality. Fear snakes through them, takes hold of their heart and drives them to do dark things in its name. That was the nature of humanity.

"Night dusted down to the song of dusk. A hot, sweaty dusk. We crammed into the courthouse, made even more miserably hot because so many concerned citizens showed up. We had people at the door that only allowed Parsons locals in. Labor leaders fine-tuned the organ of resentment for Holten to soon come play. Rumors tore through the town presenting problems only politicians promised to fix. Rumors that more Negroes were due to be imported in from others states, to steal men's jobs. The mood became more and more hostile as the night wore on.

"Then that devil Holten stood up.

"'Parsons has changed,' he said, 'and is no longer safe for good folk. Right now, in our jail, sits an animal guilty of murder.'

"'Murder?' 'Who?' The whispers scattered like crickets in the night.

"Holten paused, letting the weight of his words carry, his fingers deftly dancing along the organ. He slowly revealed how earlier that day, Samuel Demory, an ax buried in his neck, was found dead. The blade did not match the savagery of the wound, the veins almost mutilated in the frenzy but that didn't matter. The ax belonged to his long time workman, Ezekiel Walker. The same man guilty of ... deeds most vile against Samuel's daughter, Rebecca. She still rested in shock, being treated by her mother at the Demory place. Rebecca Demory. She had spark that girl did. Her aristocratic manner she used to try and put on never once hid the gentle soul that did not hesitate to reach out to people. She stirred things within any who saw her. Made it difficult for them to keep their hungers at bay, no matter how God-fearing or disciplined they were.

"'Our women, our daughters, are not safe. How long will the good folks of Parsons suffer this?' Holten asked. 'Our women desire protection and this is the only way we'll get it.'"

The man paused, stroking the curls of the sleeping girl. The rise and fall of her chest came in regular, even breaths. The way the moonlight fell on her face, swathing her like a shroud, only made her seem more winsome. More vital.

"If it hadn't have been this, it would have been something else. I know it in my soul. When you have a room full of blasting powder, the kind of spark doesn't matter. By early evening, the paper ran an editorial: 'Nab Negro for Attacking Girl.' The fact that he was already 'nabbed' and in jail eluded everyone. The article demanded—without actually calling for—the lynching of the Negro that very night. It ran beside a cartoon of Negroes bribed with beer, chicken, and watermelons carted in to be new voters to the area and steal jobs.

"Because the flames apparently needed a little more fuel.

"Holten deputized everyone. It didn't seem to matter that he couldn't deputize his big toe much less anyone else. 'Niggers were guilty of crimes against whites,' he shouted to any doubters, 'that was all the authority I need.' The women, in their Sunday dresses — all calico and sunbonnets — paraded alongside us as if on their way to a show. A town full of good people, decent people, now overwhelmed by the sudden conviction of the rightness of their actions.

"My convictions I thought were unshakeable. I lived by a simple code which kept me alive for so long. To hear people murmur, there was no doubt that come the next morning, they would be able to stand by what they did to that 'rabid beast,' Ezekiel. No one felt any sorrow over righting that wrong. But their shame was soon coming.

"Apparently word had escaped to the Scott Settlement about the storming of the jail and the justice to be carried out on old Ezekiel Walker. The people of Parsons didn't care. They wanted the Scott folk to know that any one of them could be next if they stepped out of line or forget their place. Even as the good people of Parsons were dispersing after our ... bonfire ... word got back to us that the Negroes were arming themselves. For a war. Can't say that I much blame 'em really, folks just defending themselves and their families. But niggers with guns? No one could have foreseen that. The very notion of that was disconcerting. A stand had to be taken. There had to be respect for the rule of law.

"The night color gave courage to many men who had been different during day hours. Men swarmed about, the hour too late for respectable women and children. It was a motley collection of overalls, thick tan shoes, and felt hats. They weren't thinking any more, not in the way men usually think. It was as if they were seized by a feeling, almost a presence, bigger than themselves, bigger than Holten Owensby, maybe bigger than Parsons. Like worker bees rushing about serving an unseen queen bee. I don't know what their intentions were, whether we wanted to secure our town or rush into the Scott Settlement with the common goal of beating every Negro in the area. I really think we believed it was more of the former.

"They reached the crest of the hill where their meager cabins sat like Christ seated in judgment over our town. The people of Parsons labored beneath a feast of a moon. Between bolts of pine trees, oil lamps swayed in marched unison to the flop of their feet along the dusty road. Caught up in the urge that first made Cain splinter his brother's skull with a stone.

"The pull of blood. I recognized the quickening of the pulse. The metronome of the hunt. The taste of copper on the tongue. Blood drew them like a thirsty man to honeysuckle.

A SOLDIER'S STORY

"No, not them. Us.

"The plaintive cackle of chickens first announced their presence as they neared the first farm. A shadow peered from behind the henhouse.

"'Evenin' gen'lmen,' Jim Archer said, his old shotgun, reminiscent of a Confederate provosts' musket, cradled in his arms like a bouquet he'd come a-courtin' with. He tanned hides down at the Pruitt Shoe Company. A good man. Never tried to cheat you. He should've been running a middle buster, plowing his field, not challenging them.

"'Where you going with that gun, nigger?' Holten asked. I heard the voice as clear as day, yet it sounded as alien as anything I had heard. Angry, distorted, little more than a growl, not in control of his own faculties. Like a puddle of quicksilver, each of them was a drop that pooled together in one unseemly mass. One voice speaking for the whole.

"'Thought I might stick around. Use it iffen I have to,' Jim said in that steady, unintimidated voice of his. By light of day, this might simply have been a man protecting his family's farms, but that night, right then, he was only a nigger threatening white men with a gun. Part of me wanted to cry 'Put the gun down and run, Jim. Don't be so damned proud.' But my silence, the conspiracy of silence which kept secrets long buried like cancer eating away from the inside continued to hold reign.

"'We takin' you down, boy.'

"The thing about quicksilver is that once you drop it, it scatters in little drops that you have to sweep up.

"But you could never track all the drops.

"Men pounced on Jim from the surrounding shadows. They jerked his gun high, with only a single shot fired off. Two men held him while others beat him. Others set his henhouse, and then his own house, ablaze. He must've sent his family to a neighbor's house. I could almost hear his wife pleading with his stubborn mule self to join them. Now the only voice heard was an unsteady, terrified one that cried out to Jesus.

"'Southern niggers deserve a genuine lynchin'!' Holten coaxed in mincing school mistress fashion, as if to school boys with their primers, all dirty grins and horrid chuckles. He danced about overturned chairs, climbing atop Jim's hay-filled wagon for a better view. Holten against the flames, the very picture of the devil incarnate, his features, dark and twisted a wrathful shade of red.

"Frenzied whoops of carousing, between their cheers, their howls, and their imprecations arose at his suggestion. Even as the smoke seared my nostrils, through the tumbling smoke, buried in the flames, Jim was no longer Jim. No longer human, but some vague threat wrapped in flesh. Clubs smashed his head open with brutal efficiency, the poor cuss. loody, unconscious, near death. Lofted into the air, they passed from man to man, a battered ragdoll no one wanted yet everyone wanted a piece of. 'I got some rope,' someone yelled. A noose slid around Jim's blood-slickened neck. As he was hoisted into the air, the rope broke.

"'Get stronger rope,' another voice bellowed. It sounded like one of my neighbors, but again, the voice was distorted. Ugly. Barely human. Jim, however, was none the wiser and long past caring. In order to put the rope about Jim's neck, someone (I?) stuck his (my?) fingers inside the gaping scalp and lift his head by it. What monsters we had become, to think nothing of the fact that my hands were awash in the man's blood. To drink deep of the violence to quench the thirst for blood.

"'Grab hold and pull! Pull for Parsons!' Holten yelled. We pulled Jim about seven feet off the ground and left him hanging in a grove of mulberries and locusts, a blood-smeared, sambo scarecrow. I drew water from his well. Tepid water, tasting like beech trees and old bucket, but it was wet in my parched throat. Though my thirst remained unabated. The evening had barely begun.

"We set afire the shacks of poorer Negroes who lived in the surrounding area. The flaming wood skeletons painted the night in amber hues. We stoned and clubbed Negro men, women, and children, whoever we came across. We were a mess of people tramping about in the mud; muddy despite the fact that it hadn't rained in quite a spell, but you stomp enough people, your boots'll get wet just the same.

A SOLDIER'S STORY

"I don't know if you knew or not, but I was a gunner in the war. Worked as swift as we could. Focused, we were. The labor was meticulous or so it seemed to the other calvary men. We was always asked 'how do you remember what all you have to do in that confusion?' I became numb to it, if I were ever truly conscious to it to begin with.

"The key was to concentrate on the work. Experience which came in handy that night. We destroyed any saloon or business that catered to Negroes. We overturned the tables, drank the liquor, broke the windows, then torched the place in view of hundreds of spectators.

"As the night wore on, the creature we had become had to find new ways to amuse itself. Make no mistake, on the fringes of the chaos, I fed. Blood smeared my lips and dappled my neck. But the blood on me was out of thirst. Primal necessity. No one glanced a second time in my direction. In the shadows of night, however, neighbor reveled with neighbor, spurred on by their own blood sport. We was all a-whoopin' an' a-hollerin'; having a gay ole time of things. We were heady on the intoxication of that night's pursuits, emboldened by the fine liqueur of fear. I was blood drunk. Fear — ours and theirs — swept us along. Fever infected our brains, and we were a brigade of possessed madmen; grinnin' devils, teeth looming large and yellow in the amber glow of the torches, going about the business of hell.

"The frightful din of windows breaking. The clutter and clang of fences being knocked over. The screaming. The caterwauling. Babies crying, mewling, like they were past scared tears and simply awaited what they knew was coming. Or worse. Eyes wide open taking in everything that they saw, they were just too young for their brains to know what to do with the information. Not crying a bit, just staring, with dead eyes, eyes no child should have.

"Shooting residents as they ran through smoke and flames became a game, monstrous fun, if one were to judge by the laughter, hollering and clapping. One Negro in particular, gave us quite the sport of a chase. That crazed fool dashed from his burning home. We fired by the score, not to hit him, only to scare him into running. I kept waiting for a fox hunting bugle to be blown. He zig-zagged between the few buildings that remained untorched. The men fanned out, more amused than perturbed, between the shacks and sheds, eyeing the crawl spaces and nooks that our quarry had to know far better than we. Some men had been foolish enough to follow him directly and were soon tangled up in trash.

"Unfortunately, for him, his panic at our proximity took him down an alleyway. The nearest three men or so followed him in. He regained his senses long enough to use his head. He smacked the first man on him, knocking him clean out, which gave the rest of them pause, pause enough for him to scamper past them.

"I found myself rooting, even praying, for him, but only the way you cheer for the hopeless horse in a race. God heard my prayer as well as any made for myself the night I was cornered trying to fight past just as ancient a hate on that fated battle field so long ago. Only the Negro's fate was more merciful. All it took was one well-aimed shot. The Negro leapt into the air, his sprawl met with our shouts of approval. As the flames crept toward his body, he writhed, attempted to get up. A few warning shots kept him low. The flames marched on. He looked up at me with his yellow eyes desperately searching out hope. His veiny hands pulled him away from the flames' grasp, faster than the flames moved to catch him.

"Someone shouted that his arms should be broken, see how fast he'd crawl then. A man stepped forward and brought his heavy boot down upon the Negro's arms. He stomped until a bone poked through the flesh. The terrible snap it made."

The scrape of his boots as he paced along his wood floors drew him out of his revelry. The old rocking bed creaked as she rolled over in her sleep. It neared dawn now. Soon she would wake, full of hope and promise. So often he'd visited those of his line from when he was human. Not to watch over them, but to see what he'd missed. To touch, to rekindle, whatever remained of his humanity.

The story was almost done now.

A SOLDIER'S STORY

"The soft glow of the burning moon showered the Negro shanties; a mournful luminescence over the ashen countryside. The low murmur of wind whispered through the tree branches. We had cut a bloody swathe from one side of the Scott Settlement to the other. I don't know how much was left, I only knew the one cabin that stood in front of me. Mocking as all of the Scott Settlement had mocked Parsons, and what we stood for.

"The single log cabin room was built of logs split open and pegged together. From my window-side vantage point, one window, two doors. The wind whistled through the black cracks of the wall boards. The black earth along the floorboards crunched beneath soft footfalls. A woman hummed as she tended the black iron kettle that swung above the fire. She pressed her delicate hand against the small of her back to ease whatever back strain she may have had. The backdrop of the fire against her robe revealed how full with child she was. She slumped wearily into a chair, the sole furnishing in the room except for the pallet in one corner and a spinnin' wheel and loom in the other.

"She had a wheel an' loom in one corner of the cabin. Her son scrambled into her lap, enthusiastically clutching a tattered hand-me-down children's story book. An oil lamp burned unsteadily above them as they stole a moment to read.

"Their brown eyes strained against the fine print. Her pointed nose, straight and long, set against her high cheekbones. Her skin, the color of leaves in the fall, she kissed her son with the loving affection I'd seen your mother so often show you.

"That was when we heard the scraping sound.

"They looked up, out the window, I scrambled out of view as I heard the sound. I wondered why I chose to get out of sight, though I had no reason to hide. I knew the all too familiar sound, but maybe she didn't. So far away from everyone else, she may have been too far removed from 'the trouble.' Or maybe her husband had left her there while he went out to protect them. Maybe that's who she thought she heard approach as she excitedly scanned the surrounding woods. But I knew. The woods were deathly still. A throbbing silence. A womb song. Interrupted only occasionally by the rustling of leaves caught up in the night's breeze. And the scraping sound.

"The scraping sound drew nearer.

"Apprehension must have fanned the embers of dread in her soul, with the dawning realization of the scraping sound. The sound of men on a mad march, like papal warriors on yet another unholy crusade. The scrape of gun barrels against tree branches, the early dawn of nearing torches from all sides.

"'Manna?' I heard the little boy ask. He clutched her desperately, perhaps sensing her own fright. Fear-dilated eyes frantically scanned the room.

"Holten was the first to enter probably because he knew her folk was away. 'What have we got here?' he said with a devil's drawl.

"'Nothin', suh,' she said. I truly feared for her in that moment. My soul filled with an unspeakable dread. The loose pile of bedding shifted behind her.

"'You lyin' ta me girl?' he said. His shotgun issued a single report.

"Executed for her crime of hiding her child. I felt her deep-set eyes poring over me, accusing me, as her limp and lifeless body collapsed into a heap on her floor. Her blood mixed with the dirt, making it look like she bled mud.

"The wee boy was torn in two by the second report of the shotgun. Blood sprayed the cabin walls. Shot just because ... The room filled quickly with the odor of blood. Blood smells. The hovel smelled of a butcher's shop, at the time of an animal's butchering. The thick, musky, biting aroma of blood and the earthy odor of slaughtered meat, that was what I smelled that night.

"'Look what we got here, boys,' Holten said, spying the risin' in her belly.

"'What you reckon we ought'n do with it?' someone asked.

A SOLDIER'S STORY

"'Someone here needs a doctor,' Holten said, pulling out his hunting knife, 'and looks like I'm the nearest surgeon.' The flesh made a horrific sound as it was torn, not unlike the gutting of a hog. Her open eyes were long past caring. Her insides ripped open as she lay in a pool of her blood. He paused for a moment then found my gaze. And he smiled the same terrible grin he gave me when he spied me hovering over Samuel Demory's body, my mouth buried in the open rictus of the man's throat. No revulsion, no horror, only the light of damnable opportunity in his eyes. He resumed his carving until a small purple fleshy mass was pulled from her, sputtering mewls as it gasped for breath. Holten carried it outside with the casual disdain of a man carrying one of his dog's newborn pups. 'It's over, boys,' Holten jabbed his knife through the infant into a willow tree, letting it hang. And he stared at me with knowing eyes. Leaving it for me, scraps for a dog from his master's table. 'Let's end things.'

"It didn't take long for the fire to consume the cabin. The tongues of flames wagged, swollen with the gossip of hate, serenaded by the morning song of whippoorwills. The crackling and spitting of logs, like mocking laughter; they tossed the woman into the fire. Blood splattered their shirt sleeves as if they labored at an abattoir. It was then that I realized that in the light of morning, with time to reflect on what they'd done, they would be able to meet one another's eyes without care or remorse. Unashamed. Plastered with mud, shivering in the pre-dawn air, my time drew near, an empty sort of fear all over, so I ran to beat all.

"Holten blamed the whole affair on 'Negro agitators.' The conspiracy of silence consumed everyone. From the town leadership down, no one wanted to press the matter. No copy of the newspaper that riled so many of us could be found, not even in the archives. It was as if the paper skipped a day in its publishing history. The state attorney in Jefferson County claimed that he couldn't prosecute anyone because he was unable to find a single person who witnessed any citizen committing violence that night. No one had that look, that tainted, guilty look of barely held, barely hidden secrets.

"I'm tired of the hate. I'm tired of the unceasing thirst, that soul ache, which can drive someone to depths they'd never imagine. Even those that prey in the night trembled before the malice of the human heart unchecked.

"It is almost morning. I had it in my mind to drain you. Prevent you from growing up in this cesspool. But who am I to judge.

"I'm so tired. And the sun will be up soon. It will be a beautiful view."

RATTENKÖNIG
Douglas F. Warrick

Douglas F. Warrick's short stories have appeared in *Apex Magazine, The Drabblecast, DailyScienceFiction.com*, the *Dark Faith* anthologies, and elsewhere. His collection, *Plow the Bones*, is available from Apex Book Company. Douglas splits his time between the United States and East Asia, where he alternates between teaching English and singing in punk rock bands.

When asked about vampires, he says, "I've spent time with a great many pop-cultural vampires. That's the prerogative and the imperative of anybody who ever engaged in a serious adolescent goth kid phase. And boy did I ever. I dutifully penciled in the bubbles on my *Vampire: The Masquerade* character sheet, searched high and low for a fedora to accurately emulate the one worn by David Bowie's character in *The Hunger*, harbored actual crushes on a number of the characters from Poppy Z. Brite's *Lost Souls*, and memorized the lyrics to Bauhaus's "Bela Lugosi's Dead" and Concrete Blonde's "Bloodletting." Still, of those earlier obsessions, very little interest in things vampiric really remains. Those vampires that have endured in my affection tend to be ugly, anemic, asexual, even pathetic. The brood of sociopathic social engineers in Kathryn Bigelow's *Near Dark*. Klaus Kinski's repulsive manipulator in Herzog's *Nosferatu*. DeFoe's skittering, spastic Max Schreck in *Shadow of the Vampire*. These are my dudes. These are the guys who, to me, represent the best possible semiotics that the vampire myth can shoulder. Reminders that death isn't sexy. It's nasty and unfair and inconvenient and no fun to look at. And it lasts forever."

She sat Indian-style before them in the Sudden Room. Her face ached. She'd been sitting there with her shoulders slumped and her neck craned, chewing on the insides of her cheeks. She could feel the rough nasty texture of the unsanded, unpainted planks in the floor through her jeans. It smelled like age and dampness in here, and with each breath, some paranoid part of her brain screamed out that she was probably inhaling a floating miasma of old wallpaper and crumbling plaster and prehistoric mold, a chemical buffet. She didn't want to be here, but she knew that if she left, she would just want to come back. Nothing in the Sudden Room was comfortable.

The Sudden Room. Oh, the bastard Sudden Room, the nightmare from which she couldn't wake up and from which some part of her, the self-pitying masochist recently awoke, never wanted to. It had existed in the corner of her eye, a cancer of the periphery, a door at the end of a hallway that didn't exist. For years, she passed it and never saw it. For years, she stumbled like a sleepwalker from her bed to the bathroom, tracing the wall of the second-floor corridor with her fingers, and still she never noticed the branching hallway, or the door at the end. But once she saw it, like an optical illusion, like a filmic continuity error, she couldn't unsee it. It was always there, the door to the Sudden Room. As were the things that lived inside.

She couldn't figure them out. She wanted to know them, to understand them, to catalogue them and toss them behind a partition in her brain where she filed the vast and forgettable species of stimuli called "normal." But they weren't normal. They were shaped like people, but they stared at her through eyelids fused shut, their skin thin and jaundiced and divided into uneven puzzle pieces by a lattice of thick black veins. They sniffed the air, ticking and twitching and shivering the same way she'd seen tiny dogs shiver in the arms of women blonder and more successful than her. They were hairless, or were almost so, and their not-quite-hairlessness (patches of thin white wires that seemed to quiver like insect antennae) was worse than pure baldness. They opened their mouths and made thin, wordless, bubbling noises, and even when their mouths were closed, their long, sharp teeth hung over their chins like stalactites, rotten, yellow at the ends and black at the roots, the teeth of tigers in the mouths of meth addicts. And all of them were fused together, a shared carcinoma of a body from which jutted their terrible hungry heads and twitching toes and waving, spasmodic arms.

God, she wanted a cigarette.

They couldn't touch her. Not if she sat far enough away. The far wall, framed by the sliver of light from the hallway beyond the door, consisted entirely of *them*. From floor to ceiling, a wall of flesh. There were twenty-six of them that she could see (or twenty-six heads, anyway), and sometimes she thought there must be more, that the Sudden Room must stretch backward for a thousand miles of cramped, conjoined bodies. The wall of monsters in the Sudden Room. In college, when she had been an optimist, she wrote a paper on Rodin's Gates of Hell. She spent weeks staring at the sculpture, analyzing the cramped faces and bodies of the damned, lost in thought or twisted by misery, reaching, climbing, curled into fetal clumps and crammed into alcoves. The things in the Sudden Room with their terrible teeth and their weak, reaching fingers brought her back to those Gates, a breathing representation of Rodin's masterpiece, hungry and blind. And before them, a supplicant engaged in perplexed and petrified prayer, sat Abigail Quatro, queen of failure.

And downstairs, the doorbell rang.

Downstairs, the doorbell rang, and Jim resisted the training that compelled him to answer. On the couch with the old wooden metronome in his hands, running his thumb along the pyramid angle, watching the arm tick back and forth, trying to hypnotize himself. He wanted to fill a syringe with something dark and thick, something that could numb and blind and fuzz-out, and he wanted to jam it into his brain and push the plunger down and force the whole operation into blankness for a while. Hence, the metronome. The insignificant rhythm.

The bell again, belligerent and obsequious.

There's no rule, he thought. *There's no law against ignoring a doorbell. Nobody can force you to answer it.* But the imperative to answer tugged at him. It was funny how much power people had over you. They didn't even need to know you, and they could command your attention with a pointed index finger and a tiny fucking button mounted to the left of your front door. To be in your house was to be powerless.

The doorbell shrieked again, and Jim bit down on his tongue. With the pain, the world swam back. The truth resolved, focused, became sharp. And there didn't seem to be any reason to ignore the door anymore. So (groaning, growling, glaring at the frosted glass window set into the front door and wishing sudden death upon the person behind it), he went to the door and opened it.

"Hello, homeowner," said the doorbell man. He offered Jim his hand and, not wanting to, Jim shook it. It was a thin hand, delicate, a pianist's hand with long fingers and short, clean fingernails. He wore a gray suit and a green tie and a black overcoat. He wore a fedora and a pair of circular sunglasses. He carried an umbrella, for which Jim immediately and irrationally hated him. *Affectation*, he thought. *A stupid affectation. Sun's shining. What are you trying to prove?*

They stood there shaking hands for too many empty moments. Jim's chest tightened, his shoulders clenched. He ground his teeth together. The doorbell man smiled silently.

Jim's brain rolled through its lexicon of pleasantries and settled on,

RATTENKÖNIG

"Can I help you with something?"

"Homeowner," the doorbell man said, "I understand you have a pest problem."

They sometimes said things that sounded like words. She had a little moleskin in which she took notes of what they said, time-stamped and dated, a little book of nonsense quotations.

Theramin forest – 11:35 PM October 28th.

Stinking nest – 4:14 PM November 1st.

Regards – 1:21 AM November 10th.

When she started taking notes, she told herself that she was trying to piece together the quotes, solve the mystery of the Sudden Room. But as the months wore on into nearly a year of sitting and writing, she abandoned that goal. They were mindless words, the kind of thing dementia patients said as their brains broke down, and she was sure that she was imagining at least half of them. Still, she wrote. Because she'd already started, and she needed the habit.

They were excellent listeners, the bound-together cave-fish things. She could talk to them for hours, in a low monotone gone creaky, dry, and uneven from nicotine withdrawal and depression. She could tell them all sorts of things. She could eviscerate the girl she'd been before her life fell out from underneath her, the girl who had decorated the ceiling of her college apartment with glow-in-the-dark stars and moons and planets, who sipped wine and imagined herself to be an adult, the girl who forgot that someday you had to get a job and grow old and die, and that manic optimism and bright-pink hair dye didn't change any of that. She could talk about how, by thirty, she had expected so much more than this.

Argument fish assembly – 10:10 AM December 3rd.

Paramount – 3:33 AM January 9th.

An aimless, and apparently ownerless, arm swung rhythmically. A blind and hungry head snapped its jaws at it. The whole party hissed like vipers.

"I just wish," said Abigail, "That this wasn't the most exciting thing that had ever happened to me."

Hungry hungry hungry – 6:01 AM January 13th.
Seed eating parable – 1:12 PM February 20th.
Portcullis – 12:30 PM February 21st.

Someone downstairs laughed like a radio announcer, and then was silent.

The doorbell man, sitting on the sofa next to Jim and holding his coffee cup without drinking from it, laughed like a radio announcer, and then was silent.

Jim disliked most people he met these days. Just standing within breathing distance of the debris of his ambitions could turn him against a person. He knew that it was all bullshit, that he was lashing out, taking out his disappointment on the people around him. But he was starting to think that this polite little doorbell man, whose every expression and action seemed to be rehearsed, was legitimately deserving. He carried an umbrella on sunny days. He had absolutely no hair beneath the fedora, absolutely no eyebrows either. And he had just laughed at absolutely nothing. It was as though he had read, without context or explanation, that people sometimes laugh when they sit with one another.

"What's funny?" Jim asked.

"Nothing, homeowner. Now, back to it."

The doorbell man had asked for coffee, and for information. He wanted to know about their life together, Abby and he. Were they happy? Were they really in love? Where was she from? What did she do for a living? What did he do? How often did they make love?

And you know what the fucking terrible part was? Jim was telling him. Jim had lined up their photo albums on the coffee table and he was telling him all of it because this delicate little grub worm of a man knew — he *knew!* — about the Sudden Room and its residents, and that had to

RATTENKÖNIG

mean ... something.

"Okay," Jim said. And again, "Okay." He took a deep breath, and he told the man everything. He told him how he met Abby, in a Women's Studies class in which he was one of four men, and in which they shouted at one another from across the room, Abby passionately championing Steinem, Jim aligning himself with Paglia despite not knowing the first thing about feminist theory. "I just thought," he said, "that she was fascinating to look at when she got worked up."

The doorbell man nodded and hmm-d and hrr-d and picked up a pencil from the coffee table and tapped it against his lips.

Jim told him how they'd dated, at first like silly high school kids despite being in their twenties, sneaking away from every social engagement to make out in closets or cars or behind the high hedges in the park, and then later like ancient friends, sharing stories with brief glances, holding between them a thousand esoteric punchlines and secret passwords. "Turkey-fingers," he said. "I used to ... This is so stupid, but in college I used to wrap my hands in sliced turkey, like sandwich turkey. And I used to chase her around the apartment. Kind of, you know ... warbling. 'Turkey-fingers! Turkey-fingers are coming for you! Turkey fingers!' Like a ghost. Like, I don't know, it was like a half-cocked Boris Karloff impression. You know? You know."

The doorbell man chewed off a hangnail. He said, "I know."

Jim told him how they'd forgone the vows and quoted Wilco songs at each other, because it was silly and irreverent and somehow more meaningful than somebody else's old promises. He told him they'd come to live in the big house in the nice neighborhood. "My dad," he said, "My dad is ... was ... an attorney. It was a wedding present. The house, I mean. God."

The doorbell man took off his hat and scratched his scalp.

He told him of the fall, the gradual slope away from ambition and hope toward debt and joblessness. Useless degrees, an absence of marketable skills, property taxes and student loans they couldn't afford.

The miscarriage, and the money they'd spent on a baby that never came. How they slept back to back, or sometimes in different places, he in the bedroom and she in the Sudden Room where she didn't actually sleep at all. How they couldn't afford cigarettes anymore, and how neither of them wanted to leave the house even to find a smoker from whom to bum. How they could go days without saying much to one another. How when he said, "I love you," it sounded like a plea, like a desperate dive toward her, and how he wasn't really sure he was capable of loving anyone anymore. He said, "Things were supposed to be different for us."

The doorbell man said, "I see."

Her back hurt. She had gone into the room around seven o'clock this morning, and it must have been after four by now. Her entire life story had fallen out from between her lips for the thousandth time, unheard by the slit-eared fungus of skin and limbs and teeth. She said, "Last night, Jim tried to cheer me up. I was falling asleep on the couch and he came in with, ah, the, uh ... " she sighed, snapped her fingers together. "The shirt he wore at our wedding. It was ... " a smile, weak and noncommittal, something to which she couldn't devote any patience or energy. "It was just way too small for him. He's put on some weight. We both have. His gut was pushing out the fabric, like, putting these great big gaps between the buttons, and he looked at me and he said ... he said, 'Enjoying the view?'"

She thought about laughing, decided against it. She listened to the grumbling and bubbling of her monsters, trying to figure out why she'd started this story in the first place. "Thing is," she said, picking at the cuticle of her left thumb, seeing how deep she could stand to drive her house key into the soft skin, "it was just so desperate. I could see how angry he was, how aimless and scared and angry. I'm not dumb. I felt ... insulted. How can you pretend that anything is normal?"

Pushing deeper with her house key, pushing the dry white ridge of her cuticle backward, back as far as it could go. It hurt, but what else was new? Lots of things hurt. Not smoking hurt. Looking at your checking account balance hurt. Watching your husband pretend not to hate you hurt. Walking by your diploma hanging on the wall hurt. Not acknowledging the bulk boxes of diapers or bottles of formula or untouched toys and baby books hurt. Pain stopped being such a big goddamn deal after a while.

A head close to the ceiling hissed, writhed, coughed up thick mucous the color of mustard, and said, "Turkey-fingersssss."

Every muscle in Abigail Quatro's body tensed. Her eyelids retracted, her throat went immediately dry. Her key slipped, sliced a jagged reservoir across the knuckles of her thumb. She gasped, more in shock and recognition than pain. She said, "That wasn't fair."

Now all twenty-six heads were still and silent, pointed at her, their nostrils flaring rhythmically as though some olfactory homing device had lighted upon its target. Her breath was coming faster than her lungs could handle comfortably and her brain screamed for nicotine, and she reeled. These emotions, this *fear*, was stronger and more manic than anything she'd felt in almost a year. What were they doing now? Why were they quiet, why weren't they moving, what did they smell with their terrible misshapen, uneven, grown-together nostrils?

In the silence, she could hear blood pattering from the gash on her hand to the naked floorboards. And with each drop, the twenty-six heads (oh God, no, no, perfectly choreographed, synced) twitched. She sat up straighter, snagged the moleskin from her back pocket, readied her pencil.

Turkey-fingers – 3:somethingPM March 3rd (WHAT???)

They sat there for a long time, and the only sound was the syncopated drip of her blood and the matched rustle of her rotten monsters straining toward it.

The only sound was the syncopated tick of the cat-shaped clock above the television, a relic of an era of silliness and kitsch, as Jim tried to figure out what to say next. He thought, *Stop talking to this asshole. There's something wrong with him, this hairless little freak. Have you stopped to think for one fucking second about why he's here? What he intends to do? What he has to do with the putrid secret cancer growing upstairs?* What he said was, "They're like ... mole-rat people. Have you ever seen those? Mole-rats? They're hairless and wrinkled and blind and ... ugh ... ugly. And these mole-rat people ... their skin has grown together and now they're just this big wall of mole-rat men ... In a room we never knew was there until ten months ago. Ten months ago! How do you live in a place," the words spilling out of him as though tied to a string tugged by the skinny fingers of his uninvited houseguest, "for seven years and never see an entire room of it? How can that happen?"

The doorbell man pulled a face, a bawdy parody of empathy, and reached out and patted Jim's knee. Jim lurched away from him, his pulse swelling and pulsing below his jaw. He wanted to scream at the man, to attack the man, to light a fire underneath him and remove him like a tick from his house. Except this didn't feel like *his* house anymore, and hadn't for a long time. His nerves quaked and rattled, and he curled into himself on the edge of the sofa thinking, *I look like a junky. A quivering junky going through withdrawal.* He said, "I'm sorry. Just ... I'm really sorry, I just don't want you to ... to touch me, okay? Just don't ... fucking touch me ... sir."

The doorbell man smiled, bit his bottom lip. His teeth were too long, too white. He looked like a theatrical mask. He said, "Mr. Quatro ... homeowner ... have you ever heard of the *Rattenkönig* phenomenon?"

"No. Nope. I, uh ... no."

"Hmm," said the doorbell man. "It is said that rats, when isolated together in small spaces, will fuse together at the tail. Can you imagine, homeowner Jim Quatro? A nest of trapped rats, isolated from food, from sunlight, as their tails tangle together and eventually become ... one.

Amazing, if it's true, although I myself have never seen any compelling evidence for its veracity. Imagine, then, homeowner, that a nest of some other animal becomes trapped. An animal that survives by different means, adheres to different rules."

The doorbell man stood up, stepped onto the coffee table, kicked aside the photo albums, crushed his coffee cup beneath his heel. Jim stared, open mouthed, and thought, *You're standing on my table. You're standing on my table. I don't know why, but you're standing on my table and gesturing at the ceiling like a professor lecturing to the ceiling fan.*

"Let us theorize that this species travels through secret corridors, makes its way toward new feeding grounds via an entire sequence of tunnels, much like your ... ugly ... hairless ... wrinkled ... blind ... mole-rats." He was smiling now, the doorbell man, breathing fast, haloed by the ceiling fan, lost in his lunatic sermon. "Let us further theorize that the way is one day blocked by some means, homeowner! Let us now hypothesize what might happen to such a marvelous species over decades, over centuries, homeowner, in the dark! In the bloodless, skyless dark, homeowner!"

A pause. The doorbell man stared longingly at some distant point beyond the house, out in the cold dark bloodless, skyless universe, and caught his breath. Jim realized he was digging his teeth into his tongue, gnawing on that same fat ulcer he'd made earlier when the doorbell had interrupted his thoughtlessness. It had been a very long time since he had't felt angry. But now he did not. Only scared and confused and unbearably sad. He thought, *You're the same. Same as the things in the Sudden Room. Something with a barely functional understanding of human behavior, something doing a bad impression. And you exist. The universe is huge and cruel.*

The doorbell man smoothed his suit and stepped down from the table. He took a seat, crossed his legs, adjusted his fedora. "What do you suppose would happen then?"

This was what they wanted. What they always wanted. Just this slow thick leak, these fat droplets spattering against the floor and sinking into the woodgrain, staining the teeth of her house key. She squeezed the meat of her thumb with her opposite hand, milking the blood from the wound and speeding the drip. The monsters (*No*, she thought, *not quite monsters, are they? Or not just any kind of monster. I know what they are. I know their name. They have been understood and catalogued and thrown behind a partition marked with their species and phylum*) shuddered and salivated and gnashed their rotten broken saber-teeth to match the new tempo.

"I know what you want," she said. "I know what you are."

One of them hissed, "Paaaaaglia. Sssssteinemmmmm."

Another growled, "Behhhhind the hhhhhedges."

Another, its face fuzed into profile, its mouth almost filled with the metastasized flesh of its fellows, said, "Ennnnjoying the view?"

"I could give you what you want," she said, and wondered what would happen if she did. Wondered if it could somehow erase the bad decisions and the worse luck, the tense and unpleasant marriage, the dead baby that never lived, the ghost of which floated between her and Jim. She wondered if she'd finally feel like she'd done something worthwhile. Each of the faces in the wall salivated in expectation, wet from lips to chin with thick foamy spit. Could she refuse them? Could she disappoint them like that?

She would tell one more secret. And then she would see.

"When we were in college," she said, squeezing the gash, "Jim asked me what I wanted to do. With my life, I mean. We were spent, exhausted. We had just finished, you know … fucking, I guess. Making love. I don't know. We were satisfied with ourselves. We felt philosophical. So he asked me … 'in the cosmic sense,' he said, whatever that means, what I wanted to do. And I took a deep breath, and I imagined that I was inhaling the whole universe, the stars and the planets and the dark matter, and I told him what I wanted to do. I wanted to make an impact. I wanted the world to bend a little under my weight. To never be the same after me."

RATTENKÖNIG

She lifted her thumb upward, offering it to the chomping mouths in the wall of the Sudden Room. They strained and gurgled and roared, and the house shook.

Jim could hear them gurgling and roaring upstairs, louder than they'd ever been. And here he was, downstairs, listening to the doorbell man, whatever he was, stumble through his best estimation of what human conversation might sound like. He wasn't sure how much more of this his brain could take.

"Now imagine," whispered the doorbell man, "that some homeowner just ... stumbled onto the secret corridor where that *Rattenkönig* had become stuck. It would have to have been a sleepwalking homeowner, a homeowner catatonic with despair and disappointment. Sound familiar, homeowner? Sound like anyone you know?"

"Okay, enough!" Jim was standing. "Enough, man, alright? Now what?" He was leaning over the doorbell man, shaking his fists, gesturing, shouting. "Why are you here? Are you here to help? Can you help us? Can you, what, kill those fucking things?" He grabbed the doorbell man by the lapels, shook him. "Can you do fucking anything? Huh?" He crumpled, came down onto his knees before the doorbell man, buried his head in the doorbell man's chest, wept.

The doorbell man caressed the hair at the nape of Jim's neck and shushed him, rocked him back and forth. "No," he said. "No, I'm not here to kill them. I just wanted to ... see. I wanted to see, homeowner. I've never seen a *Rattenkönig* before."

Upstairs, someone screamed.

Abigail Quatro screamed. She tried to pull herself away, but she was trapped, held by dozens of scrambling arms and legs against the pulsing wall of skin. She felt their razor fangs at her wrists, her thighs, her shoulders, felt their dry, sore-covered lips wrap around the wounds and suck, drinking desperately from her, and it hurt, it hurt, God, it hurt. She struggled, kicked, squirmed, but even piled into a single gigantic body, they were stronger than anything she'd ever known. They weren't letting her go. Her vision was getting hazy, and the part of her with the will to fight back was shrinking, fading. It wasn't fair. None of this was fair.

She heard the door to the Sudden Room slam against the wall, felt the hall light burst through onto her skin, saw two silhouettes through the haze. One of them was shouting her name, rushing toward her. Jim. It was Jim. It had to be Jim. She was so very tired. And this wasn't fair.

The other silhouette clapped his hands, bounced on the balls of his feet. It said, "Marvelous. Absolutely marvelous."

Jim was at her side now, pulling on her, trying to remove her from the wall of mean mouths and blind eyes. He was screaming. He was struggling.

When they finally let her go, she knew that Jim hadn't saved her. Her monsters just ... weren't hungry anymore.

Her vision was coming back to her now. The pain was receding. She felt numb and betrayed. She kept trying to speak, but her throat wouldn't let the words pass.

"God, Abby. Oh Jesus, Abby, it's okay," Jim, above her, faking his way through normal again, "it's okay, baby, I'm here. I'm here. God damn it, god damn it. Okay, it's okay. I'm going to call the hospital, baby, okay? Everything is going to be ... "

She hated to be called Abby. Always had.

The other man ... the bald man with the sunglasses and the fedora and the umbrella hanging from his arm ... put his hand on the back of Jim's head. She watched all of this from the floor. She didn't like the floor. It was so dirty. So uncomfortable. The bald man said, "Well, that was fun, homeowner. Bye, now."

Jim's head jerked up to stare at the bald man, watched him

strolling through the door, down the hallway. Out. She stared at the slope where his jaw became his throat. She watched his pulse announce itself in the throbbing vein there. It seemed to be beating so much faster than hers.

"What?" he screamed. "What?" Loud, raw, unhinged. "What?" A real question. A question to which he desperately expected an answer.

For many moments, they listened to the bald man's footsteps. They listened to the door slamming on his way out. And then all there was to listen to was the gurgle and slurp of the wall of monsters.

When her voice returned, Abigail Quatro said, "Nothing changes. Nothing is different. Everything is always the same."

VAMPIRE NATION

Jerry Gordon

Jerry Gordon is the co-editor of the *Dark Faith* and *Last Rites* anthologies. His fiction has appeared in *Apex Magazine*, *Shroud*, and *The Midnight Diner*. His apocalyptic thriller, *Breaking The World*, will be released through Apex Publications in 2013. When he's not contemplating the end of the world, he's blurring genre lines at www.jerrygordon.net.

His favorite vampires overwhelmed humanity in Richard Matheson's classic, *I Am Legend*.

"*Africa?* When are you going to pick a cause you can actually win? From what I hear the continent has maybe two months at best."

"That's about right." I poured myself a scotch and walked along the wall of captures that adorned Senator John Mitchem's office, stopping in front of one frame that showed him and his older brother as college students. The low-res motion clip followed their volunteer group as it worked to restore oil-ravaged beaches on the Gulf Coast some twenty years ago. I handled most of the camera work for that trip. It was my first and only adventure as an honorary member of the Michem family.

"So what's to save?" John darted in and out of his senate office's private bathroom, fiddling first with his tuxedo jacket and then with a mangled excuse for a bow-tie. "I mean the Chinese have a pretty good handle on containment."

"Come on, you know the Chinese have a vested interest in Africa's demise."

"Sure, they get the land. We've agreed to that much, but you're assuming anyone will ever use it. The Chinese are going to have a hard time convincing their people to build on vampire central."

"I thought you guys were only allowed to refer to it as the quarantined zone?" I smiled and took a quick sip of scotch to hide my nerves.

"Did you see the footage of that human rights group in Johannesburg? The vampires ripped out their throats and drank their blood. On camera. Once the networks got hold of that footage, fangs and all, the name ship sailed."

I glanced at the capture above the Gulf Coast trip. It was a more modern clip of John taking his oath of office. While the rest of our Yalie cronies had comfortably settled into middle age, John's thick black hair and deep blue eyes belonged to a man ten years his junior. Standing tall with his right hand raised, he embodied our college pact to change the world. Two years into his second term of office, it was time to see if he actually had the guts to do it.

"They have a vaccine, John."

"What?"

"The Chinese. They have a vaccine, and they're choosing not to use it."

John came out of the bathroom, pulling the loose bow-tie apart. I could see my old friend measuring the likelihood that this was some kind of perverse lobbyist joke.

"Are you sure?" he asked.

"I have the ambassador from the African Union outside. He flew directly from their emergency headquarters in Paris."

"Damn it, David." John glanced at the backdoor to his office, considering a quick escape. "It's one thing for you to sneak up here to say hi, but don't corner me with something like this right before a state dinner. I'm the foreign relations chair for God's sake. There are channels for this sort of thing."

"There isn't any time for that."

John gave the backdoor a second look. "Has this ... *vaccine* even been tested?"

"Yes."

"And you're sure it works?"

"Of course I'm sure. I wouldn't be here if I wasn't sure."

"Fine, you've got five minutes." John took off his jacket and punched the antique intercom button on his desk. "Liz, let the ambassador in."

The door opened and a distinguished African statesman entered the room. His dark, shaved head framed a graying goatee.

"I hope you will pardon our rather unorthodox meeting, Senator Mitchem."

"Call me John." He offered the ambassador a heartfelt handshake. "Your people are in my prayers, Ambassador ... "

"Hounsou."

"Ambassador Hounsou, of course. Please, sit. Can I get you anything? Coffee? Scotch?"

The ambassador looked past him, sizing up the tattered colonial flag that suspended itself on the wall behind John's desk. Before fading into the state flag of Pennsylvania, the simulacra morphed from a stained relic of the Revolutionary War to a spotless, fifty-two star standard.

"I thank you for the offer, Senator, but that will not be necessary. I am well aware your time is limited."

"Of course." John leaned against the front of his desk and motioned me to take a seat next to the ambassador. "I understand that you may have found a cure to the terrible plague ravaging your country."

"A member of your Gates Foundation smuggled the original formula and its antigen vaccine out of India."

"*India?*" John straightened his tuxedo shirt, shooting me an angry glare before returning to the ambassador. "I was told this was about China ... and what do you mean *original formula?* Are you suggesting this is somehow man made?"

"That I am, sir. The Indian scientist that created the formula committed suicide shortly after the plague appeared in Benin. One of his former aids helped the foundation obtain the technical information necessary to stop it."

"That's a very serious accusation, Ambassador."

"It is not an accusation. It is an unfortunate fact for both our countries. India has been providing bio-weapons research and technical support to the Chinese. The documentation that accompanied the antigen vaccine is proof enough of that."

John closed his eyes, pinching the bridge of his nose. "And you've actually tested it?"

"We dispatched two of our remaining SANDF teams into Africa through the Mediterranean. The Chinese blockade shot down both helicopters, but one managed a hard landing in the foothills of Tipasa. The team captured and treated five test subjects in various stages of transformation. Within forty hours, all but one of them had stabilized and was beginning to exhibit non-violent cognitive thought. I personally linked into the operation from our headquarters in Paris."

"How much time does your team on the ground have left?" John asked.

Ambassador Hounsou met his gaze with cold, dark eyes. "Their makeshift compound was overrun twelve hours ago. They held out as long as they could."

I could see the pain on John's face. For all his flaws, he understood this type of loss better than anyone. We both did. John's older brother Sam was killed the summer after our sophomore year when militants overran his UNICEF operation in Darfur.

Three college summers, three causes. That was our freshman pact. The idea had been Sam's, but he let John pick first. That's how we ended up spending two months cleaning beaches in the wake of the Gulf Coast oil spill. Sam's passion for Africa made it our sophomore destination. He spent two years there with the Peace Corps before joining his younger brother at Yale.

When the three of us were tapped to be Bonesman, just weeks before the trip, Sam was the only one to say no. Instead of joining Yale's most prestigious secret society, he boarded a plane for Africa. I never chose a third destination. I left the university shortly after Sam's death.

"With the help of the French," the ambassador continued, "we have set up a facility to mass produce the antigen vaccine. But we are in no position to challenge this blockade. The only military assets we have left flew President Mobunte and his cabinet out of the capital city. China and India are bursting at the seams, and it appears our continent is the perfect solution to their population problems."

I knew the vaccine put the United States in a difficult position. Africa had plenty of natural resources left, but their most valuable one was space. In a world of eight billion people, disease and war had conspired to under-populate their continent. The vampire plague, properly contained, went a long way toward mitigating a whole host of population problems.

"With India's support," I began, "the Chinese have a dominate position, but they can't afford to ignore us on this issue. We could —"

"Just stop, David. It's not fair of you to get the ambassador's hopes up. As much as I wish it wasn't the case, the President's not going to go for this. He's as isolationist as they come, and there is no way he'll risk pissing off China and India over a country with, I'm sorry Ambassador, little to no strategic value."

I shook my head, unwilling to accept John's cursory dismissal. "If this was happening in the Middle East —"

"We'd be deploying troops out of the Iranian Protectorate. I don't disagree. This isn't the turn of the century. Our nation building days are behind us. The Chinese played it smart and let us exhaust our resources trying to change the world. Now they're on top, and we play by their rules."

"What about the Grid? We could take this to the people."

"Come on, David, nobody on the Grid cares about Africa or anything else. They're all too busy wasting away in their private virtual worlds. Why fight to make this or any other country a better place when you can just link-in and have it any way you want? If we didn't make them pay to be on the Grid, we wouldn't have any ditch diggers left. Outside of the rich, nobody cares what we do."

"But we're talking about half a billion people." I put down my scotch. "There has to be something you can do."

"I can talk to the President about asylum and maybe even provisional citizenship for the refugees that made it to Paris. I feel for the African Union, I truly do. What's going on there is unspeakable, but you're gravely mistaken if you think the United States is going to challenge another nuclear power's military blockade. In that respect, Africa is on its own."

"I feared as much." Ambassador Hounsou stood, extending his hand. "I thank you for your candor and your time, Senator Mitchem."

"I really wish I could do more."

"Oh, I believe you will."

"Excuse me?" John tried to pull his hand away, but the ambassador held tight, cutting his fingernails deep into the palm. The whites of Hounsou's eyes turned red as blood vessels swelled to the surface, nearly bursting.

"My country has had less experience with democracy than yours, but I have come to believe, from personal experience, that politicians only care about problems that affect them. For that reason, I injected the vampire plague into my body shortly before this meeting. Now, my problem is your problem."

John pulled away from the ambassador, his hand red with blood. "For your sake, this had better be a joke."

"I would not joke about such things." The ambassador leaned closer, exposing the beginnings of nicotine-stained fangs. "Depending on your individual physiology, the virus will take between sixty to ninety days to permanently destroy your brain. The first forty-eight hours will be the worst for you. You will begin to feel the blood in your veins boiling. It will become progressively difficult for you to think clearly. Your reactions will become more violent. Your thought processes less human and more, shall we say, animalistic."

"Why would you do that to me?"

"As you so eloquently stated, we have no strategic value to your country. That makes it easy for you to sit in comfort while we die. Aids. Ebola. Genocide. Your government has turned a blind eye to Africa in our greatest hours of need, never offering more than token sentiments and inconsequential donations. It's time for your country to pay for its indifference."

"Do you really think infecting me helps your cause? What part of avoidable nuclear confrontation do you not understand? There are seven and a half billion people on this planet that don't live in Africa. David, tell him this isn't something I can talk the President into."

"You don't have to talk the President into anything, John. You just have to go to dinner tonight and shake his hand. We've taken care of the rest."

John turned to me in disbelief. "You really think I would knowingly infect the President?"

"To save your own life, and the lives of half a billion people, yes I do. I chose you for this. If you let Africa die, everything Sam believed in, everything he gave his life for, will die with it."

"Don't you dare bring my brother into this, you bastard."

"He wasn't just your brother, John. He was my best friend. There is no way he would let this happen to Africa and you know it."

"Look, even if I helped you get the President, I wouldn't have any control over the policy decisions he'd make. I'd be sitting in a quarantined jail cell right next to you. What makes you think he won't just use this cure to save America and then turn his back on Africa?"

"Because I have taken that choice from him." The ambassador stood tall, resolute in his statement. "The Chinese militarized their border before we could act, but the African Union used my diplomatic status with the United Nations to disperse several teams across your North America. These teams carry with them vials of a mutated strain of the vampire plague, one for which the Chinese have not engineered a cure.

"So now, Senator, my country's problem is your country's problem. Either you will help us convince your President to challenge this blockade and save Africa, or my people will open those vials ... and we will all live in a Vampire Nation."

CURTAIN CALL
Gary A. Braunbeck

Gary A. Braunbeck was born in Newark, OH (the city that serves as the model for his Cedar Hill Cycle stories) and currently lives in Worthington, OH. He has published 24 books, evenly split between novels and short-story collections, including *In Silent Graves, Coffin County*, and the forthcoming *A Cracked and Broken Path*. His work has garnered 6 Bram Stoker Awards, an International Horror Guild Award, and a World Fantasy Award nomination. That is the end of anything remotely interesting about him.

Some of his favorite vampires include both film versions of *Nosferatu, Francis Ford Coppola's Dracula,* Kathryn Bigelow's *Near Dark*, and the little-scene, Richard Matheson-scripted television adaptation of *Dracula*, starring Jack Palance.

(From the unpublished papers of Charles Fort)

I have been, for most of my life, a collector of notes on subjects of great diversity — such as deviations from concentricity in the lunar crater Copernicus, to the great creature Melanicus and the super-bat upon whose wings it broods over the affairs of Man, as well as stationary meteor-radiants, the reported growth of hair on the bald head of a mummy, the appearance of purple Englishmen, instances of amphibians and blood raining down from the heavens, apparitions, phantoms, the damned, the excluded, wild talents, new lands, and "Did the girl swallow the octopus?"

But my liveliest interest is not so much in things as in the relations of things. I find now, in the twilight of my life, as I pour over the endless data that I have assembled throughout my days, that I think more and more about the alleged pseudo-relations we call "coincidences." What if these events, rather than being happenstance, are the final result of great, secret, dark machinations of the Universe interacting with the subconscious to produce an event or events which guide humanity down certain roads certain of its members were destined to take?

I am writing now of a brief period I spent in London when I was thirty-six, in the early months of 1912 (nearly ten years before I decided to move there), and of a most singularly peculiar bookshop, its even more peculiar proprietor, and a bit of London Theatre history which none before me has ever recorded.

I was staying at a very comfortable rooming house in Bedford Place, just around the corner from the British Museum in Great Russell Street (since my visit to London was solely to search through the Museum's vast archives of manuscripts, the location of my rooms could not have been more advantageous for my purposes). On this particular day — kept from my research at the Museum by a cryptic note delivered to my room early that morning — I was exploring the narrower, less often traveled streets of the vicinity, in search of an address which seemed more and more to me a flight of fancy in the mind of whomever had composed the note, when the heavens opened wide and within moments the rain was pounding down violently. I was in Little Russell Street, just behind the church that fronts on Bloomsbury Way, and there was no way for me to find immediate shelter from the storm. The address written on the note was obviously someone's idea of a joke, for I had been up and down this street no less than three times.

So why had I not noticed the little bookshop before?

CURTAIN CALL

It seemed that as soon as the sun was obscured by the rain clouds, the tiny edifice simply appeared out of the rain, set between a baker's and a haberdashery where before there had been only, I am certain, a cramped alleyway.

I shall state here that, despite the path of research my life has been dedicated to, I am not a man who is given to either hallucination or flights of fancy. I neither believe nor disbelieve anything. I have shut myself away from the rocks and wisdom of ages, as well as the so-called great teachers of all time; I close the front door to Christ and Einstein and at the back door hold out a welcoming hand to rains of frogs and lands hidden above the clouds and the paths of lost spirits. "Come this way, let's see if you can explain yourselves," I say unto these phenomena, always taking care to look upon them with a cold clinician's eye. I cannot accept that the products of minds are subject-matter for belief systems. I neither saw nor did not see a bookshop hidden away on this street. It simply *was*, at that moment, where the moment before it was not.

I crossed the street and entered the place, nearly soaked through.

The first thing that assaulted my senses was the so-very-right *smell* of the place. Perhaps you have to be a true lover of books to understand what I mean by that, but the comforting, intoxicating, friendly scent of bindings and old paper was nectar to my soul.

I called out, asking if anyone were there. When no response was forthcoming, I removed my coat, draped it on the rack near the door and — after patting down my hair and shaking off the remnants of rain from my shoes and sleeves — proceeded to browse through the offerings.

The walls were lined from floor to ceiling with sagging shelves full of books, and I could see at a glance that, though the stock contained everything from academic texts to the usual classics, its primary focus was on matters philosophical and occult; everywhere I turned there were books such as Agrippa's *De Occulta Philosophia*, the ancient notes of Anaxagoras of Clazomenae detailing his conclusions that the Earth was spherical, *The Gospel of Sri Ramakrishna*, the Hindu *Ris Veda*, the poems of Ovid, the plays of Aeschylus, Lucan's *De Bello Civilia* ... my heart beat with tremendous anticipation. What treasures would I find here?

It was only as I was admiring an ancient copy of the *Popol Vuh* which sat under a glass case in the center of a great table that I became aware that I was no longer alone. How I knew this I could not then say, though what was soon to follow would make the reason clear.

I turned and saw the proprietor.

Though he appeared to be only a few inches taller than I, there was, nonetheless, a sense of power and great, massive presence about him. His fierce, dark eyes stared out at me from underneath thick eyebrows that met over his knife of a nose. His heavy white moustache drooped down past the corners of his mouth, drawing my attention at once to his red and seemingly swollen lips, which were flagrant and somehow femininely seductive against the glimmer of his face. Though he was obviously an older gentleman, he carried himself with the grace and power of man fifteen years my junior.

"Mr. Fort," he said, in a heavily-accented, full, rich *basso* voice the New York Opera would have swooned to have sing upon its stage, "I am so very pleased you were able to accept the invitation." He offered his hand. "It is a great honor to meet a gentleman such as yourself, who shares my interest is matters of data that Science has excluded."

I shook his hand. His grip was steel. I winced from the great pressure and the pain it sent shooting up my arm.

"I beg your pardon," he said, releasing my hand. "I sometimes forget that, in my enthusiasm, my handshake can be a bit ... "

"Formidable?" I said, massaging my fingers.

His smile was slow in its appearance but total in its chilling effectiveness. "What a kind way to put it." He turned and started toward a door near the back of the shop. "If you'll be kind enough to follow me, sir."

I did, though somewhat reluctantly. After all, what did I know of this fellow or his intent? True, in my studies I had come across many strange tales told by sometimes stranger individuals, but (at this point in my life, at least) I rarely had to meet any of these people face to face. Still, I must admit, my curiosity was stronger than either my anxiety or trepidation.

I need speak in a bit more detail of the cryptic note which was delivered to my room as I was readying myself for the day's research at the Museum. It arrived in a heavy envelope which contained — aside from the letter itself — several newspaper clippings, which I will summarize momentarily. It read as follows: "My Dear Mr. Fort: I know that you will read the enclosed with great interest, but also with your Intellectual's eye. Come to the address written below before the noon hour and I will give you irrefutable proof that these incidents are, indeed, based on fact and not myth. I urge you to keep this appointment."

Below the body of the writing were these words: *Denn die Todten reiten schnell* ("For the dead travel fast," a line from Burger's "Lenore").

The letter was signed only: *A.S.*

Having read with great delight Mr. Jules Verne's famous novel, I found myself smiling at the thought that I might encounter the fictitious Arne Saknussemm at the end of my own "journey."

The clippings came from newspapers such as *Lloyd's Sunday News*, the *Brooklyn Eagle*, *Ottawa Free Press*, and the *Yorkshire Evening Argus*. All of them detailed stories of various bodies which were discovered to have died from massive blood loss — often the bodies were drained totally of their blood supply. All of the deaths had another fact in common: each victim, though at first thought to have been the target of a robbery-related assault, was found to have " ... tiny puncture marks" near or on a major artery. Sometimes there were more than one pair of these marks (a body found in Chicago had at least thirty such puncture marks on her legs) but, in each case, saliva was found within these punctures, leading, naturally, to the conclusion that each of these victims had been killed by " ... mentally disturbed" individuals who suffered " ... the delusion of vampirism."

My hope is by now you will understand why my curiosity overpowered any anxiety I might have been experiencing.

GARY A. BRAUNBECK

The proprietor opened the door and led me down a long stone stairway which emptied out into a surprisingly cavernous basement. Lighting a kerosene lantern, he proceeded to lead me down a slope in the floor to an area which I can only describe to you as being a sort-of hidden theatre; there were a few rows of seats (which smelled of old fire) and a raised stage, more than a few of whose boards still bore the black marks of a fire.

As I sat where the proprietor directed me, I noticed the insignia of the Lyceum Theatre on the back of the seat in front of me, and realized at once that these seats — as well as portions of the stage before me — had been scavenged from the great fire which destroyed the Lyceum in 1830. (That they might have been scavenged from the wreckage of the 1803 fire did not, at the time, seem a possibility to me.)

The proprietor wandered away into the darkness, the light from the lantern growing smaller and more dim as he made his way through a curtain off to the side. I heard him moving around back-stage, then a few squeaking sounds, a cough, and then the curtain fronting the stage rose slowly to reveal a series of chairs and small podiums, each on different levels, arranged in a manner befitting a "dramatic reading"--what is often called "Reader's Theatre" in America.

There was, however, only one person on the stage as the lights came up, and he was neither standing nor seated behind one of the podiums.

He was in a wheelchair, down-stage center, illuminated by a spotlight from above. His face was half in shadow, even after he raised his head to look out at his "audience."

Newspaper clippings of blood-drained victims.

The Lyceum Theatre.

A.S.

I knew even before he spoke in his watered-down but still musical Irish brogue that I was in the presence of none other than Abraham — better known as "Bram" — Stoker.

"Mr. Fort," he said, barely above a whisper. "Thank you for coming.

CURTAIN CALL

Have you paper and pen?"

"I do," I called from the darkness of the theatre, then produced said items from my jacket pocket. (Fortunately the light from the stage bled forward enough that I could see to make notes.)

"Excellent," said Mr. Stoker, then wiped at his mouth with a dark-stained handkerchief he clutched in one shaking, palsied hand.

I knew — as did many of his admirers — that Stoker had been in seclusion for the last few years. Ill health was rumored — a rumor which I saw now to be sadly true (though whether or not he was suffering from the final stages of untreated syphilis I had not the medical knowledge to ascertain). I can tell you that the rumored feeble-mindedness was true, for several times during his narrative did Mr. Stoker begin muttering gibberish for minutes on end, until he would fall into something like a brief trance from which we would emerge lucid and articulate.

"I am a great admirer of your writings," he said from his place on the stage. "You must assemble your articles into a book for publication one day."

"That is my intent," I replied, suddenly aware of the single bead of perspiration that was snaking down my spine.

"May I suggest, then," said Stoker, "that you call your work 'The Book of the Damned?'"

"Why?"

He laughed. It was not a pleasant sound. "Because all so-called 'unnatural phenomena' comes from damned places, sir. Speak of damned places and you speak of places where powerful emotional forces have been penned up. Have you ever been within the walls of a prison, Mr. Fort? Where the massed feelings of hatred, deprivation, claustrophobia and brutalization have seeped into the very stones? One can *feel* it. The emotions resonate. They seethe, trapped, waiting for release, waiting to be given *form*, Mr. Fort. What you might call an 'unconscious confluence' were you to label it in one of your articles.

"You now sit in the remnants of one such 'damned place,' sir: the charred remains of the Lyceum Theatre. These stage boards, the curtain above me, the very seats which surround you and the one in which you now sit, were discovered by myself in a basement storage area of the Lyceum during my time there as manager — along, of course, with Sir Henry Irving, my own personal vampire."

He spoke Irving's name with a level of disgust that was absolutely chilling to hear. Even though Stoker attempted to hide his true feelings about Irving in his biography of the famous actor, it was now well known that, during the twenty-seven years he worked as stage manager at the Lyceum, Irving treated Stoker little better than a slave, paying him so very little that, upon Irving's death, Stoker was forced to borrow money from friends and relatives in order to survive; when he was no longer able to borrow money, he was forced to write such drivel as his latest (and, I suspicioned, what would be his *last*) novel, *The Lair of the White Worm*.

I could not help but share the sorrow of this broken man on the stage before me; there had been a potential for true literary greatness there, once, but no more ... and the late Sir Henry Irving was as much to blame for that as were Stoker's so-called "personal indulgences."

"Remember as you listen, Mr. Fort: emotions resonate. They seethe, trapped, waiting for release, waiting to be given form."

I wrote down his words, though they seemed more the ramblings of mind surrendering to the body's sicknesses.

Stoker coughed into his handkerchief once again. Even from my place in the "audience," I could see that he was coughing up blood. His handkerchief was useless to him now. I took my own, unused handkerchief from my pocket and rose to approach the stage and give it to him, but was stopped by the appearance of a great, dark wolf by Stoker's side.

It wandered on from stage left and seated itself next to his wheelchair. Even sitting on its haunches, it was nearly as tall as he. I had never seen such a magnificent and terrifying creature in all my life. It looked upon me with pitiless eyes that, in the light of the stage, glowed a deep, frightening crimson.

CURTAIN CALL

I returned the handkerchief to my pocket and took my seat once again.

"You'll come to no harm, Mr. Fort," said Stoker, reaching out to rub the fur at the nape of the great wolf's neck. The beast growled contentedly. I thought of a line from Stoker's most famous novel, about the Children of the Night, and what sweet music they made.

What follows is my transcription of Stoker's narrative. I have taken the liberty of removing the sometimes-prolonged pauses he took between words, as well as excising those instances where his crumbling mind led him down rambling paths of incomprehensibility.

I ask only that you remember this was a man who could have achieved true literary greatness, but who is now only remembered as the author of " ... that dreadful vampire book."

Even now, I still sorrow at the thought of What Might Have Been, had Fate been kinder to him.

The Narrative of Abraham (Bram) Stoker, as told to Charles Fort. Little Russell Street, London, 1912.

I was born in Dublin in 1847, one of seven children. Though I was a very sickly child, I was nonetheless my mother's favorite. During those years I spent in my sickbed, my mother tended to me with great and loving care. Having fostered a lifelong fascination with stories of the macabre, she entertained me with countless Irish ghost stories — the worst kind there is, I should add. As a child I was lulled to sleep each night with tales of banshees, demons, ghouls, and horrific accounts of the cholera outbreak of 1832.

My mother was a remarkable woman — strong-minded, ambitious, proud, a writer — she hoped that I, too, might one day become a person of letters — a visitor to workhouses for wayward and indigent girls, and above, she was a proponent of women's rights — much like her close friend, the mother of Oscar Wilde. I sincerely believe that, were it not for her kind ministrations on my behalf, I might have surrendered to the illnesses that plagued my early years. But she gave me strength and a sense of self-worth, and for that alone I shall always cherish her memory.

When I became of college age and was accepted at Trinity on an athletic scholarship — you would not know it to look at this pathetic body now, but there was a time when I was a champion. I was a record breaker, in my day ... and, I must admit, I gained a reputation among the members of my class for a somewhat exaggerated masculinity — some would even call it polemical. But I assure you that I was never less than chivalric toward the ladies with whom I kept company. I often wonder now if my way with the ladies back then is not the reason I am being punished in my final days with a wife so distant and frigid I might as well be wed to a corpse.

In 1871 I graduated with honours in science — Pure Mathematics, which enabled me to accept a civil service position at Dublin Castle. That same year I began to review theatrical positions in Dublin, and in 1876 I was privileged to review Sir Henry Irving's magnificent performance in "Hamlet." Shortly thereafter, we became great friends — or so I thought.

The great actor is a strange beast, indeed, Mr. Fort, for his ego is such that it requires — nay, *demands* — constant feeding. Sir Henry was much like a child in that way. He took more of my friendship than he ever did return, but I was simply too awestruck by the man's genius to take notice of this.

I became his stage manager when he took over management of the Lyceum Theatre. That same year, I began to publish my writings — *The Duties of Clerks of Petty Sessions in Ireland*. It was released to unanimous indifference from critics and the public alike. Sir Henry urged me to explore more 'universal' themes in my work, much as Shakespeare and Milton and Marlowe did in theirs. The man was simply hoping that his lap-dog assistant would, perhaps, compose a play in which he might once again take center stage and be the focus of attention ... but I digress.

CURTAIN CALL

I served Sir Henry well and loyally over the years. His opinion of my writing remained, as always, dismissive ... until I wrote *Dracula*. On this, he at last expressed an opinion. 'It is absolute, pandering rubbish,' he said. Still, in 'reward' for my many years of service and friendship to him, he agreed to allow me to stage a dramatic reading of the novel before its release from the publisher.

The novel was, as I'm sure you know, quite dense, and so several long, sleepless editing sessions were required in order to make the work an acceptable length for theatrical presentation. During this period in the latter part of 1896, I insisted on being able to rehearse with a cast so as to determine the success of my editing process. Sir Henry would not allow his personal company of actors to be 'inconvenienced' — his word — with a 'work in progress,' and so left it up to me to assemble a cast of unknowns with whom to rehearse the piece. It took me several weeks, but at last I had my cast — with the exception of an acceptable actor to portray Abraham van Helsing. But I shall come to that.

You need to understand that, during this period of intense concentration, the character of Count Dracula became even more alive to me than he was during the years of research it took to create him and write the novel. He was so alive to me, in fact, that I often found myself talking with him as I would stagger home nights after hours of emotionally draining rehearsal. 'My dear Count,' I would say, 'have I lost all perspective where you are concerned?' I did this to relieve my anxiety: if the novel were not reduced to an acceptable three-hour theatrical entertainment, Sir Henry made it quite clear to me that he would not permit me to present the work to the public ... not in his precious theatre. And so the Count became my constant companion, sir, my father-confessor, my only true friend.

I began to realize that they only way for the work to be made right, it was necessary for me to make the cast believe in the Count as fiercely as did I. I spoke to them one night of my imaginary conversations with the Count, and though they were at first amused, they came to understand that my dedication to the project was unflappable. I have to say, they were far more accommodating to me than Sir Henry's personal players would ever be with him; being unknowns, there were no egos to soothe or feed. Until the last rehearsal, it was the purest, most enjoyable theatrical experience of my life.

Soon, all of the cast were holding conversations with the Count. I recall encountering the actress who portrayed Mina Murray one night during a break in the rehearsal: I found off-stage left, sitting with her book, eyes closed, whispering, 'Why does someone as remarkable as you, dear Count, have to be so very, very wicked?' It *moved* me, sir, to hear that — and not only from her, but from all of the cast members. Oh, the stories I could tell you of their recountings of their conversations with the Count. They came to believe in his existence as much as I.

Remember: emotions resonate. They seethe, trapped, waiting for release, waiting to be given form.

The deadline for my final draft of the performance text was rapidly approaching, and still I had not found an actor who I felt would adequately convey the essence of Van Helsing. It may seem a somewhat selfish point, but the other actors had so refined their vocal interpretations of my characters, had given them such life, that to bring in an actor who would less than their equal would have been an insult to them.

Then one evening, after having ended rehearsal early, I found myself in this area of Little Russell Street, and came upon this very bookshop. As I wandered among its many volumes, the proprietor took my aside and asked, 'Are you Mr. Bram Stoker, author of *After Sunset?*' 'I am,' I replied, seeing with some delight that he held a well-read copy of that very short story collection in his hands. 'I am a great admirer of your stories,' he said, offering the book to me, 'and I would be honored if you would inscribe my copy.'

I took the book from him with thanks, and proceeded to uncap the pen he offered, but somehow I managed to cut the tip of my thumb in the process. I bled a little upon the first page — not enough to ruin it,

CURTAIN CALL

but enough that it could not be easily or neatly wiped away. 'Please do not worry yourself,' said the proprietor to me as I signed my name to the title. 'It can be taken care of.'

After I returned the volume to him, he took it behind the counter and knelt down behind a shelf of books. A few moments later he emerged and showed me — much to my surprise — that the blood had been successfully removed from the title paper. I noticed — but did not think much of — his licking his lips several times after emerging from behind the counter. 'I must say, Mr. Stoker, that I am greatly anticipating the release of your new novel.' 'You may be one of the few persons in England who is,' I replied, and we shared a jovial laugh at my remark.

Something about him seemed terribly familiar to me, and as I listened to his voice with its weary, sand-like quality, I came to realize that I was looking at my Van Helsing. I proceeded to tell the proprietor of my problem, and asked him if he would be willing to read the part of Van Helsing for my presentation to Sir Henry at the end of the week. He was deeply flattered, and of course accepted my offer.

When the time came for the rehearsal, I found him outside the theatre, nervously pacing by the performers' entrance. 'My dear fellow, we are all waiting,' I said. When he said nothing in reply, I opened the door wider and said, 'Please, come in and join us.' He did so, and the rehearsal began.

It was the most magnificent reading of the novel I have ever witnessed. He captured not only Van Helsing's weariness, but his near-mad drive to destroy Dracula, as well. His performance was a prism of compassion, fury, wariness, dedication, sadness, and strength. When it came time for his 'This so sad hour' speech, he had all of us transfixed. He *was* Van Helsing.

Then, at the conclusion of the scene, he began to laugh.

It was the sound of an ancient crypt door being wrenched open.

The spell was immediately broken. 'My dear fellow,' I said to him. 'May I inquire what you find so humorous about this very tragic scene?'

'That you see it as tragic at all is what amuses me,' he replied, only this time his voice was not that of either Van Helsing or the sandy-voiced proprietor I had met at the bookshop the previous day: it was the voice of Count Dracula — not only as I had heard it in my imaginary conversations with him, but as the others in the cast had heard it, as well. I looked upon all their faces and knew that *this* was the voice of the Count as we had come to believe it would sound.

Speak of damned places, Mr. Fort, and you speak, on some level, of belief. Emotions resonate. Electrons dance. Equations collapse and are replaced by newer, equally possible equations. Call it the collective unconscious or the hive mind of the masses, but the emotional charge had built and surged down the cumulative lines of our psyche and found not only focus but *form*.

He changed before our shocked eyes; from man to bat to wolf to rodent to owl to insect, then back again, then a hybrid of all creatures plus man — a sight so unspeakable I have never been able to bring myself to put its description onto paper for fear of being labeled mad.

Count Dracula rose up before us in all his dark, majestic, terrifying glory. 'My thanks to all of you for our little talks at night,' he said, smiling a lizard-grin and exposing his awful teeth. 'I have searched for centuries for a proper form in which I could enter your world, and you have so thoughtfully provided one for me.'

We began to run for the doors, but he became shadow and beast and speed itself: none of the cast made it any farther than the stage-left dressing room entrance before he fell upon them and opened their veins with his teeth. His strength was super-human, his speed that of the wrath of God Himself — if indeed such a Being exists at all.

I huddled behind a stack of risers, listening to the terrified and soon-silenced screams of my cast as the Count fed on each and every one of them. After what seemed an eternity, he found my hiding place and lifted me up as easily as one would a newborn child.

Holding me by the throat, he glared at me with his glowing red eyes and said, 'I wish to thank you personally, Mr. Stoker, for giving me life. But you have also made it necessary for the others who populated your novel to enter this world behind me, and so I must take my leave of you for now. Since I now know the ending of your story, I feel it is my duty to change it on this side ... but you needn't worry about further revising your manuscript. I think it will be satisfactory to have the world believe that I am a fictitious creation who was summarily dispensed with at the conclusion of your little melodrama.'

And with that, he released me, and disappeared into the night.

Shortly thereafter, the members of my cast rose to their feet, undead all, and made their way down into the basement of the theatre and, from there, into the sewers of the city. They are still there to this day. And I sorrow for what I unleashed upon them and the world. Dear God, how I sorrow.

I sat in the darkness of the theatre in stunned silence for several minutes after Mr. Stoker finished telling his incredible tale. The man was obviously mad ... but there still lingered in my mind a whispering doubt. And there was, after all, that unearthly wolf on the stage with him.

"How can I help your unbelief?" came a voice.

I had been staring at Mr. Stoker. His lips had not moved. I looked, then, at the wolf by his side.

It spoke again: "Your unbelief, Mr. Fort. How can I help it?"

The wolf moved forward, hunkered down as if to pounce, and at once became an army of rats that swarmed across the stage and into the orchestra pit and emerged in the aisle as the proprietor who had led me down here. "Does this help?" he asked of me.

I rose to my feet and began to frantically make my way over the seats toward what I believed to be the staircase I had descended earlier. My heart was pounding against my chest with such force I feared it would smash through my ribs and tissue.

The proprietor became several bats who quickly swooped down and around me, assaulting me with their wings. I fell to the floor and the bats collided in a flash of darkest shadow and became the proprietor again, only now he was much younger in appearance, taller, stronger.

Eternal.

"Look upon me and fear, Mr. Fort. For I am as real as you dread I am."

He reached down and grabbed onto my jacket with one hand, lifting me off the floor with unnerving ease so that my feet dangled above the aisle like some marionette left hanging on a peg.

I could not take my eyes from his blood-red gaze.

"My biographer, my creator, wishes for his cast to be given their proper curtain call, the one denied them so many years ago." He slammed me down into the nearest seat and held my there with one mighty hand on my shoulder.

"Nothing less than your most enthusiastic applause will ensure your safe exit from this place," snarled Count Dracula in my ear.

An iron grate in the floor near the foot of the stage shifted with a nerve-wracking shriek and was cast aside by a hand that was more bone than flesh.

And the parade of the dead began.

How to describe what I saw? How to convey the pathetic, terrifying, sad, depraved sight which my eyes beheld?

Their flesh — what remained of it — had the color and texture of spoiled meat. Worms and other such creatures of filth oozed in and out of the holes in their faces where once their eyes had resided. The stench of death was sickly-sweet in the air. Some shambled, a few crawled, and one — a woman — had to be carried by another cast member because much of her lower torso was gone, leaving only dangling, tattered loops of decayed intestine which hung beneath her like a jellyfish's stingers.

I wept at the sight of them, but I applauded them; oh, how I applauded!

CURTAIN CALL

And I was not alone in my efforts.

Surrounding me, each of them as decayed and pathetic as the sad creatures who were assembling on the stage before us, were all the characters from Stoker's novel, all of them flesh and blood, all of them — thanks to the Count's actions — now equally un-dead: here was Mina Murray and Jonathan Harker; there was Dr. Seward and Lucy, Lord Godalming and Quincey and every last character from the novel who had participated in Dracula's destruction, only now they were the destroyed ones ... even the great Abraham Van Helsing. All un-dead and applauding those whose portrayals and belief had brought them into this world and given them life — albeit briefly.

I became aware of several women clothed in white encircling me as I continued to applaud and the cast to take their individual bows.

The brides of Dracula surrounded me, caressed me, touched me with their lips and hands. My temperature rose in depraved want for them, and I applauded all the harder for it.

"My cast," intoned Stoker from the stage, gesturing to each member of his troupe. "My fine cast, my dear friends."

Dracula smiled and wiped something from one of his eyes. Looking at me, he smiled his awful, bloody grin and said, "I am moved, are you not the same?"

"I am," I said, quite dizzy.

The applause from the audience grew deafening. Dracula parted his arms and became a giant man-bat thing with slick flesh. He flew above stage and proceeded to land gracefully in the center of the players.

"Let my brides pleasure you, Mr. Fort," he bellowed above the noise in a voice part human and part beast, "and worry not, for they will not feed on you. You are our messenger now. Leave here, and tell the world, if you have the courage, that I am real, and that as long as men read my story, I shall never die. With the coming years and centuries, my story will be read by thousands, millions more, and each time the book is opened, each time a page is turned, I grow stronger and more eternal! Tell this to the world, sir, if you dare! For in the centuries to come my followers will grow, they will read of me, go forth, and multiply, and there will come a night when the entire earth will awaken and pull in the sweet damned breath of the un-dead, and then I will be as I should have been from the very beginning: The true Prince of Night, the king of my kind! Go, then, and tell them, if you dare."

One of his brides fell on her knees before me whilst another began to tear at my shirt.

The applause swelled as Dracula himself took a bow, and then I fell down into a dizzying pit of desire and darkness.

When I regained consciousness, I found myself outside the Lyceum Theatre, some good distance from where I was staying.

I cannot say for certain how I came to arrive safely back at my rooms at Bedford Place, only that I did find my way back there and was at once taken by the arm and led to an office where I was given a stiff drink of whiskey while a constable was called to take my statement.

"Robbery and Assault" was the official explanation for my condition. I saw no reason to argue their conclusion.

The next day, no fewer than three bodies were discovered around London, the blood drained from their veins.

The next day, I discovered reports of several other deaths in Canada, The United States, and Germany.

I returned home soon after, and for the rest of my life continued to gather such stories of bloodless bodies.

I am now an old man and my time is short. It has taken me a lifetime to muster the courage to set this tale to paper. Whether or not you choose to believe this is a matter between you and your conscience. I can no longer say I neither believe nor disbelieve nothing. Belief or unbelief, the dark forces of the Universe will have their way, regardless.

At my window last night I beheld the countenance of Mr. Bram

CURTAIN CALL

Stoker, himself among the un-dead now; beside him was his creation, the Count, and in his eyes was a promise: *Soon.*

I fear I may not be alive come morning.

Not that I would have lived that much longer, anyway.

So I take my leave of you. Do with this recounting what you will. The night is nearly upon us.

An article in yesterday's *New Yorker* listed *Dracula* as one of the best-selling books of all time. To this date, it is estimated that somewhere around five million copies in twenty different languages have been sold.

So many readers. So many pages turned.

And he grows stronger with each word read.

There will come a night, he said.

I fear it may be sooner than we think.

I shall lay down my head for the last time now.

God go with you in all the damned places that you walk.

Soon, such places shall be all there are.

—*Charles Fort, the Bronx, May 3, 1942.*

ABOUT THE EDITOR

Michael West is the critically-acclaimed author of *The Wide Game, Cinema of Shadows, Spook House, Skull Full of Kisses,* and *The Legacy of the Gods* series. He lives and works in the Indianapolis area with his wife, their two children, their bird, Rodan, their turtle, Gamera, and their dog, King Seesar.

His favorite vampires reside in Stephen King's classic novel, *'Salem's Lot*, and in the films *Fright Night, Near Dark,* and *Let the Right One In.* When sunlight hits them, they all burst into flames, as it should be.

Check out the following pages to see more from

All Seventh Star Press titles available in print and an array of specially priced eBook formats.

Visit www.seventhstarpress.com for further information.

Connect with Seventh Star Press at:
www.seventhstarpress.com
seventhstarpress.blogspot.com
www.facebook.com/seventhstarpress

Now Available from Seventh Star Press, the horror stylings of
MICHAEL WEST
Featuring illustrations and cover art by
acclaimed artist Matthew Perry!

Trade Paperback ISBN: 9780983740209
eBook ISBN: 9780983740216

Trade Paperback ISBN: 9781937929718
eBook ISBN: 9781937929725

Trade Paperback ISBN: 9781937929954
eBook ISBN: 9781937929831

Epic Urban Fantasy-The Rising Dawn Saga

A shadow falls across the world, and realms beyond, as a war that has raged since the dawn of time itself draws closer to a decisive clash. As groups aligned with a movement called The Convergence speed up their efforts to bring about a global economic and legal order, resistance mounts after the host of a syndicated radio show, Benedict Darwin, discovers the true nature of a virtual reality device that has come into his possession. The Rising Dawn Saga will take you into mythical, supernatural realms as it unfolds, as the most unlikely of individuals rise to confront powers that have existed since before the world began.

Book One: The Exodus Gate
ISBN: 978-0615267470

"With The Exodus Gate author Stephen Zimmer sets the stage for an adventurous new science fiction fantasy series that is sure to entertain the reader from beginning to end. Zimmer has weaved a tale of fantastic realms populated with exotic creatures. Keep a sharp eye out for this new series."

-Mark Randell, Yellow30 Sci-Fi

"…a book that Fantasy Book Review recommends for lovers of thoughtful-fantasy. It is also a book with an ending that is near-prophetic, written as it was before the world's economic meltdown."

-Fantasy Book Review

Book Two: The Storm Guardians
ISBN: 978-0982565636

"This novel transports me from my bedroom to the edge of an upcoming storm — a battle to be fought by incredible villains and noble heroes of all forms. I love Zimmer's imagination, as each of his creatures play a pivotal role in the bigger picture. Unfortunately, for every auspicious being there is an ominous beast lurking in the shadows. Zimmer's weave of fantasy and religious fables leaves the reader sated"

-Bitten By Books

"The scope of The Storm Guardians is massive, opening up and expanding on the conflict only hinted at in The Exodus Gate. The intrigue and action promised in the first book is fully developed and mercilessly exhibited. The Storm Guardians is a non-stop thriller that lives up to the promise of The Exodus Gate and points at an even more amazing denouement in the final book of the series. Once again, Zimmer has used his command of cinematic imagery to give us a spectacular vision of war both heavenly and hellish. Two thumbs up on this one."

-Pure Reason Book Review

Book Three: The Seventh Throne
ISBN: 978-0983740247

NOW AVAILABLE!

Now Available from Seventh Star Press, H. David Blalock's newest urban fantasy, featuring illustrations and cover art by fantasy artist Matthew Perry!

Trade Paperback ISBN: 9780983740230
eBook ISBN: 9780983740285

Why do bad things happen to good people? Simple. In the ancient war between the Angels of Light and Darkness, the Dark won. Now it is the job of an undercover force simply known as The Army to rectify that.

Using every tool available, The Army has worked to liberate our world from The Enemy for thousands of years, slowly and painfully lifting Mankind out of the dark. On the front of the great Conflict are the Angelkillers, veterans of the fight with centuries of experience.

Jonah Mason is an Angelkiller, and his cell is targeted as part of plot to unseat a very powerful Minion of The Enemy. Mason and his troop are drawn into a battle that stretches from real-time to virtual reality and back. The Conflict is about to expand into cyberspace, and if Mason is unable to stop it, The Enemy will have gained dominion over yet another realm.

Now Available!
R.J. Sullivan's
HAUNTING OBSESSION

Trade Paperback ISBN: 978-1-937929-87-9
eBook ISBN: 978-1-937929-88-6

SHE WANTS TO BE LOVED BY YOU ... ALONE!

Daryl Beasley collects all things Maxine Marie, whose famous curves and fast lifestyle made her a Hollywood icon for decades after her tragic death. Daryl's girlfriend, Loretta Stevens, knew about his geeky lifestyle when they started dating, but she loves him, quirks and all.

Then one day Daryl chooses to buy a particularly tacky piece of memorabilia instead of Loretta's birthday present. Daryl ends up in the doghouse, not only with Loretta, but with Maxine Marie herself. The legendary blonde returns from the dead to give Daryl a piece of her mind—and a haunting obsession he'll never forget.